A BILLIONAIRE FOR CHRISTMAS

JO LYONS

B

Boldwood

First published in Great Britain in 2025 by Boldwood Books Ltd.

Copyright © Jo Lyons, 2025

Cover Design by Alexandra Allden

Cover Images: Shutterstock

Interior Images: Boldwood Books and Shutterstock

The moral right of Jo Lyons to be identified as the author of this work has been asserted in accordance with the Copyright, Designs and Patents Act 1988.

Every effort has been made to obtain the necessary permissions with reference to copyright material, both illustrative and quoted. We apologise for any omissions in this respect and will be pleased to make the appropriate acknowledgements in any future edition.

A CIP catalogue record for this book is available from the British Library.

Paperback ISBN 978-1-80557-173-5

Large Print ISBN 978-1-80557-174-2

Hardback ISBN 978-1-80557-172-8

Ebook ISBN 978-1-80557-175-9

Kindle ISBN 978-1-80557-176-6

Audio CD ISBN 978-1-80557-167-4

MP3 CD ISBN 978-1-80557-168-1

Digital audio download ISBN 978-1-80557-170-4

This book is printed on certified sustainable paper. Boldwood Books is dedicated to putting sustainability at the heart of our business. For more information please visit https://www.boldwoodbooks.com/about-us/sustainability/

Boldwood Books Ltd, 23 Bowerdean Street, London, SW6 3TN

www.boldwoodbooks.com

For the Lyons boys

'You only live once, but if you do it right, once is enough.'

— MAE WEST

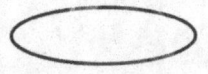

Ava's Bucket List (RIP)

Drink champagne with a billionaire while naked in
a hot tub overlooking the Alps

Bark loudly every time someone round
the table says your name

Crash a wedding and give an
uplifting toast

Ride a camel dressed in
a costume

Speak in third
person all day

Solve a mystery

Conquer a fear

Fall madly in love

Spend the day blindfolded

Make your own face out of sausage meat

Publicly eat vanilla pudding out of a mayo jar
(with gusto)

Spend ten minutes naked in a sauna standing like
the Vitruvian Man

1

AN EXCEPTIONALLY BAD START

Billionaires aren't like buses. Which is unfortunate because talented chef Molly Johnson needed one. And not just any old billionaire. She was after a nice one that she could drink champagne with. In a hot tub. Overlooking the Alps. While naked. Very, very naked.

Her best friend and late business partner, Ava, had written a will leaving Molly sole ownership of their restaurant and the apartment above it, along with a request to complete the bucket list she'd never got to finish. But because of some unfortunate wording, the request and the bequest seemed to have got entangled in the eyes of the law and Molly was set to lose everything if she didn't complete the list before the end of the day on Christmas Eve. And this was no ordinary set of tasks. Ava had been outrageously specific. Which was how Molly found herself spending the festive season preparing high-end cuisine for the rich and fabulous at a very glamorous ski resort in France, while she looked for an incredibly handsome yet (and this was crucial to her plan) incredibly *blind* billionaire to tick off the list.

Molly glanced once more at the letter in her hand, forwarded from Paris. Only Ava's solicitor sent letters to her these days, and they were never good. She reread the (heart-stopping, panic-inducing, gut-wrenching) reminder that she had twelve days left to comply with the legal requirements before all her and Ava's company assets were due to be liquidated and the deeds to their beloved restaurant along with them. With the words blurring on the page, she sagged against the industrial steel kitchen bench. 'I'm so stupid,' she groaned to herself. 'How did I let this happen?' She knew how. She'd left the unopened letters to pile up for months.

She deeply regretted not getting round to formalising the business partnership with Ava. It was always on their to-do list but once their quaint little restaurant, Le Petit Ange, nestled in the heart of the French Alps, took off, they were so incredibly busy, seven days a week, that there never seemed any time. And then when Ava was diagnosed with ovarian cancer, it was the last thing on their minds.

Molly pulled out her phone and dialled the solicitor's number. He picked up on the third ring. 'Hello, Monsieur Fournier. It's Molly Johnson here... Yes, again. It's about the letter... Yes, of course I've read it properly. I'm doing my best, but it just doesn't seem fair that—' Molly bit her tongue.

Monsieur Fournier was prone to reminding her of the obvious.

'Yes, I'm aware that we didn't write a transfer of ownership into the contract before Ava died. Yes, I know the bank accounts are frozen, because I ran out of money to pay the bills and the staff two months ago. Why do you think I'm working two jobs? I'm running the restaurant single-handedly during the day *and* working in a hotel kitchen every night.' Molly heard the irritation rising in her voice. She took a deep breath in before continuing. 'Look. Let's be reasonable. I own half of the business. How am I supposed to —? I'm not angry with you. If I'm angry, it's at the French legal system. It's ludicrous. No one in their right mind could achieve even half of the things on that bucket list, never mind *want* to!'

Molly was almost screeching down the phone as

panic soared through her veins. 'I know I've had months to try and complete them. But in case you hadn't noticed, I've been running myself ragged! Ava is...' The words caught in her throat. 'Ava *was* my best friend. More than a friend. My soulmate. There's no way she would have foreseen this happening.'

Molly wiped a tear from her cheek with the back of her hand. How was this her life now? Desperate, broke and about to lose her home and livelihood?

'Sorry. Sorry, I just... Okay. I understand. It has just been *the* toughest time and to be honest, I'm not coping very well... Oh. You're busy... Okay, thank you for your time, Monsieur—' He hung up before she could say goodbye.

So that was that. Thanks to spending the best part of the year grieving and staring into space instead of just getting on with it, Molly's only option was to work her way down Ava's bucket list in the next twelve days, ticking off every bonkers thing Ava had left her to do while somehow collecting proof in the form of signatures and selfies. To be quite honest, she wasn't a million miles away from giving up completely so that she could enjoy a catastrophic breakdown in peace, watching back-to-back tear-jerkers on Netflix while squeezing cheese down her throat.

Footsteps across the cold stone tiles dragged Molly from her thoughts.

'Molly, can you drive this lot up to the Cigar Lounge before you finish your shift, please?' Petra, the hotel kitchen manager, asked, pointing to a stack of crates. 'Sorry to ask but apparently things are getting a little wild up there, and the porters have clocked off. Looks like it might go on through till morning, so the boss wants the place fully stocked, just in case.'

Molly's heart sank. 'The Cigar Lounge?' She'd heard enough rumours about what might go on up there to know that she'd much rather not.

Petra, a pristine-looking woman in her early thirties, not much older than herself, gave her a sympathetic look.

Molly fought the desire to refuse. The Cigar Lounge was for sophisticated rich people, whereas she had grown up on a council estate in the north of England. It was as far out of her comfort zone as the bucket list.

'You'll get paid double for the extra hours.'

A prickle of exhaustion crawled up her spine. She quashed it down. With the future of her restaurant hanging in the balance, she desperately needed the extra money to keep it afloat. At the end of a gruelling fourteen-hour day, some food, a hot steaming bath and her soft bed was all she craved, but she would have to wait. She smiled politely at her supervisor. 'Okay. Sure. I'll do it.'

'Thank you so much. I owe you one.' Petra inspected Molly's work. 'These hors d'oeuvres are divine. Take them all with you.'

Molly stuffed the solicitor's letter into her pocket and gazed longingly at the trays of delicate, mouthwatering canapés that had taken her three hours to create.

'Shame they've been such a huge hit,' Petra said, holding one up before devouring it. 'You'll probably be stuck in this kitchen forever.'

Molly did not need reminding. She nodded weakly at the compliment and reflected on how far she'd fallen in such a short time. Less than a year ago, she'd been juggling running an up-and-coming restaurant with nursing Ava. Sharing in the pain and injustice, raging against the world, and now, here she was, failing to fulfil a promise made on her friend's deathbed and still raging. It was all so unfair.

Molly snapped to attention as Petra handed her the keys to the snowmobile. 'And don't forget, as it's your first time up at the Lounge, try not to make eye contact with any guests at the parties, no matter what the circumstances. Restock the bars and replace the canapé trays as discreetly as you can. Most of them are famous celebrities, so do not repeat a word of anything you see or hear, okay?' Petra looked coy. 'It's Burlesque Night. The host expects maximum privacy.' She shrugged by way of explanation.

Molly bristled. Going to the Cigar Lounge was one thing. Going during its annual Burlesque Night was quite another. Especially as she was in the midst of an excruciatingly long dry spell. It had been years since she'd had any physical contact with a man. Her hands felt immediately clammy at the thought of what could possibly be going on up there.

As Petra went to push open the exit doors, both women stared out across the resort's lively village plaza as thick snowflakes whirled around the many après-ski revellers scampering back to warm, cosy hotel rooms. The Val D'Amore ski resort was one of the most exclusive and breathtakingly beautiful resorts in the world, with an unrivalled reputation and alpine views. It was built around a picturesque square, lined with twinkling lights, exclusive high-end luxury shops and restaurants, infamous rooftop bars with world-renowned DJs that drew crowds from around the world, and a guest list of *seasonnaires* to rival any celebrity red carpet. Molly followed Petra's gaze up to the Cigar Lounge, the infamous members-only club nestled further up the mountain, reached only by a single-track road designed for snowmobiles for staff access. Guests were ferried back and forth in a private velvet-lined gondola ski lift, straight from the Cigar Lounge doors down to the plaza and the luxury suites that only the super-rich could afford.

When she and Ava had decided to move their UK-based catering business to the resort, they'd had no idea that it was a billionaires' playground. They'd aimed high and worked ridiculously hard to compete with the other Val D'Amore restaurants, neither of them knowing that Ava would die before she got the chance to see the business flourish. And that Molly would be left to run it alone, so soon.

A sadness swept over Molly as she hurriedly piled the crates of canapés onto the trailer attached to the snowmobile. Her friend had loved this place. She had been enthralled at the majestic snowy peaks of the mountains by day and the blaze of stars by night. But none of it sparked joy in Molly any longer. She was too grief-stricken to feel anything but numb.

Her weary thoughts were broken by the steep and treacherous drive up to the Lounge. Much better to travel on the gondola swinging high above her like an ornate royal carriage rather than on this dimly lit, icy track. Especially in this weather. The snow was coming down so heavily and being blown around by a howling gale with such force that she could barely see two feet in front of the snowmobile and had to fight to keep control of it. Molly made it to the top of the track with some effort. She was just able to make out a small covered area, and she pulled up to the back entrance of the Cigar Lounge.

Up close, the whole place was lit up like a Christmas tree with the slow, rhythmic thrum of music seeping from the large wooden doors. The huge shutters over the windows were closed. There were no outward clues as to what was going on inside, or how many people were in there. Molly checked that the pallets of food piled high on the trailer and the crates of fine wines, champagnes and spirits were intact. There was enough for at least two hundred people. She fell on the staff door gratefully, bursting through into the warmth. As she removed her helmet, she was immediately greeted by two other staff members relieved she'd come to the rescue.

'Thank goodness you're here! We've got so many different events on tonight. Things are getting quite messy. They're all trying to drink each other under the table. I'd have sent the gondola down for supplies, but the sheaves and cables have frozen over. We'll unload the pallets while you prep the canapés.'

Molly politely acknowledged the frazzled woman in front of her as she got to work.

'You're a star. Thank you. Oh, and did Petra tell you about the no phones policy and the no unnecessary eye contact or flirting thing when you go into the parties? We've got some big names in upstairs, so security is super tight and staff down to the minimum. Just keep your head down and you'll be fine.'

While she could hold her own with the best of them when it came to preparing delicious food, she was way out of her depth when it came to socialising and mixing with crowds of happy, drunk people. Blending into the background was second nature. 'Not a problem.'

'I'm Keela, by the way. I work exclusively up here. You must be new. Where have they got you working? Private, corporate or main hotel?'

'I'm Molly.' She decided not to reveal that she was the current owner of a struggling restaurant tucked away in a corner of the square, that she was working two jobs just to scrape by and hadn't felt a man's touch in over three years. 'Main hotel. Catering contractor. I've hardly left the kitchen.' Since Molly had started six weeks ago, demand for her skills had skyrocketed. Her speciality hors d'oeuvres had gone viral around the resort.

Keela gave her a sympathetic shrug. 'Work, eat, sleep is pretty much the standard here, unless' – she gave Molly a conspiratorial wink – 'you've been here for five years like we have.' She waved a hand in the direction of a friendly-looking barman who was heaving a crate of bottles onto his shoulder. 'We know where all the fun is to be had.'

Molly managed a tight smile. She wasn't here for fun. She was here to fulfil a promise, the only thing that mattered to her right now.

'Here. You'll need this costume.'

'Costume?'

'Yeah, sorry. We are "required" to blend in. You can change out of your snowsuit in there.' Keela pointed to a door on the far side of the stockroom. 'Help yourself to any stuff you need. It's all brand new. Pick whichever shoes you want. They all scream high-class stripper but at least they're designer and you get to keep them.'

'Thanks.' Molly took the outfit out of the bag, unfolded the delicate tissue paper and gasped. She held the fragile material in her hands. Where was the rest of it?

She tilted her head anxiously. 'Is this really necessary?'

'First time in burlesque?' Keela grinned at her. She

reached for a bottle from a nearby crate and untwisted its top. 'House rules. Here, have one of these. It'll help you relax.' Keela handed her a shot glass. Molly downed it and immediately coughed. Keela laughed gently. 'Dutch courage. You'll need it.'

Peeling off her snowsuit, Molly inspected herself in the large mirror standing against the tiled wall. She was much thinner than she was used to due to all the grief and stress, but at least she was strong from all the running around she had done over the last year. Her thick, long, dark brown hair hung around her shoulders, framing her green eyes, which looked huge in her slightly gaunt face. She knew she had a haunted air. Every time she could bear to look at her own reflection, all she saw was her friend gazing sadly back. Molly unhooked a cotton robe and wrapped it around herself. It was warm and instantly soothing. As she picked up her snowsuit, the letter fell from her coat pocket as though reminding her why she was here. She gingerly picked it up and unfolded the damp sheets of paper.

She regarded the bucket list that came with the letter. A copy. Molly already had the original, one hundred dreams and goals crammed into a battered journal documenting her friend's final year of life in photos, scribbled memories, dates and places. It was

dotted with affirmations and such a precious reminder of all the things that shaped the person Ava
had become. Brave, courageous, kind and generous, a
positive force of nature, smiling right to the bitter end.
Emblazoned across the front page was a famous quote
by Mae West, Ava's favourite of all the quotes inside:
You only live once, but if you do it right, once is enough.

The last twelve pages of the journal were yet to be
filled. Twelve challenges remained. Twelve promises
yet to keep. Twelve days to do them. And for the millionth time, Molly closed her eyes and whispered,
'Ava, what were you thinking?'

2

SO MANY BOXES, SO LITTLE TIME… TICK, TICK, TICK

Stepping out of the staff changing room moments later, Molly was transformed. She had managed to brush her matted hair into a blanket of silk that fell into waves down one side while the other had an ornate feathery creation pinned to it. Thanks to all the make-up lying around, she'd created the face of what she hoped was a worldly-wise catering expert. One who was decidedly *above* all of this dressing-up nonsense; bold red to her plump lips, dark smoky eyes, strong eyebrows and a golden shimmer to her skin.

The costume was more elaborate than any she'd ever worn. She was wearing a tightly fitted blood-red corset with black lines running up the front that accentuated her curves. There was a sweetheart neckline with a black silk bow in the centre drawing the eye to her ample cleavage, the ridiculously tiny skirt and knickers a mix of ruffled red silk with black lace – but at least the frill covered her bottom, if nothing else. Theatrical, sheer black striped stockings ran the length of her long, lean legs up to her thighs and were each topped with a small, red satin bow. A sharp contrast to the milky white smoothness of her legs that disappeared beneath the ruffle of the skirt. In her long black gloves to the elbow, she appeared dramatic, vampish, emboldened, as though she did this every day of the week. She looked the opposite of how she felt inside.

The things one had to do to save one's business!

She swallowed her nerves, threw a nearby apron over her costume and began prepping the food.

Once the platters of bite-size gourmet appetisers looked like a prize-winning art installation, Molly stood back to observe her handiwork. She inspected the blaze of colourful, delicate petals and swirls of intricate purées on top of sumptuous hors d'oeuvres. All carefully designed to take the breath away, before melting in the mouth. When Molly and Ava had set out to impress with their fledgling business, they wanted to be twice as good as their competitors, and it showed. The complex designs and the implementation of cutting-edge ideas had been the perfect distraction for Ava during treatment for her illness. The friends had spent hours and hours perfecting the art of world-class molecular gastronomy – in particular, culinary aphrodisiacs. But Ava had always been the driving force behind making smart and risky business decisions and pushing boundaries, while Molly revelled in the safety of being the behind-the-scenes creative. When they had taken over the struggling restaurant from Ava's great-aunt, they had given the old French menu a fresh, new, scientific twist, and customers seemed to love it.

She carefully placed the trays on a trolley.

'Wow, you look fantastic,' Keela said, bustling through the door. 'It's manic out there. I've just restocked the bar, up in the Stockings and Garter Room on the first floor. Can you take that trolley up there, please? Then come and meet me downstairs.'

In a daze, Molly pushed the trolley through the kitchen door. Her costume (along with her remaining vestiges of pride) was well and truly hidden beneath her catering apron, where it would stay until the very last second. As the lift pinged to signal the first floor, Molly took a deep breath and stepped out onto the sumptuous carpet and turned left. The corridor was wide and brightly lit with a mix of wooden panelling and luxurious silk fabric wallpaper. Expensive-looking artwork hung between large, heavy wooden doors. It had an atmosphere that oozed the extravagance of old money. She caught sight of her reflection in a huge mirror hanging on the wall and barely recognised herself.

What the hell am I doing charging around like an underdressed pantomime dame?

Nerves and curiosity were starting to get the better of her. She tried to forget she was an award-winning chef as she took off her apron, folded it neatly and stuffed it onto the lowest shelf of the trolley. She knocked tentatively on the first door she came to and opened it cautiously. In the split second on entering, the warm smell of cigar smoke, brandy and cinnamon hit her. Gentle music filled her ears. She wasn't at all prepared for the sight that greeted her. She took in a hazy room full of women sauntering around with stockinged legs and designer sky-high heels, their pert bottoms in black lacy thongs on display and ample breasts housed in expensive, couture lingerie and balconette bras. More men and women, in varying degrees of undress, lounged on huge wide sofas. The scene was as decadent as an eighteenth-century portrait, and as sizzling as a high-class brothel.

Molly lowered her gaze and wheeled the trolley further into the room, silently closing the heavy door behind her. With her pulse racing triple time, she made her way to the elaborately decorated banquet table at the side of the room, and keeping her back to the sizable crowd of semi-naked people, she deftly replaced the empty canapé trays with full ones. As she worked, she heard amiable chatter rising above the low hum of music, and soft bursts of giggling. When people approached the banquet, she overheard a variety of compliments for the exquisite culinary delights she was speedily setting out. She had no urge to take any credit, preferring instead to get out of there as quickly as she could.

She wheeled the trolley full of empty trays to the corridor outside. As she bent down to retrieve her apron, she spotted a forgotten plate of canapés. She grabbed it and went back into the room to put it with the others on the table. Her stomach growled, reminding her that she had yet to eat today. Sure that no one would notice her, she took an hors d'oeuvre and popped it quickly into her mouth. She was pleased with the burst of flavour, the texture and the smokiness of the apple crisp against the sweetness of the fig leaf oil. These half-naked, randy swingers would have to go a long way to find food as tasty as hers.

'These are amazing,' said a woman in a low, cordial voice next to her. 'I've never seen anything so extraordinary. Really, darling, this place is always full of surprises, isn't it? These are Michelin-star standard.'

Since Ava's death, Molly had felt no great pleasure in receiving compliments, but she turned around out of politeness without thinking. Suddenly time slowed. Nothing in her life so far had prepared her for the bolt of lightning that now struck. The lady was standing next to the most handsome man Molly had ever laid eyes on. She only caught a glimpse of his profile each time the lady moved, but she was instantly captivated by the way his eyes crinkled, the straight nose leading to the full lips and a jaw covered in stubble. When he turned, it was enough to knock the breath from her lungs. She clutched the table, averting her gaze.

She remembered Petra telling her that only the super-rich were allowed to stay at the members-only Cigar Lounge. The billionaires, the celebrities, the politicians. Her mind flew to the bucket list and the first of the remaining twelve challenges. *Drink champagne with a billionaire while naked in a hot tub overlooking the Alps.*

What were the chances of this man being super-rich, single and in the mood to skinny dip while drinking champagne? Against her better judgement, Molly dared to sneak another look at him. He had kind, intelligent eyes, and a tanned face framed with dark, neatly trimmed hair. She stared just long enough for him to sweep it casually away from his forehead. Before she could help herself, her eyes wandered the length of his body. He was tall and lean, his arms strong and muscular beneath the tailored jacket. She'd never seen a man so well proportioned. Ever. Molly tried, and failed, to tear her eyes away. It was such a shame he wasn't blind, or she'd have frog-marched him straight to the nearest hot tub.

'And putting in that pit-stop halfway down the red slope was a genius idea,' the lady rattled on. 'I'm always desperate for an espresso martini by the time I've lugged myself all the way to the top. No one could accuse the staff of not pouring generous measures.'

'We can't have people skiing sober, can we? It's just like golf; they'll realise it's an expensive waste of time,' he replied drily, tossing a canapé down his throat. 'You're right. These are delicious.'

The lady honked with laughter as pride bloomed unexpectedly in Molly's chest. He gave a small bow and disappeared deeper into the room. The lady gazed after him with a contented sigh.

'Don't even think about it,' said another woman, approaching. The two ladies exchanged air kisses. 'If ever I was going to seduce a man, surely it would be him.'

'Levi? Get in line. Anyway, I'm not sure your husband would agree. You look fantastic by the way.'

'As do you. It's a pity Levi is such forbidden fruit. He's uncommonly handsome.' The two women stared after him longingly.

Adrenaline was coursing through Molly's veins. 'Handsome' was something of a major understatement. Maybe it was just because she'd been cooped up in the kitchen all year, but every one of her nerves was on end.

'At thirty-six, he's too energetic for you, my dear. Think of your new hip. Besides, he's the despair of women the world over. If you're going to pick a billionaire to have a casual affair with, might I suggest Old Walt over there?'

Molly, not usually one for eavesdropping, was transfixed at the conversation the two ladies were having, labelling Levi a billionaire as casually as if they'd called him a plumber. She followed their gaze to an oldish gentleman openly enjoying the attention of a much younger woman.

'That randy goat? I'd rather stick with my husband, thanks. And that's saying something.'

They giggled quietly.

'Walt took me and Elsie to New York shopping last year and then flew us all to Hawaii. If you can ignore the inappropriate jokes and the glaucoma, he's very generous.'

Leaving the ladies to gossip, Molly scanned the room for her handsome billionaire. Her pulse quickened at the thought of finding out more. She slipped in and out of the crowd, subtly glancing around, pleased that the party was in full swing and everyone was in various states of intoxication. The smell of logs burning and spicy aftershave mingled with expensive perfumes, filling the air of the various nooks and crannies. That was when she came across a giant Christmas tree, heavily decorated with glittering tinsel, bright gaudy baubles and burlesque figurines. Bearing an uncanny resemblance to herself, the angel on the top was wearing a red sparkling basque and suspenders. And next to the tree stood Levi, like the world's best Christmas present just waiting to be unwrapped. Her heart skipped a beat when she saw him casually talking to a scantily-clad woman adorned with what looked like a few million pounds' worth of gaudy baubles around her neck. Molly gave herself a mental slap. She must not get carried away. Someone was paying her good money to do a job, not to gape lustfully at exceptionally attractive party guests. But before she could tear her eyes away, Levi caught her gaze.

Christ Almighty.

He tilted his head with a quizzical expression as they made eye contact.

She'd broken the one and only rule she'd been given, and it felt overwhelmingly worth it. Smiling shyly at him, she swivelled around and made her way back across the crowded room on trembling legs. She desperately wanted to turn around, sure his penetrating gaze was trained right on her. She paused in the doorway, a sixth sense pulling at her, and risked a glance back at him.

She breathed a sigh of relief.

He was talking to a group of men. He wasn't looking at her. He wasn't paying her attention. It was all in her imagination. She was behaving erratically. It was very unlike her. Maybe it was this ridiculous costume. Maybe it was the excessive dry spell. She would have a word with herself as soon as she got back to her lovely apartment, down in the square.

Just as she was about to close the door, he suddenly turned and caught her staring again. Molly froze. The next few seconds happened as if in slow motion. He raised his glass, lazily downing the drink without once breaking eye contact with her. One rule!

He was staring back at her with unashamed interest. She had one rule and she'd broken it twice in as many minutes. She felt herself blush down to her toes. She noticed him taking in the corset clinging to her curves before placing his empty glass on a nearby tray.

In her peripheral vision, voluptuous women moved around the room dressed in theatrical burlesque attire, but their costumes were in stark contrast to the man before her. She looked him over one more time with satisfaction. He was dressed in a tux, his shirt unbuttoned at the collar, his bow-tie knotted loosely, but otherwise, he was fully dressed and did not seem as though he was taking part in whatever was going on. Unsure why, Molly nodded her approval.

This seemed to amuse him, causing her stomach to flutter as they locked eyes. This man fancied her.

And in that moment, she realised that she was experiencing lust. Overwhelming rip-his-shirt-right-off lust. It rocked her to her core. With a gasp, she swiftly closed the door.

Once outside, she took a moment to calm her

breathing. It was hot. Her head was in a spin. Molly would feel at home in any kitchen, anywhere in the world, but put her in the middle of what looked like an aristocratic orgy and she was certainly a fish out of water. She began fanning her face before bolting back to the lift with her trolley and down to the kitchen to retrieve the rest of the platters. The sooner she delivered them and got out of there, the fewer rules she might break.

'That bad, huh?' laughed Keela as Molly approached. 'Honestly, you wouldn't believe the half of what goes on in this club, but my lips are sealed, and I get well paid to keep them shut.' Her eyes were twinkling with mischief. 'This place is a magnet for the world's horniest people. A lot can happen in one night.'

At the thought of Levi, Molly experienced a warm flush. 'Where next?' she asked.

'Hen party for some famous French actress, in the Chambre Rouge. It's at the end of the corridor from the Stockings and Garter Room. Should be straightforward. They've got entertainment booked, so if you can get in and out before it starts, you might be spared some blushes. Oh, and whatever you do, don't go behind the stage curtain. It's hiding some priceless antique display that's part of the act and was a total pain to get up here. But what the super-rich want, the super-rich get.'

Molly was used to being invisible. 'Got it. They won't even notice I'm there. I promise.'

As Keela disappeared through the kitchen door, Molly was desperate for information. Her handsome stranger was called Levi. She needed to find out more. In a state of excitement, she made sure no one was around and whipped out her phone. She would search the internet for details about him. How many billionaires called Levi could there be? In her hurry, the phone slipped from her hand and landed with a crack on the tiled floor.

Molly stopped. What was she doing? Googling hot men was *not* the sort of distraction she needed right now. She needed to focus on the task at hand, delivering canapés to hungry hens. She picked up her phone, thankful to see it unbroken, and marched through to the dressing room to put it securely in her coat pocket. The copy of the bucket list was poking out. A reminder to get started. A reminder that she had until Christmas Eve, only twelve days, to tick off as many boxes as possible. Perhaps there was a small easy one that she could do once she finished her shift? She stared at the challenges on the list, but it was as though the first item kept looming from the page, dragging her eyes back to it time and again. Daring her to be courageous. Daring her to be spontaneous. Daring her to break a few rules. *Drink champagne with a billionaire while naked in a hot tub overlooking the Alps.*

It triggered an instant flashback of Levi and his incredibly symmetrical bone structure. Okay, so maybe this *was* the sort of distraction she needed right now.

3

RULES ARE FOR FOOLS

With the kitchen to herself, Molly decided on the spot that after she'd laid out the buffet for the hen party, it was almost her civic duty to go in search of Levi and somehow end up in a hot tub with him. This was a ski resort. And not just any ski resort. It was full of hot tubs and, more importantly, drunk billionaires. Besides kidnapping one, where else would she find a billionaire, never mind a smoking hot one, at such short notice?

She'd be a fool not to at least try.

Feeling dizzy with excitement, she surveyed the crates she'd brought. This hen party called for something special. Something romantic. Something audacious. She opened the crates and took out the pallets she was after and got to work. Once the trolley was loaded, she headed for the first floor.

When she arrived at the correct door, Molly smoothed down her costume. What little there was of it. She knocked on the door and entered. The room was tastefully decorated, every light fixture and fitting oozing high quality, and she was comforted to see that all the hens were in costume like her, although some not quite as sober or as dressed. The group was bigger than she had expected, and she was thankful she'd brought more than enough food.

Molly recognised a few famous faces straight away and as the women delighted in watching her create a swirling tower from the aphrodisiacs, canapés and edible alcoholic shots, they took turns elaborately feeding each other. It was all harmless fun, and Molly felt an unusual glimmer of pleasure at how excited these celebrities were to taste her creations.

The music was throbbing out of the speakers, the lights low and the champagne fountain in the corner was doubling as an excuse to toast the bride and bride. Molly hid her shock at the high number of Butlerettes in the Buff wearing nothing but tiny French maid-style aprons while they served drinks from trays. The party atmosphere was heating up in the room. A discreet knock on the door announced the arrival of a stunning woman in a black silk cape, looking as though she had swept in from the set of a Broadway musical. Molly busied herself putting the final touches to the buffet and tried not to stare as the hens made a huge fuss of her. As the lights dimmed, the music changed, and a single spotlight shone down on the woman in the cape, who began an intoxicating slow dance for her captivated audience. The rumbling beat of the song was mesmerising, the atmosphere suddenly charged with sexual anticipation. Molly had never seen anything like it. Burlesque was very sensual and arty to her eyes. She tried not to stare at two of the women kissing in the shadows while the show went on. She gulped as the lady taking centre stage, with striking red hair, batted her thick eyelashes at them and sauntered over to trail a large black feather down the hen's cheek and across her cleavage. Then, while the tune thumped out its slow beat, the redhead reached out a gloved hand to tease at the hen's corset before unhooking one of the buttons to free a single pert breast. She brushed the nipple with the feather, teasing it to a peak, before winking at the hen with a heavily made-up eye. The ladies were whooping and cheering, and the hen became instantly flustered. The mood in the room was electric.

While the redhead was dancing seductively round

the dimly lit room, Molly didn't know where to look as women paired off to openly enjoy each other, licking, teasing, caught up in the heat of the show, easing one another back onto the sumptuous cushions of the giant, richly coloured sofas dotting the room. Above the pulsating harmony, Molly heard murmurs and kissing noises, the popping of suspender snappers and the low hum of sex toys being administered. As she kept her eyes trained on the buffet in front of her, her libido fluttered unexpectedly into life, creating a tingling sensation to flow through her body. She couldn't remember the last time she'd felt like this. Well, she could. It was three years, two weeks and four cosmopolitans at a Christmas party ago. Not that she was keeping track.

Molly popped a canapé in her mouth as a quick quality check – it was absolutely scrumptious – and decided it was time to leave. She was brilliant at what she did for a living, but she had a restaurant to save, and now an errant libido to dampen. And that was when she saw it. Hidden behind the stage area, curtained off, an Arabian-style tent had been erected, made of silk veils, with giant embroidered cushions scattered around, and there, right next to the tent, was a giant life-size model of a camel. It was too good an opportunity to miss. It was almost as though her friend was pulling heavenly strings from above. *Ride a camel dressed in a costume.*

When else would she get the opportunity to ride a camel while dressed in a costume? Molly checked that no one was watching her and grabbed a chair, ready to take a selfie of herself. She clambered from the chair onto the model camel, wedged herself between the two humps and took a photo. The first of the impossible boxes ticked! Her heart soared in triumph as she completed the mission. And although it seemed very likely a certain degree of pride would have to be swallowed with each task, she had a strong urge as to what the next one should be as she attempted to slide down.

Nobody ever tells you this, but once your suspender belt gets caught on a camel's hump, they are notoriously difficult to unsnag. Molly clung to the camel's neck, one leg almost on the floor, the other hooked over its hump. She'd never done the vertical splits in her life, and now she understood why. She let out a quiet whimper.

'What are you doing? Get down from there!' bellowed someone with a sharp, angry, Italian accent.

Molly twisted round to see the redhead performer standing a few feet away with her hands on her hips. 'Don't you know that was shipped in from Hollywood

Studios? It's from the set of *Lawrence of Arabia*. It's a surprise gift from the bride's father who starred in it!' She marched over and reached out to unclip Molly's stocking. 'Show some respect.'

'No, don't!' yelled Molly. She had nothing to grab onto for balance but the camel. Ignoring her, the redhead popped open the fastening. Molly's weight immediately threw the camel off balance. As she tumbled backwards, she grabbed onto the nearest thing to her – the curtain.

An almighty ripping sound announced the poor workmanship of the flimsy frame and its curtain rings. Molly and the camel thudded to the floor in a heap, followed by a collective shriek of alarm from the hens.

Molly clambered to her feet, shrugging off the heavy curtain. She shook the hair from her face and straightened up. 'Sorry about that,' she told her captive audience, whose horrified eyes were drawn to the four stumps that used to be the camel's legs. Keela's reminder not to touch the priceless antique behind the curtain suddenly swimming in her ears, Molly looked down at the poor camel, snapped off at the knees, its humps no longer majestic looking.

The redhead shook her head, aghast. 'Ah, you're British.' There was no mistaking the level of disappointment in the tone. 'That explains it.' She jabbed at her phone, perhaps to alert Interpol or Hollywood Studios or her team of animal rights activists over the shameful dromedary desecration. 'Is that a phone in your stocking? You will get into a lot of trouble for this. A lot of trouble. Who are you? What's your name?'

Molly panicked. 'I'm no one. I'll sort it. I'll tell reception. I'll hand myself in.'

With the party atmosphere ruined beyond repair and the redhead screaming after her, Molly picked her way out of the debris, apologising profusely to confused couples, many of whom had their heads jammed between a pair of thighs, and bolted from the room. She took a beat outside to gather her thoughts. Molly could not afford to be sacked or slapped with a huge bill. That bloody bucket list. She needed to flee this place. Adrenaline coursed through her veins as she ran along the corridor with her trolley and turned the corner in this maze-like building. She had accomplished one of the most difficult challenges. And while it was by no means a positive experience, a flicker of hope ignited in her chest. Maybe this list was not going to be so impossible to achieve after all. A thought formed in her brain. Before she fled the Cigar Lounge, did she have it in her to attempt one more? Searing flashbacks of the handsome stranger invaded her thoughts.

Molly wanted to find him. Maybe he was still at the party. She'd have to hide from the staff and the hens and any security guards who no doubt would be looking for her. Perhaps it would be too difficult. Although, seeing that almost all the women in this place were wearing burlesque-style outfits, it might not be completely impossible to blend in with the crowd. When she was sure she wasn't being followed, she leaned against the wall for support, closing her eyes to take stock. Was he thinking about her the way she was thinking about him? Just as she was contemplating the wisdom of acting on this impulse, she heard the lift door ping, and as though she'd manifested him to make the decision for her, Levi appeared, walking in her direction.

His eyes travelled the length of her stockinged legs, hovering over her cleavage before raking slowly upwards. She was almost swimming with desire; it was dizzying. Any brief fantasy she'd allowed herself did not compare to the real thing standing in front of her.

'Didn't I see you earlier at the burlesque party?' A half-smile hovered on his lips. 'You're not following me, are you?'

Oh dear. He was a real triple threat. He was clearly an American and yet there was a hint of French to his accent. Then there was the small matter of his being a billionaire. If he declared that he liked nothing better than to snuggle up in front of the fire with his pet pooch and a good book, she'd be in real trouble.

Molly tried to pull her thoughts together. Here was her chance. He was exactly what she needed. Never in a million years did she think she would be capable of such a thing, and yet she was gazing into his dreamy chocolate-brown eyes, thinking there was nothing she'd like more than to get him into a hot tub.

He gazed back as though she was bewitching him. 'Are you staying here at the Cigar Lounge?' he asked when she failed to answer.

Molly looked up at him through her thick lashes, Keela's warning about not flirting with the uber-rich guests fresh in her ears.

'No. Not really, no.'

His interest was growing by the second. 'Not really?'

'I mean no. No, I'm not.' Molly teased a curl of hair round her finger. 'Are *you*... staying here?' She couldn't have dragged the sentence out any longer. And why was she making it sound like a proposition? Her hand went to her hip, and she stood as though on the corner of a red-light district, leaning a shoulder towards him. *This is probably how they do it in Amsterdam*, she thought briefly. She continued to curl a strand of hair. Disturbingly, she was taking to it like a duck to water.

'Yes. I stay here a lot.' His eyes were as dark and twinkling as the night sky. 'Where are you going?'

Everything about him drew her in. It was as though she no longer had use of even a single functioning brain cell. 'I'm not sure.'

She made an elaborate attempt to bite her lip seductively. It appeared not to work. 'Are you lost?' he asked.

How could she admit to desperately needing to escape the scene of a crime?

Levi squinted, his eyes roaming hers. 'I haven't seen you before. Is this your first time as a guest here?'

Not ready to correct him, she attempted to explain her hasty departure from the room without sounding too guilty. 'I was at a party,' she said quietly. 'But things got a bit, erm, intense.'

'Intense?'

How awkward. Molly blinked, heat rising from her neck.

'And you can't go back in?'

Molly shook her head. 'No because...' *Because it is*

full of angry lesbians who hate me for kneecapping their famous camel and spoiling their sexy show. '...because they've started to get intimate... licking each other's... well, it doesn't matter what they are licking, but I'd hate to interrupt. In fact, I really need to get going.'

'Did you say *licking* each other?'

Did she? Did she say licking? What was wrong with her?

'Yes.' Images swam in her mind. 'Like ice creams.'

It felt very playgroundy, like she was telling tales.

Levi took a beat before his face creased with laughter. It took him a few moments before he composed himself. 'Sorry,' he said, quick to apologise. 'So is the plan to wait out here until they've finished?' He took a deep breath in, his eyes sparkling with amusement.

She could barely look him in the eye. It was late, and Molly was shocked to imagine him licking *her* like an ice cream. She blinked the image away. 'No. I just got the wrong room, that's all. It was the wrong party.'

'Which room did you mean to go in?' he asked, loosening his already loose bow-tie. Her eyes were drawn to the perfectly neat fit of his shirt across the chest. His voice sounded husky and warm. It was playing havoc with her ability to tell the truth.

'That room there.' She pointed to a random door further along the corridor.

'Really?'

Molly needed to come up with a way to seduce him quick, so that perhaps he'd ask her back to his hot tub.

'What a coincidence.' Levi raised his eyebrows and swept his arm down the corridor. 'I was on my way there too. We'll go together.'

Shit.

Molly walked beside him trying to think up a billion excuses as to why they shouldn't go into that room and why they both should in fact go back to his room, away from angry lesbians and away from further trouble. The door loomed ever closer. What if she ruined another perfectly good orgy?

No excuses sprang to mind during the thirty-second walk.

Levi tightened his bow-tie and straightened his tux jacket, tugging at the sleeves, before he flung the door open. Molly was surprised to see that a wedding party was in full swing. The soundproofing in this place was out of this world. A nuclear device could go off and you wouldn't hear a thing. All the guests were in glamorous glittering evening gowns. Molly stood out like a sore thumb in her burlesque costume, and their entrance caused an immediate stir. People eyed them both with interest.

'Well, you seem popular,' Levi murmured in her ear. 'Do they all know you?'

Panic came at her like a charging rhino. A light film of sweat formed on her upper lip. She was simply a chef gone rogue and not used to all this. She flapped her hands around, trying to deflect attention. 'Goodness. Why is it so hot in here?'

Levi put a hand to her elbow and guided her to a less crowded spot. 'Better?'

They were at a wedding! She slid her clammy hands over her corset. She needed to somehow brazen it out and persuade him to invite her back to his room. 'So, are you here for the bride or groom?'

He gave her an amused look. 'Groom. You?'

Why was he so handsome? It really wasn't helping.

Molly smoothed her hair to calm her nerves. 'Erm, the bride.'

What was she doing? She'd have no idea who the bride would be. Suddenly, she caught sight of a huge wedding cake and the names Bev and Wyn on a swirling cake topper.

Which one was the bride?

'Actually, I'm a friend of both Bev's and Wyn's.' She

was rambling. Words spilling unfiltered from her lips. 'Lovely couple. Lovely. So young and in love.'

Molly glanced around the room. The average age was at least eighty.

Levi tried to stop himself from laughing. 'Seriously?'

'I meant young at heart.' There was no way she could go through with this. Stupid bucket list. She was going to have to abandon this mission before things got too out of hand. A lump formed in her throat. 'Actually, I forgot my... erm, my gift for them. That's it. I'll go back and get my gift.' Molly prayed that Levi wouldn't ask where she was going back to. Or what the gift was. All this lying had her nerves in shreds. 'Perhaps we could meet up tomorrow? If you're not too busy skiing or partying or...' *Attending orgies for posh people?*

Molly stopped talking as two elderly gentlemen approached. They shook hands with Levi and welcomed him. 'Is this your date?' one asked. 'Hello, dear. Don't you look divine? Simply ravishing.' He gave a small bow, maintaining eye contact with Levi. 'But then, you've always had exquisite taste.'

Molly's blood pressure skyrocketed. Pretending to be a guest at a wedding wasn't as easy as it sounded. If only she could ask which of their grandchildren was getting married without Levi hearing.

Levi's eyes were sparkling as he turned to her. 'I presume you've met the two *grooms*, Bev and Wyn?'

The words left Levi's mouth but took an eternity to reach Molly's ears and settle in her brain. From the amused way he was regarding her, he knew she didn't have a clue who they were. The cat was out of the bag. Luckily, a survival instinct kicked in from out of nowhere as the third challenge on the bucket list sprang immediately to mind. *Crash a wedding and give an uplifting toast.*

'I've come to give your toast,' she said shamelessly. 'As a surprise.' Keeping her voice steady, she continued the lie. 'This lot hired me.' She thumbed to the crowd of people dancing. Before Bev and Wyn could reply, Molly spotted a microphone by a small stage area and darted towards it. A DJ was playing hits from the 1950s. His eyes nearly popped from his head as he took in her costume. She hurried towards him and reached out to grab the microphone, held it up and tapped on it. Feedback squealed everyone into silence.

'Can we pause the music, please? Just for a moment.' Molly had no idea what she was doing. Perhaps some evil spirit had taken possession of her body. 'Let's all stand to toast the happy couple.' Molly spotted a couple of wheelchair users. 'Sorry, not you two. You don't have to stand.' She spotted a whole table of disgruntled geriatrics, huffing and puffing as they struggled to scrape back chairs. 'In fact, let's *not* stand if you're not already standing, and *stay* standing if you can manage it. Or seated if you prefer.'

It wasn't rocket science but somehow she'd managed to cause confusion. Half of the dance floor had emptied, scrambling to grab the nearest seat. Levi was looking on with a puzzled frown.

Molly cleared her throat. 'The main thing is we're all here to celebrate this wonderful union.'

'Will the dance take long?' a frail voice called out. 'You're not going to take off *all* of your clothes, are you? I've recently had a pacemaker fitted, you see.'

'And I'm on beta blockers for my blood pressure,' another guest cautioned.

Molly felt every pair of eyes on her. She smoothed down the tiny ruffles of her skirt, pulling at them to see if she could make the outfit a little less revealing. She really couldn't. This miniscule costume wasn't doing her any favours.

'I'm not here to dance.' She grabbed a flute of champagne from the tray of a passing waiter. 'Besides, I'm strapped in pretty tight. This thing won't come off without a fight.' Why did she get a sudden urge to look at Levi while she said that? Why? 'Can we all raise our glasses to the happy couple, Bev and Wyn? May they enjoy a long and healthy life together...'

A ripple of sniggers ran round the room. It was then that Molly noticed Wyn's walking frame, and that Bev was attached to an oxygen tank on little wheels. She wished the ground would open up and swallow her whole.

'To Bev and Wyn. To everlasting love. Or however long you have together.' Molly felt herself falling down a rabbit hole. She tried to recall the affirmations from Ava's journal. 'We have to live in the moment, don't we? I mean, you never know what's around the corner.'

Was her corset getting tighter?

No. It was the air. It was hot in here. Hot and stuffy. She wiped the back of her hand against her brow.

The crowd stared at her as though waiting for her to make sense, perhaps hoping for a few pearls of marital wisdom.

'We just have to take each day as it comes and be thankful. You just don't know when your time will be up.' Molly exhaled gloomily into the microphone. 'Life can be so short.' She should know. Just take poor Ava. 'Very, very short.'

Eerie silence.

She felt herself spiralling and began rapidly fanning her face. 'To the grooms, everyone. You only live once, but if you do it right, once is enough, as someone famous once said.' Molly cast her eyes around at the forlorn and slightly confused-looking crowd and swept a hand towards a worried Bev and Wyn. 'Here's to only living once!' Grateful that everyone clinked glasses, Molly quickly whipped out her phone to take a selfie before giving the microphone to the DJ, who started the music back up. Slipping her phone back into her stocking top, she rushed towards the door. At least that was another challenge completed. But she was going to have a stroke at this rate.

'Going somewhere?'

It was Levi.

'Yes. I'm leaving. My work here is done.'

'Work? You're a professional at this?' He was trying not to snigger. 'I should have guessed. That was quite the speech. Very powerful. Intensely thought provoking. You almost had me reevaluating my life.'

Molly relaxed. 'It was a... I did it for a friend. So you can cut the sarcasm.' She would have to give up on the idea of persuading him to get naked with her. She was not coming across at all well. She needed to lie down somewhere cool and dark and re-examine her values. She had finally hit rock bottom. 'I guess I should be getting back now. Down to the main square.'

'Ah. I'm afraid the gondolas back to the square have been stopped due to the snowstorm. It might be best if you wait here. Explain to me in a bit more detail about this only-living-once theory you have. It's triggered something of an existential dilemma for me.' Levi seemed to have enjoyed her display of buffoonery a little too much. 'In fact, here come Bev and Wyn now. They're probably keen to know who gifted them such an inspirational toast.'

She would rather have poked her own eyes out than stayed here to face the poor grooms whose wedding she had crashed. Plus, the longer she spent in Levi's company, the quicker she'd blurt out that she wasn't a wedding guest or any other sort of guest, that she was technically an employee, and not a very good one at that, and she had a perfectly serviceable snowmobile waiting downstairs, outside the kitchen door. 'That's okay. I'll find a way back.'

'Wait. I was only...' she heard him call.

She darted quickly from the room, resisting the urge to glance over her shoulder at Levi as she closed the door behind her. What had she been thinking? She scurried down the corridor before stopping to lean against the wall. Hanging her head, she rubbed her forehead, closing her eyes against the sting of tiredness. Her entire body ached. She needed to take off this ridiculously tiny costume and these towering, spindly heels and go straight to bed.

Her eyes snapped open at the sound of some extremely loud, raucous voices.

'Well, what have we here, gentlemen?'

Molly took in four very large, very drunk, very leery men sauntering down the corridor towards her and froze in panic.

4

A STEAMING PILE OF REGRETS

Molly's heart was pounding in her chest as she fought to stay calm. She scanned the corridor. No other people were around. The group of men was advancing slowly, all of them clearly inebriated, wolf-whistling loudly and making their desire to see her perform some sort of X-rated routine, especially for them, *very* obvious. She could either bolt towards the lift, hoping they didn't reach her before it came, or she could run back to the wedding and pray that she'd reach the door before they did.

Precious seconds ticked by while she tried to get her frozen body to move in time with her thoughts. Ava had always been the one who dealt with difficult and rowdy customers. And while Molly appreciated she needed to get better at confrontation, tonight was not the night to try. Just as she decided to race back towards the room, the door swung open.

Levi emerged, his head swivelling between the group of men and Molly, clocking the situation. With a thunderous look on his face, he barked out a command. 'Leave her alone or I'll have you all thrown out. Show some respect, you drunken imbeciles.'

The men stopped. They seemed to recognise him instantly, and they scurried away in a babble of apologies, leaving Molly and Levi facing one another. She was relieved beyond measure that he'd come out when he did. Perhaps he was a well-known billionaire politician? Or on the television?

'Thank you.' Molly's mouth felt suddenly dry.

'Are you okay?' He stood in front of her, his face concerned. His voice soft.

Molly blew out her cheeks. 'Yes.'

'Some guys can be real jerks. Especially on a night like this. No one is quite themselves. Can I escort you somewhere? Are you here with friends?'

Molly didn't know what to say.

'Or were you just here to crash a wedding as part of a dare?'

Terribly handsome *and* terribly astute. Such a lethal combination.

Molly decided not to dignify his accurate assumption with an answer. 'That's very kind. But it's late, and I'm sure I'll find my way back to my... *hotel* room somehow.'

She shivered even though her cheeks were on fire. She really hadn't thought this through. Weaving a web of lies was utterly exhausting.

'Are you cold?'

'Yes.'

See? She was still lying. What was the matter with her? The place had to be about fifty degrees. It was as hot as a furnace.

Levi whipped off his jacket, placing it gently around her shoulders before stepping back to give her some space. 'Maybe it's the shock.'

Her neck tingled where he'd grazed it with his knuckles. 'Maybe.' She caught his manly scent. A stark contrast to the perfume-filled room she'd left earlier. Something weird was happening. Molly had never felt this drawn to a man before. At a loss for what to say, she stood staring at him.

He stepped towards her.

She stepped towards him.

They were an inch apart. She had never wanted to kiss a man so badly. Levi's eyes roamed her face before dropping to her mouth.

'Is it me or is the universe drawing us together this evening?' His voice was enticingly soft and low.

If she was entirely honest, Molly wouldn't have been surprised if it was Ava, incessantly trying to matchmake from beyond the grave. Ava with her many failed attempts to fix Molly up on dates.

From the way he was looking at her, Levi was interested. Very interested.

Molly's morals got the better of her. Yes, he was handsome. Yes, he was a billionaire. Yes, the opportunity to persuade him, or someone like him, to take off all their clothes and drink champagne with her in a hot tub overlooking the Alps might never come around again in her lifetime. But something held her back. He seemed like a decent man. She did not want to deceive him. Besides, he had just come to her rescue. She owed him.

A clicking sound jolted her out of the trance. A few feet away, the burlesque entertainer closed the door to the hen party quietly, swept her pillar-box red hair into the hood of her black silk cape and lifted her smiling gaze to Levi. He stepped away from Molly as though she was on fire. He fiddled with his bow-tie, clearly embarrassed.

'Nice to see you again... Angelo, mi amore,' she said lazily in what sounded very much like a fake

Italian accent, now Molly was hearing it for a second time. The woman flicked her uninterested eyes to Molly and back to Levi. When he didn't respond, she did a double take, screwing her eyes at Molly. 'Wait. It's you, isn't it? Aren't you the one who broke the famous camel?'

Mortified, Molly tried to deny it. 'No. Absolutely not.'

'Yes, it was you.' The redhead put her hands to her hips. 'That was a priceless antique. Over a hundred years old. It came all the way from the film studio in America.'

Molly's neck prickled. 'It was a health and safety hazard. I was testing it.'

As though that was any better.

The redhead tutted loudly, turning to Levi presumably for some sort of agreement. 'She should be sued! Wilful criminal damage.'

Shitting hell. There was nothing like being made a fool of in front of France's most handsome man to make you want to fill your pockets full of rocks and walk into the nearest lake. Luckily for Molly there were no lakes within a hundred-mile radius.

Instead, Levi gave Molly a mischievous grin. 'You have had an eventful night, haven't you? I'm sure my team of lawyers can reach some sort of amicable agreement.' He nodded curtly to the redhead. 'Leave it with me. I'll sort it.'

'Fine. Call me,' the redhead demanded brusquely in a sulky voice, flapping her silky cape with annoyance.

Molly was pleased Levi did not reply. He gave her a cursory nod, and they watched her saunter away. A proper saunter, Molly was disheartened to see. She took in a deep breath to regain her composure. 'A friend of yours?'

She noticed Levi's cheeks redden slightly. He cleared his throat. 'No. She works here. Occasionally.'

'Well, it's very nice to meet you, *Angelo*.'

Intrigued, Molly wondered why he didn't correct her. More to the point, Levi obviously did break the rules from time to time. Perhaps he was not so *angelic* after all. She held his gaze. The energy between them was obvious. It was causing a major about-turn. If he was withholding his true identity, should she do the same?

They stood gazing at each other.

'Would you like to get a drink? Shelter from the storm together?'

Molly held her breath as she contemplated what was being asked. The sentence was loaded with sexual tension, its meaning unmistakably clear. And it was a few moments before Molly realised that she was the one who had spoken. They were her words, not his. *She* was propositioning *him*, not the other way round.

Levi visibly swallowed. 'Like I mentioned earlier, I have a room here. We could *shelter* there.'

Shel-ter:

(noun) A place or sanctuary to provide protection (against further interruptions)

(verb) To find temporary refuge (in a bubbling hot tub quaffing champagne)

Besides, it was the *way* he said it, thick with a sexual undercurrent. At least, that was what she was telling herself. Molly stepped towards him and reached out to press a gloved hand lightly on his chest. She looked up at him through her lashes. 'Let's go.'

Levi took her hand, and they walked quickly to the lift in silence. The moment the doors opened, Molly was in such a state of excitement that she pressed against him as he jabbed the button, both of them wide-eyed and slightly panting. She had never felt so alive.

When the door closed, she looped her arms around his neck. He reached down to trail his fingers up her stockings, inhaling sharply as they connected with the smooth, silky flesh of her thighs. He let out a low groan as though he was incapable of stopping. The sensation caused pangs of lust to shoot straight to her nether region.

Molly's eyes were drawn to his lips. 'Kiss me.' He was having a catastrophic effect on her, and as he dipped his head, she launched at him, hungry for his kisses, desperate with desire.

He hoicked her leg up to his hip, holding it in place while he kissed her neck, her throat, her lips. He tangled his hand lightly in her hair, gently pressing her against the wall of the lift so that their limbs entwined. Running her hands up and down his back, she spread her fingers out wide to cup his rock-hard buttocks. She brought him closer, causing him to moan against her mouth. She felt him harden through the soft fabric of his expensive tuxedo as their kiss deepened. She liked the effect she was having on him. It made her feel powerful and sexual. He seemed to want her as much as she wanted him.

'Who are you?' he whispered, sounding unravelled to his core.

At this point, it was anyone's guess. She barely recognised herself. 'Does it matter?' she answered breathily. Had he not heard of a holiday fling? A crazy, regrettable one-night stand?

Levi stopped briefly to murmur in her ear, 'Yeah, it kinda does.'

'Milly,' she moaned as his lips trailed kisses down her neck and across her collarbone. He was reducing her brain to mush. 'My name's Milly. No. I mean Molly. Christ Almighty. My name's Molly.'

'You sure about that?' He chuckled. It was the sexiest sound she'd ever heard.

Now really wasn't a good time for a quiz. Especially if she couldn't answer the basics.

Levi clamped a hand to her breast, letting out a small desirous moan as he rolled his thumb over the corset, laced tightly, keeping everything in place. 'What do you do, Molly?'

Besides crashing weddings, humping camels and throwing myself at handsome strangers?

'I'm a chef,' she managed to say, her breathing ragged. His hand slid tantalisingly down to her waist, causing her to shiver from top to toe. 'I run my own...' Her entire body tingled. '...catering...' She was on fire. '...company.'

Not technically a lie, just because the assets were currently frozen and it was on the verge of fiscal collapse.

'And you?' she purred, weak with longing. This had to be the slowest lift ride in history. His image was reflecting off all the mirrors. From any angle, he was breathtakingly gorgeous in a kind of striking playboy yet ruggedly down-to-earth way. 'What do *you* do, Angelo?'

Between counting your billions every day and fighting off sexual advances from every woman on the planet, life must be so exhausting.

He stopped mid-kiss, a question in his eye. It was almost a challenge. 'You don't know who I am?'

'No.' She stared back. 'Should I?'

Her question hung in the air. Now Levi was the one struggling to find the right words and looking flushed.

PING. They sprang apart as the lift doors opened.

'Oh, there you are...' Keela stopped talking. Her eyes flickered briefly to Molly, expertly devoid of any surprise. She trained her eyes on Levi. 'I was just about to bring these to you, Monsieur LeRoux. The hors d'oeuvres you ordered, sir.'

Stepping out of the lift, Levi took the tray from her. He seemed uncomfortable. 'Thank you, Keela. I'll take them to my room.'

'Enjoy. Have a lovely evening.' As though purposefully not making eye contact with Molly, Keela flew back down the corridor towards the kitchen.

Levi waited until Keela had disappeared before

facing Molly. 'I'm sorry. I should not have lost control like that.' He was clearly flustered, as though being caught by Keela had brought him to his senses with a sharp slap.

Molly understood. She felt completely out of control herself. What was she doing? Surely she'd be sacked once Levi found out who she was. Keela was bound to tell him eventually. Molly put a hand to her chest. 'It's fine. I understand. We were both caught up in a moment of madness.'

They took a beat to regain their composure.

'Exactly. Forgive me, Molly.'

'Nothing to forgive, *Angelo*.'

She gave him a moment to come clean as their eyes met.

He didn't.

With the atmosphere becoming increasingly awkward, they hovered in the corridor. Levi could be anyone. He might even have shares in the place for all she knew. Plus, there was the small matter of the angry redhead determined to sue her into the ground. Molly decided to leave before she caused any more trouble. Even in a treacherous storm, the snowmobile seemed the better option. 'So, anyway, thanks for the kind offer but it's probably best if I just go and wait in the bar.'

'Probably.'

He was clearly having a change of heart about her going back to his room anyway. Molly went to take off his jacket.

'No. Keep it. That bar might be full of...' Levi stopped talking.

'It's fine. I'm sure I'll be able to handle a few drunks. Besides, I'll probably wait in the kitchen.' Molly looked down at her skimpy outfit. She would immediately go and change into her comfortably padded, libido-crushing snowsuit and moon boots.

'Kitchen?'

'No, not the kitchen. I mean the guest waiting area. Where guests usually wait. For the gondola.'

He fumbled in his pocket for his room key, balancing the tray Keela had given him in the other. 'This is silly. Why don't you at least hang in my room until the gondola is back up and running? The engineers couldn't even make it up here on their snowmobiles.'

The storm was too bad for snowmobiles? 'How long do you think it'll take?' Molly had depressing visions of herself sleeping standing up in the kitchen, propped against the freezer cabinets.

'A while. It's a bad one.' Levi opened the door to his suite for her. 'I'm sure we can behave like civilised

adults while we wait for the storm to pass,' he joked
weakly.

Molly took a moment to appreciate the ridiculous-
ness of what he'd just said. They had barely survived a
thirty-second lift ride without wanting to act on
impulse.

'You're right. I'm sure we *can* behave like civilised
adults.' She had doubts even as she was saying it. It
would take just shy of a horse tranquiliser to calm her
thumping heart. She was all but dressed for a night of
wild sex, and he was a raging pile of pheromones. Her
eyes wandered the length of him. One twang of her
garter and he'd be salivating.

With her mind in a whirl, she walked through the
doorway into a luxurious living room. She took in her
surroundings. Three giant sofas with tasteful cushions
surrounded the flickering fire. The immaculate
wooden décor accentuated the stone walls. Candles
burned discreetly on all surfaces, the smell of jasmine
and bergamot filling the air as though she had
stepped into a luxurious spa. 'This place is amazing.'

'Please make yourself comfortable,' Levi said in a
formal tone as he placed the tray down on the coffee
table.

Molly waited to see which of the giant sofas he

would sit on and was disappointed when he chose to remain standing. She perched on the nearest sofa.

'I'll ring reception for an update.' He spoke on the phone in fluent French, which she immediately found horny and distracting, but she managed to catch the gist of what was being said.

Levi clicked off the call impatiently. 'Sorry. Looks like you'll have a bit of a long wait. They still need to clear the cables and do a test run. Even the helipad is out of action.'

Thank goodness for her fear of rotating blades. She'd rather stay stranded at the Cigar Lounge in her bone-crushingly tight corset than face getting airlifted out by helicopter.

She shook her head vaguely as Levi paced around the room sounding like he'd come straight from the Met Office. 'Storms of this severity don't usually happen too often, thankfully. Something to do with a low-pressure system sweeping in from the Atlantic.'

The romantic atmosphere was waning dramatically as they engaged in what was arguably the most stilted and self-conscious exchange between two people desperately trying to pretend they hadn't just had their tongues down each other's throats.

'I know what you mean. The snow.' She pointed

outside. 'There's way too much of it.' Honestly. Where were her words? The longer, sophisticated words?

He stopped pacing and faced her with a bemused expression. 'And snow wasn't something you expected to see holidaying in a ski resort at this altitude? At this time of year?'

Molly wondered whether this undercurrent of sarcasm was strictly necessary, but she could barely look him in the face, he was so ridiculously good-looking. She needed to stop acting as though she had a schoolgirl crush. 'I can think of worse places to be trapped during a storm. Not that I'm trapped here. Obviously not. Great view.' She was babbling. Her thought processes were all over the place under the pressure to show him she was a rational and civilised adult. Without sex on the brain. *Three whole years!*

Levi followed her gaze to the window. Apart from snow pounding unnervingly against the glass, it was pitch-black outside. All she could see was her own reflection staring manically back.

'I mean, probably. It's *probably* a great view. Through that *great* window that you have. It's... it's a great size. For viewing through.' Her words petered out as she anxiously smoothed down her hair, aware that she was hardly going to win any literary prizes any time soon.

He seemed to take that as a sign to point out the obvious. 'Oddly, I always find the view is better during daylight hours.' His eyes crinkled slightly. 'What with you being a member here, I'd have thought you were familiar with it. You are an *actual* member here, aren't you?'

She made what could only be described as a yipping sound. *Must lying be quite so stressful?* Her corset suddenly felt too tight. She tried pulling it up, managing only to jiggle her breasts at him, causing him to politely look away. She pulled his jacket around her. She had just yipped at him like an injured chihuahua. She had no idea what was going through his mind, other than he must be starting to have deep and undeniably justified reservations about her being in his room. Common sense was poking at her brain. If she was going to be trapped here with this Greek god for the next couple of hours, she may as well try and complete the most difficult of all the bucket list challenges while she waited.

When she didn't answer, Levi walked over to the coffee table, where an ice bucket with champagne and several crystal flutes stood. 'Drink?'

'Please.' She watched him expertly open the champagne, deftly pour two glasses and hand her one. He then proceeded to knock his back and repour it. She wondered if she was making him nervous.

'These look amazing.' Molly pointed to the platter of her creations that he'd placed next to the ice bucket.

'You mentioned that you're a chef. How is your knowledge of fusion gastronomy?' Levi seemed grateful to grasp at any conversational bone thrown his way.

'Uh-huh. I cook. I create things. I bake. I invent new recipes. In the company that I own. That I run. By myself.'

Please shut up and answer the question.

Levi leaned over and popped one of her canapés in his mouth. 'Help yourself. They're quite nice.'

Molly felt a pang of pride as his eyes widened with appreciation, but ideally, like any chef worth their salt, she always hoped for far better than *quite nice*. The man might be drop-dead gorgeous, but he clearly had something wrong with his tastebuds. It was almost a relief to realise he might not be so incredibly perfect after all.

'As you're a chef, I'd value your opinion. These little things have been causing quite a stir.' He swooped another one up, inspected it for less than a nanosecond and threw it down his throat. It scarcely had time to touch the sides.

Little things? Obviously, he had no inkling of how to correctly ingest molecular gastronomy or the effort that went into each and every single creation. Did he think the delicate compositions, the viscosity, the chemical reactions were a happy accident? Thrown randomly together by some lazy butt-crack of a chef?

Molly blew out a deep breath. This was very much an opportunity for her to come clean and admit she had made them herself. She could teach him a thing or two about culinary appreciation, but she took one look at his stubbled jawline and thick eyelashes and decided against it. Surely men this attractive shouldn't be expected to keep abreast of everything, she reasoned. 'Are you in the catering business yourself?'

She watched as he picked up a remote control and increased the flames in the stone fireplace. They roared to life, instantly restoring the romantic vibe. 'Not exactly, no, but I'd usually consider acquiring any company that draws people in with a novelty like these have. They're supposed to be aphrodisiacs. Very clever. They've gone viral around Val D'Amore. This place is full of randy sods who will pay extortionate amounts for anything that gets them laid.'

What?

Molly needed a second to think. Apart from wrongly calling her life's work a *novelty* and pacing up and down like he was in a lecture theatre, did he just say he might want to buy her company?

5

WARNING: HOT MESS INCOMING

'Is that what you do? Buy up small businesses?' Molly asked, trying to keep her voice calm. An actual billionaire was interested in buying her company. How could that even be possible? Yes, she'd been slaving away in the resort's main hotel kitchen for weeks. Yes, she'd had orders up to the eyeballs, day and night, with hotel guests ringing up to request party platters and bottles of fizz as though she was doing Deliveroo. But surely that wasn't enough.

Levi shrugged. 'Sometimes. Although I hear the company responsible for these tasty bites is a local restaurant, which is unusual.'

Tasty bites?

'Better still, my sources tell me that the restaurant

owner is currently working in the main hotel kitchen herself, which is even more dubious. Makes me wonder if the business is in trouble if she's taking on more work to keep financially afloat. She'll be getting a basic wage while they charge a fortune for something that she's making. She clearly has no idea how to run a business. Now *that's* a good time to buy someone out. Anyway.' He leaned over once more and threw a couple more canapés down his throat. 'Tell me more about you.'

Stunned silence.

He had basically called her an idiot.

Molly was flabbergasted at the rudeness.

He obviously had no idea it was her, but still. Molly did not care for his rather disturbingly accurate depiction of the financial ruin her culinary business was currently teetering on the brink of. The business that wouldn't even belong to her if she didn't get that bucket list done.

She took a deep calming breath. She would play along. She took off his jacket, folding it carefully. 'What's unusual about a restaurant owner taking on outside contracts? Lots of restaurants do it. Perhaps her coworker signed an agreement without her knowing about it?'

Levi shrugged. 'Doubt it.'

'Or maybe she just felt like getting out from be-hind her desk and getting her hands dirty for a change? Connecting with real people. Finding out what they want. Discreetly checking out the competition perhaps.'

'Highly unlikely. Would you work all day in a restaurant and then all night in a hotel kitchen? There will be more to it than that, I guarantee. I've been in business a long time.'

He was depressingly close to the bone.

'Or maybe she's just supremely talented and wanted to show off what she can do?' Molly tried to sound matter of fact. 'I mean, look at the craftsman-ship. These are among the best appetisers you'll find anywhere.'

'I'll look into their finances. They'll be struggling. Poor business decisions probably, or bad manage-ment, because you're right, there's certainly nothing wrong with the product.'

She watched him toss another highly innovative, cutting-edge masterpiece of scientific food technology down his throat as though it was a dry-roasted peanut. She would have to rise above it. 'As mentioned, I'm an expert in the food industry.' She shifted her weight. It was time to change the subject. 'What industry did you say you're in?'

'This and that.'

'Sounds awfully vague,' she said, handing the jacket back to him.

He took it from her, causing her to quiver as his fingers grazed hers. 'It *is* awfully vague.' A grin tugged at the corner of his mouth as he casually flung the haute couture jacket over onto the opposite sofa before turning his gaze back to her.

Molly wondered whether he could feel the energy crackling between them, but Levi was giving nothing away. He pointed to the floor-to-ceiling window, the snow still thwacking against the glass in waves. 'I might as well pick your food industry brains while we wait for the storm to die down.' He seemed slightly on edge, clutching for something to say. Perhaps he was politely switching to business mode to ensure they didn't try to rip each other's clothes off with their teeth. 'Okay. Talk me through these. They look well thrown together.'

Thrown together? Molly nearly choked. Ava had once compared Molly's ability to take an age over every precise detail to that of a bomb disposal expert. Molly took a glug of the fizzy liquid. The hit was instant. Before tonight, she hadn't touched a drop of alcohol since the day Ava died. Christmas Day. Of all the days. Molly felt her chest tighten as, for the billionth time, the guilt at being 'alive' seeped through to her bones.

'Are you okay?' Levi asked, concern in his voice.

Molly shook the heaviness from her mind. It was never going to go away. She just had to find a way to live with it. Or she could fill her life with distractions. Like the one right in front of her, currently making her stomach flutter.

'Is it the champagne?'

Molly blinked herself back to the present. 'Yes.'

'Yes?'

'No.'

'No?'

She needed to get her act together. She took another sip and pretended to swill it in her mouth. 'I fear it may be a touch on the dry side. The tasting notes are too...' She sucked in her cheeks. '...too flowery.' Molly sat back. She knew nothing of champagne, per se, but she sounded like an expert. Confident. Knowledgeable. Superior. Firmly on solid ground conversation-wise. 'It's vitally important to cleanse the palate and stimulate the tastebuds in order to fully appreciate such exquisite canapés.'

Levi inspected his flute and drained it. 'But at 3,000 euros a bottle, you'd expect it to go with almost anything, wouldn't you?'

Molly nearly spat out her champagne, but at almost 200 euros a mouthful it was too expensive to waste.

Levi glanced at the mini artworks. 'These canapés must be something else.'

Yes, her canapés were good, but perhaps not *that* good. She really must get this newly developed penchant for low-level lying under control. She flicked her hair from her face, nervously tucking it behind her ear before Levi raised an eyebrow with interest. She dropped her free hand into her lap as they locked eyes.

'I'm hoping to take my business in a more gastronomic direction,' he said. 'Solo travel and culinary hotspots with Michelin stars are the latest emerging trends. I'd value an expert gourmet's opinion.' His gaze tore right through her as though she were an open book, the pages flicking back and forth in an icy wind. 'How long have you been running your company? Do you have a Michelin star yourself?'

'Long enough. And not yet.' She carefully picked up a canapé from the tray, willing and praying to all the gods that she would not drop it on the expensive carpet. 'Try this.' She pretended to inspect it. 'It looks like a hand-crafted *panino nero* bun, with lobster meat, assembled on puréed gherkin and wild keta caviar.' She hoped her voice was not shaking as much as her hand. 'It's molecular gastronomy at its finest, I'd say.' As she held it out to him, she realised that he was not making any effort to take it from her.

'High praise indeed.' His eyes were twinkling, reflecting the lights from the candles dotted around, but his face remained impassive.

'Are you going to take it? Or do you want me to feed you like a baby?'

Her words hung worryingly in the air, causing Molly to, once again, wonder if she was experiencing early onset dementia of some sort or whether a demonic influence really was at play. She hadn't sounded like herself since she stepped foot in the Cigar Lounge.

Arching his brow in surprise, Levi straightened up, taking the morsel from her. 'I doubt these snacks are even aphrodisiacs. Probably just a marketing gimmick.'

Molly knocked back her drink, holding it out for a top up. There was nothing that she did not know about food, the making of food, the putting together of flavours, the effects of food on the mind and body and, in particular, how to combine food groups to encourage the flow of endorphins. In other words, she was a master when it came to creating culinary aphrodisiacs.

'It's a question of stimulating the love senses.'

'Go on.' Levi shuffled a little closer to her, his eyes wide with interest.

Whenever she was in the company of a food enthusiast, she became a completely different person. The shyness seemed to fade without her even trying. 'So, even though the ingredients on their own wouldn't increase a person's sexual appetite, putting them together in such a way that all of your senses, your sight, taste, touch and smell, are stimulated at the same time does often produce the desired effect.'

'So this is an actual aphrodisiac?' Levi turned it this way and that.

'Only if you roll it gently on your tongue. Release the flavours against the roof of your mouth. Really take your time to experience it fully. As though it was a sexual act.' Molly cringed at how unnecessarily erotic she was making the simple art of eating sound.

'Okay. I'll roll it on my tongue.' He devoured the delicious bite-sized treat more carefully this time, his face changing as the flavours burst onto his tongue. His eyes lit up. 'You're right. That's amazing. There have to be at least twenty different aromas in there.'

Molly beamed with relief. Perhaps she was in with

a chance to get this rodeo back on track. 'Obviously, some of it has to do with the placebo effect. If people think they're eating an aphrodisiac, the psychology of their sexual desire is so multifaceted that they'll naturally experience an impact.'

Molly felt she was overusing the words *sexual* and *desire* to an unnecessary degree and wished that she'd stop. However, it appeared contagious.

Levi regarded her with glee. 'When should I be experiencing an increase in sexual desire? How many of these things would it take?'

'That depends. Are you *hoping* for an increase in sexual desire?' Molly gulped anxiously. There really was no scientific basis to her culinary creations. They were essentially an edible metaphor for desire. At that moment, she couldn't even be sure if this whole conversation had been reduced to a mere metaphor, such was the verbal foreplay going on between them.

Levi removed gold and diamond cufflinks. The movement captivated her. His hands were tanned and manly, deftly rolling up his sleeves to reveal strong forearms. He undid his bow-tie, sliding it slowly from his neck. Molly felt her heart racing and tried to shift her focus to the glass in her hand. Levi dropped the bow-tie onto the coffee table in front of them and shifted his weight to face her dead on. 'Sex sells. You only have to see how much the tickets cost for the party upstairs. All on nothing but a promise. It's basically Tinder for the super elite.'

'Exactly.' Molly had no idea what extortionate price people would pay to attend a Burlesque Night at the Cigar Lounge, but she had heard rumours that the tickets were so prohibitively expensive, only the super-rich could afford them. This was so far from her world. 'Who wouldn't want to dress up like this every year for a date?'

It was an unintentional invitation to check her out, and Levi took it. As his appreciative gaze roamed across her body, it sent her temperature soaring.

Her mind flew to the bucket list and the pressing need to get it completed before close of play on Christmas Eve. 'Mind-blowingly expensive tickets demand mind-blowingly good food.'

'Exactly. What's next?' Levi asked as he topped up their glasses.

The champagne was doing a brilliant job of relaxing her. *Me, I'm next*, she thought, eyeing his impossibly toned shoulders and biceps as he placed the bottle back in the ice bucket. They were magnificent.

Unused to flirting, she had had very little practice and had never tried to do it while drinking champagne or while hiding an ulterior motive. But if she couldn't succeed at it now, dressed in the sexiest costume she'd ever worn, then when could she? She made a big deal of crossing her legs, making sure her stockings were centre stage. She mirrored his movements, propping her elbow on the back of the sofa, twirling her hair suggestively.

Molly dragged her teeth slowly over her lower lip. She needed to get him on the same page and hoped he couldn't read the turmoil going on in her mind. She inspected the tray with a forensic eye and slowly picked up one of the more delicate pieces. A spectacularly ornate creation made with cured salmon gelatine in the shape of a diamond, rolled in bright green wasabi dust, topped with a watermelon purée and a pensée flower. Feeling brave, she leaned across and fed it to him. The gesture was intimate enough to create instant tension.

Levi opened his mouth to accept the offering and chewed slowly, not taking his eyes from hers.

She leaned a little closer to him. Still, he held her gaze. She licked her lips. It reminded her of those poor women in romantic novels, constantly licking their lips every five minutes to get a man's attention. Levi instinctively dropped his eyes to her mouth. This had to be the most sensual experience of her entire life. She was now but inches from his face.

She lowered her voice a full two octaves. 'The techniques that go into it are very specific. Like, spherification... and, erm, the one that you are currently taking forever to eat... has been emulsified.'

'Fascinating,' he said, a hint of delight in his voice while he rolled the food around his mouth.

Chew. Chew. Chew.

Pursing her lips, she waited for him to stop chewing and start kissing her. She couldn't make it any more obvious, but as the seconds ticked by, Levi kept chewing.

Her lips hovered millimetres from his. It was intrusive at best. She had crossed a professional line. The poor man was hungry for food and culinary advice, not her. She eased back into her seat and guzzled her champagne.

Levi, with a final swallow, observed her silently as though he was toying with her, while she felt borderline manic, consumed with a need to seduce him.

Infuriating.

What would tempt him? She would need to try harder. This situation called for romancing at the highest possible levels. She tore her eyes from his and glanced down to see her breasts rising above the corset. She caught Levi following her gaze. She was comforted to see he had a lustful glint in his eye, for all he was trying to restrain himself. It would have to do. Emboldened by the scandalously expensive bubbly, Molly parted her lips and thrust out her chest. She hadn't read a thousand Mills & Boon novels over the years without learning a thing or two. Perhaps she could wear him down with sheer determination. She swept her hair seductively to the side in her most alluring manner. 'I'm just trying to, you know...'

Silence.

Oh, for God's sake.

Molly let out an exasperated sigh.

Levi leaned closer to her, their eyes colliding in a heated gaze. He reached out to cup her face. 'You're an incredibly beautiful woman. It's very late. You've had almost an entire bottle of champagne, and I'd hate for this to go anywhere you'd later regret.'

There was nothing she'd regret less. Shaking her head, she searched his face, hoping for signs that he felt the same way. She saw his pupils dilating and decided that would have to do. She leaned into him and whispered against his ear. 'Do you have a hot tub?'

6

THE WORST DECISIONS OFTEN MAKE FOR THE BEST MEMORIES

Levi hesitated as though momentarily startled. He shifted in his seat. 'A hot tub?'

'Erm, yes, that's right. For warmth. To warm up. That I could use,' Molly said hastily. 'That *we* could use. While we wait for the gondola to start working.'

Levi jabbed at the remote. 'I'll turn the fire up.'

'A hot tub would be better.' She took a deep breath and closed her eyes briefly. Maybe she was reading the room wrong. She never was, and never would be, any good at being sexy. It just wasn't in her nature. When she opened them, he was still looking at her.

'You want to get in the hot tub right now?' Levi glanced at the snow beating against the window.

Molly glugged her drink down. This was no time to play the shrinking violet. 'Yes.'

'Okay... if you're absolutely sure,' he said, getting up and backing out of the room. 'I'll see if it's on.'

'Please do.'

She'd never have another opportunity to do this. She'd been stuck in the kitchen for months. She'd not even so much as seen another human being that was remotely attractive, and here was a spectacular-looking specimen stood right in front of her, and she was all but chasing him physically from his own room. She leapt up and followed him out of the patio door, over some decking, to a hot tub. It was frothing and steaming away. It was partially sheltered from the snow falling and had the most breathtaking view across to the twinkling lights of the ski runs.

'Wow. That view is incredibly... incredible.'

'You should see it on a clear night when the sky is full of stars.'

Of course it is. That's what you get when you're a billionaire. A billion stars.

Molly felt a sudden urge to write a poem. 'It's magical.'

'And you're really sure you want to get in right now?' Levi still seemed unconvinced. 'You seem a bit...'

Pissed? Yes, she was. She was utterly shit-faced. But she was hiding it very well.

'I want to get in that hot tub more than anything in the whole world.' Molly smoothed her hair from her face, swaying slightly. 'I love them so much.'

Levi let out a small laugh. 'I think you are a bit too tipsy. Why don't you come back into the lounge?'

'Nope.' She edged further away from the patio doors.

'Besides, you can't go in wearing that.'

Molly let his words sink in. Was she confident enough to suggest they strip off and go in naked?

The thoughts swirled intoxicatingly round her brain.

No. No, she wasn't.

But she had it in her to be. She wanted to be daring and risk-taking. Molly scrambled around for a few words that would be suggestive without being too forward, but before she had a chance to collect them together, Levi spoke.

'Just give me a second,' he said, sounding exasperated, disappearing back through the door. He returned moments later. 'My sister often has swimming costumes and clothes sent over just in case she pops by.' He handed her a bathing costume with an expensive price tag, approximately a week's wage, hanging from it. 'There's a bathroom through the lounge. I'll get you some coffee.'

Maybe the chance to get him naked would come up later.

'I'll be right back. Don't you dare go anywhere!' Her sing-songy attempt at humour had red flags all over it.

With the sexual tension well and truly popped like a balloon, Molly slipped into the bathroom to change. All of a sudden, she wasn't happy with the status quo. Here she was with a million-to-one shot of drinking champagne in a hot tub overlooking the Alps, practically word for word her friend's dying wish. And now, she had gone out of her way to turn him right off her. *Well*, she thought determinedly, *I'll just have to think of a way to turn him right back on again.*

Molly slid apprehensively into the bathing costume, which she was pleased to find fit her perfectly but was also depressingly modest for the activity she had in mind. Covering herself in a robe, she sauntered back into the lounge. She could do this. How hard was it to seduce a man?

Levi was waiting by the fireplace, fully clothed. In fact, it looked as though he'd put on more clothes while she was getting changed. A protective layer, a barrier if you will. There were two mugs of steaming coffee in front of him as he finished up a call. 'Good news. Reception reckon that the gondola will start running again soon. Very soon.'

Molly's confidence drooped like a wilting flower. She was running out of time. She pointed to his many clothes. 'Erm, I thought you could join me in the hot tub.' Even to her ears her voice sounded faraway and lacking conviction.

'I'd rather not. I'm expecting a call.'

She smiled uncertainly. 'Please?'

Levi rubbed the back of his neck as he regarded her.

She would have to be far more convincing. 'I might drown.'

'Sorry?' he said, alarmed. 'Did you just say you might drown?'

'No. No. Not drown. I mean, what if it gets too hot? Too cold? Won't I need supervision?' She was flailing, drowning in a sea of unnecessary details. Fully aware that she was making a bad situation worse, Molly continued. 'You should come in with me in case I break it or something.'

Levi tilted his head as though asking himself, *Who is this imbecile? Didn't they do a full background check before letting her in to this exclusive club?*

Before he could answer, Molly clarified, 'Not that

I'd touch anything. I'm just saying, rather badly, that I'd like you to stay and keep me company. Please.'

Levi took forever and a day to reply. And even then, it was extremely half-hearted. 'Okay. I guess I can spare half an hour. But you need to drink this first.'

Under normal circumstances, she'd back down and run a mile at how embarrassingly forceful she was being. But these were not normal circumstances. She had a business to save. Years of hard-earned profit to claim. And a promise to keep. Plus, she was drunk, and she'd never fancied anyone in her entire life like she fancied Levi. She held out a hand gratefully, taking the coffee from him. 'Thank you. I really appreciate it.'

'Give me a second,' he said resignedly, quickly disappearing down a hallway into what she presumed was the bedroom. She heard the clicking of a door. He really wasn't taking any chances. She would have to tread very carefully with him. He seemed conflicted. Within minutes he was walking back through the living room towards her.

She took one look at him, his robe hanging open to reveal a pair of neatly fitted swimming shorts, his muscular legs tanned and lean, his smooth torso bare, and went immediately to pieces. He stole her breath away, and the excitement she felt racing through her veins could not be hidden. Desire must have been shining from her face like a Belisha beacon. Her mouth opened and closed like a goldfish, and yet she was powerless to stop it.

Outside, Levi lowered himself gingerly into the hot, steaming water, while Molly tried and failed not to gawp at his muscular, toned physique. He busied himself pressing buttons. Music flowed out of the speakers, decking lights glowed brighter, flames sprang from patio heaters dotted around and an awning stretched out above them.

'Well?' He was right to wonder why, after all the nagging, she was still standing, ogling him from the decking.

She threw her dressing gown over the nearest chair and clambered into the hot tub as quickly as she could. She slipped on a step hidden beneath the foamy surface and promptly sank, gurgling, to the bottom. *Sweet baby Jesus.* It was as though she had suddenly developed severe dyspraxia whenever she was within a hundred yards of Levi.

'Well, that's one way of doing it,' Levi said as she resurfaced, gasping for breath. 'Anyone would think it was your first time in a hot tub.'

Wiping foam from her eyes, Molly appreciated

that this was very much the right circumstance for sarcasm.

After a brief calming down period, where Levi outlined the rudimentary basics of how to step carefully into and out of a hot tub using the handrail provided, Molly inwardly cringed, her entire body rigid despite the relaxing heat of the silken water. She forced a laugh. 'I'm not normally this clumsy, I assure you. I have a reputation for being notoriously precise when it comes to my craft. I'm a perfectionist in the kitchen.' Molly's staff used to joke about her being unnaturally lifeless at times. Every movement purposeful. Often studying her work for hours on end to get it just right.

'And breaking the priceless camel?'

Ah. He was making a very valid point, but still. 'That wasn't entirely my fault.'

'It survived over a hundred years and probably generations of entertainers, film crews and circus folk before you came along.'

He was teasing her. And she liked it.

'I'll have you know I was once described in *The Great British Sausage Weekly* as a cooking robot so... I'm far from clumsy.'

Levi suppressed a smirk. 'A cooking robot? You must be so proud.'

'The British Sausage Bureau gave me an award and everything. It was a big deal. A *huge* deal in fact.'

It wasn't, but her parents had framed the article anyway and hung it above the fireplace.

'I don't know what to be more surprised at. The fact you were in a magazine dedicated entirely to sausages or that it comes out weekly.'

Cheek.

She flicked some foam at him. 'Do you have an award for inventing a sausage?'

'Do you always fidget with your hair when you lie?'

Like a rabbit caught in the headlights, Molly's eyes widened. 'Yes. Always.'

A burst of laughter escaped Levi as he shook his head slowly. 'I am already *so* regretting this.' With an easiness that she felt she'd never be able to obtain, Levi lounged his arms against the sides, water dripping from his toned biceps. His eyes crinkled with amusement. 'What else do you do, Molly, apart from win awards and tell lies to complete strangers in hot tubs?'

Good question.

Molly took her time answering. She liked what she saw. The silky foam dripped from his smooth skin, his hair was ruffled, and he had a playful tone in his voice.

He was much less imposing out of the tuxedo. She shuffled closer to him, her head suddenly empty of clever things to say. Velvety foam gently lapped over her as the bubbles caressed her skin. She may as well be honest. Making up lies was too draining. 'I read a lot. Cosy crime. Nothing gory. I just like to solve the puzzle before the main character does. I'm overbearingly fastidious in the kitchen. The product of having two full-time working parents. It's why I learned to cook at such a young age. And when I bake, I like to sing to the ingredients.'

Too much information.

'Anything else?'

She shuffled even closer. 'I play Sudoku. Advanced Expert level. The result of being an only child.'

His lips twitched.

'And I can roller skate to an almost Olympic standard. I can go from scissors straight into a grapevine.'

Levi chuckled. 'Very impressive. I've always wanted to learn.'

'Oh. And I can fix almost any machine.'

'You're a qualified engineer?' He sounded genuinely impressed.

'No. But my dad is.'

'So, if you do break this hot tub, what you're saying is that you'll also be able to fix it.'

'Yes.'

'Good to know, Molly...?'

'Johnson. Molly Johnson.'

Molly was now sitting so close to him they were almost touching. His gaze dropped to her mouth. Suddenly the atmosphere was turbo charged. Molly felt herself quiver against him. Every nerve ending was on fire. She stared into his eyes, whirlpools of desire reflecting her own. When he reached out to trace her cheek gently with the back of his knuckles, she thought she'd died and gone to heaven.

Levi cleared his throat. 'I better get that.'

'Better get what?' she breathed huskily.

'The door,' he said. 'Someone's been banging on it for the last few minutes.'

'Have they?' The distant sound of knocking penetrated her lust-filled brain as she watched Levi haul himself up from the hot tub in one languid movement, foam dripping from his body as he pointed out the handrail with a cheeky grin. 'Whoever it is, I'll get rid of them.' He grabbed a towel, drying himself off as he disappeared through the patio doors. 'Try not to drown before I get back.'

Molly, putting her fingertips lightly to her lips, stared at the snowy scene before her. It was all suddenly surreal. Here she was, sitting in a hot tub with

Europe's most attractive male. Not a soul in the world knew they were here. A tingling sensation swept through her body, her brain fizzing with excitement at the adventure she was about to embark on. This was no longer about the bucket list. This was all her. That long, long, dry spell was finally at an end.

Molly didn't just want to get naked with Levi, she wanted to wrap herself around him and feel every inch of her skin pressed against his. Lust ripped through her, emptying her mind of all else. She tugged at her bathing costume. Really, it was like something out of the 1920s it was so modest, and as she peeled down the straps, she wondered what the protocol was for having sex with a virtual stranger in his hot tub.

Without wanting to think too heavily about the logistics, she wriggled out of the swimsuit and flung it towards the patio doors. Hopefully, Levi would see it and join her. The sensation of being naked was instantly gratifying. Her breasts floated easily to the surface as dopamine flooded her brain. This was without doubt the most daring she had ever been. She tried to arrange herself in a tempting manner. She leaned back, nipples poking above the foam, legs crossed against the ledge. She lifted herself up a fraction to reveal more leg and swept up a blob of foam to cover her nether regions. This was no different to a reverse Pilates plank in some ways. She could hold the uncomfortable position until Levi had time to get a proper look at the goods. Plus, the steam rising from the tub would disguise her flushed cheeks and any embarrassment she felt about putting herself so obviously on display. For all Levi knew, she did this sort of thing every day of the week. As footsteps approached, Molly arched her back, thrusting her boobs from the water like floating jellies with cherries on top.

'Molly, this is my brother... Oh my fucking word, what the hell are you—' Levi stopped bellowing at around the same time Molly began screaming.

7

YOU MUST MAKE A CHOICE TO TAKE A CHANCE OR YOUR LIFE WILL NEVER CHANGE

The two men couldn't have run away from the scene fast enough. Molly was reeling. What had she done? In fact, if she hadn't flung her costume so far out of reach, she would have leapt from the hot tub herself and fled the scene. As it was, she had an excruciating wait of what seemed like a thousand years before she heard Levi yelling through from the living room to enquire whether she was decent or not. 'I hadn't re-alised you would be so... quite so, uh, on display like that.'

Horrific. Simply horrific.

'I threw my costume too far away,' Molly yelled back miserably. 'And now I can't see it for the steam and the snow coming down. In fact, I might have flung it over the balcony altogether.' She was rambling, her self-esteem plummeting to new depths. 'I misjudged the situation. I thought you... I thought that we'd...' The words caught in her throat as she unexpectedly burst into tears.

Levi raced through onto the patio. His eyes were wild and wandering, looking anywhere but at Molly. He threw a hand over to cover them. 'I'm sorry. Please don't get upset. None of this is your fault. It was an easy mistake to make.'

'Mistake?' Molly bawled. 'So you *aren't* interested in me?'

'No. No, I am. I was. I mean, who knows what could have happened?' Levi sounded unconvinced. 'I'm really not in the habit of doing this sort of thing. I should never have got in the tub. But the point is, please don't get upset about it.'

In all honesty, Molly thought, *he could have sounded a bit less adamant about not sleeping with her.*

'I'm decent. You can take your hand away.' Covering herself with her arms and up to her chin in the water, she smiled weakly at him, but Levi was clearly on edge. He was flustered, his words tumbling out as he backed away from the hot tub, hands splayed in front of him as though she was a wild tiger on the loose. 'Okay, I'll find your robe, you can get covered up, and we'll get you straight out of here.'

Oh Christ, he thinks I'm a liability.

Another wailing sob escaped from Molly. This wasn't just about her being *laid bare*. This was about her feeling lost. Her inability to come to terms with Ava's death. Her inability to let go of a life that was obviously slipping away. Her inability to carry on without her best friend there to guide her.

Levi picked up her dressing gown and knelt at the side of the hot tub. He waited for her sobs to subside. Poor man. He must be wondering what the heck was going on. Thank goodness he had kind eyes and a warm-hearted nature.

'Take your time. I'll be in the living room when you're ready to come out. My brother's gone. And if you want to talk about this, we'll talk.' His voice was surprisingly tender. 'I take it this is about more than a hot tub.'

Molly nodded her head slowly. If she started talking about Ava, then they'd be in real trouble. She had been known to burst into tears and not stop sobbing for days on end. So far, she'd not mentioned her circumstances to a single soul since she'd been working at the hotel, for fear of that happening again. The grief needed to stay buried deep inside her.

'That's very kind of you.' Her lips were trembling so much she could barely speak. 'I'm so embarrassed that I read the signals all wrong. You must think I'm such an—'

'No. Don't do that. Don't second-guess yourself. Everything you thought was going to happen...' Levi paused.

Molly dared to meet his gaze. Her vision was blurry as she sniffed up her tears.

Levi's tone was soft and reassuring. 'Everything you thought was going to happen would have happened. I'm sure of it.'

Molly's heart stopped as his words sank in.

It actually stopped beating.

So kind.

So lovely.

She stared gratefully at him until he began to shift uncomfortably. He cleared his throat. 'So, anyway. I appreciate the moment has well and truly passed. So I will leave you to get dressed and you can keep the robe. I have a ton of unworn sweatshirts and sweatpants if you don't want to get back into that costume.'

Oh. This was him politely asking her to leave and never come back. She should take the hint. She looked from his utterly gorgeous face to the hot tub bubbling away. The champagne bottle was lying empty next to her abandoned glass. When would she ever get another chance to tick this off the bucket list? More importantly, when would she ever get another chance to make him see that she was more than the hot mess sitting before him? She took a deep breath in and decided to take the plunge. 'How about if we start over? Just give me a second chance. Maybe if you got back in, we could—'

'No,' he said firmly. 'No, thank you. I'm sure you have family or friends who must be wondering where you are.'

Mortifying. Molly shook her head.

'You're here alone? For the Burlesque Night?' Levi sounded shocked. 'You're a lot younger than most of the women members who come here for... well, that kind of thing.'

Molly inwardly cringed. Why had she lied?

'Honestly, I'm not as young as I look. I'm thirty-five.' Molly felt a stab of guilt as he let out a small sigh of relief. *Lies upon lies upon lies.* She would seek professional help. 'Well, no, I'm twenty-nine. I've just led quite a sheltered sort of life for the past few years. But, honestly, I'm quite sane and mature for my age, trust me.'

Levi remained sceptical. She wouldn't blame him if he marched away as desperation seeped from her every pore. Molly felt sure he would have women throwing themselves at him constantly.

Levi studied her, his shoulders sagging slightly. 'Sorry. As tempting as it seems, I just don't think it's a good idea.'

Molly hung her head. This was embarrassing on so many levels. This wouldn't even make a funny tale to tell the grandkids, and the only person she would ever have wanted to share this humiliation with was dead. Molly had never felt so alone. Why had she ever allowed Ava to persuade her to leave her home country and embark on such a wild adventure?

'I'll leave the gown here for you. Don't forget to use the rail when you get out,' Levi said, getting up from his crouching position. 'I'll go to reception and see about getting you down to the hotel safely. Then I'll be back to talk if you need to.'

Was there anything worse than pity after the lethal sting of rejection?

Molly's whole body was ablaze with shame. As soon as he disappeared back into the room and she heard the door to the suite close, she scrambled out of the hot tub and into her dressing gown. Sniffing up her tears, she scurried to the bathroom with the angry force of a woman who was very annoyed with herself and who was still very much sexually unfulfilled. And while she was far from happy about it, she only had herself to blame. Three bloody years and two weeks, almost to the day, but who was counting? She rapidly towelled herself dry, grabbed her ridiculous burlesque costume and rammed her limbs into it, determined to be long gone before Levi returned. And as for borrowing his clothes, she could do without a souvenir of this hideous night. But most of all, she hoped she'd never set eyes on him again.

Catching sight of herself in the mirror, she realised she had mascara running down to her chin, her hair was a giant nest sticking out at all angles and her cheeks were on fire with humiliation. She decided there would be no more nights at the Cigar Lounge, no more nights in hot tubs. Bucket list or no bucket list, she wasn't sure her nerves would survive another moment in the company of that man. He was *too* remarkable. *Too* confident. *Too* perfect. Everything about him oozed sex appeal. *Too* much sex appeal. She'd stay safely tucked away in the kitchen for the rest of the season. She'd just have to throw herself at the mercy of the solicitor and hope that she could come up with an alternative way to save the restaurant and her home.

Once she was fully dressed, she stealthily made her way out of the suite into the plush corridor, every nerve ending on edge. She noticed signage on the wall pointing the direction to the spa and pool area, the Bar Rouge, the Billiards Room, but most importantly to the kitchen. She raced along and flung herself inside, taking a moment to catch her breath and wipe the remaining tears from her eyes. She'd rather risk crashing the snowmobile than spend one second longer at the Cigar Lounge.

She heard footsteps behind her. Was he following her? What would she say to him? Her mind raced as the door opened and Keela followed her in shaking her head. 'Of all the rules to break.'

'What do you mean?' Keeping her back to Keela, Molly knew exactly what she meant.

'The hot billionaire in the lift?'

Molly busied herself with the empty trays, clattering them loudly as she piled the trolley high, her damp hair swinging down to hide her flushed face. 'Nothing happened. That's me done. I'm off now.'

'There's a weather warning. You'll have to stay here. Wait, have you been crying?' Keela asked as she hurried to help her.

Molly shook her head.

'Are you sure you're okay?'

'I need to go.' Molly sniffed, rubbing her hot eyes with the palms of her hands.

Keela sighed. 'Honey, you wouldn't be the first, but let me warn you now, that one is strictly off limits. You'll only get hurt.'

This did nothing to quash the sinking feeling, her skin crawling with shame. If only Keela knew that Levi had rejected her before anything had even begun. Molly was desperate for this conversation to end. Her whole mind was becoming numb with embarrassment.

'Promise me you'll stay until the storm is over?' Keela soothed.

Molly nodded but as soon as Keela left the kitchen, she yanked open the changing room door. She kicked off the ridiculously high shoes and stuffed them into her backpack. Speedily pulling on her snowsuit over her costume, her boots, a hat over her damp hair and some still damp gloves, she heaved open the outside door. She was met with an icy blast and a sea of darkness.

A security light sprang on to reveal the snow, while piled high, was no longer coming down as thickly. The main plaza below was still lit up but empty of life. She had no idea what time it was, only that she wanted the comfort of her own soft bed in her own tiny room. Steeling herself against the freezing cold, she stepped out into the snow and trudged towards the snowmobile, yanking at the handles.

The vehicle roared to life as if powered by her fury. How could she embarrass herself like that! She felt it strain against the snow blocking its path, the trailer caught in the drift. Molly let out a frustrated scream. She unhooked the trailer and hopped back on the snowmobile. It surged forward with force, and within ten minutes of what felt like a terrifying sheer drop down the mountain, she was sliding to a stop outside her charming, rustic, Alpine restaurant made of wooden logs and a thatched roof and hurling herself through the door with the big CLOSED sign. She deftly wove through the wooden tables with their quaint red-and-green Christmas tablecloths and glittering candle holders, thumped up the stairs and into her safe and cosy apartment. She slammed the door shut, shaking the walls. She was fuming with rage and humiliation in equal measure. She threw herself into the shower in the small ensuite and let the boiling hot water and soothing conditioning shampoo wash away her temper until her breathing returned to normal and the pain in her chest subsided.

She dried her hair and collapsed into bed, exhausted. A throbbing between her legs reminded her of how much she'd wanted him. Her breasts felt tender, aching for his touch. Her whole body, her entire being, felt different. She was tortured by images of her arching into him, her hair falling onto his chest, his eyes burning into hers as she more or less *begged* him to kiss her.

She'd *begged* him for a second chance! How desperate!

Molly felt the tears slide slowly down her cheek as she rolled over onto the pillow and implored sleep to take her.

* * *

The alarm went off what seemed like five seconds later. Molly's dreams had been full of traitorous images of Levi. She dragged herself down to the restaurant kitchen to start the breakfasts and bottomless brunches. She inspected her pasty complexion and red puffy eyes staring back at her from the mirror. The only consolation would be that she would never have to run into Levi again. She would stay safely tucked out of sight and away from the ski resort guests. She opened up the restaurant and as always, no matter how hard she was finding things, the picture-perfect square bustling with skiers heading for the slopes against the backdrop of the snow-peaked mountains stole her breath away. Light flooded in through the wooden window shutters, illuminating the quintessentially French décor, the beams across the ceiling, the huge fireplace that dominated the main eating area. Molly and Ava had knocked a wall through, making the kitchen semi-open, so that the customers could enjoy the delicious aromas of Molly's cooking. Often, if they were glued to what she was doing, she would talk them through the process, politely answering questions on her unconventional techniques.

After a slow morning cooking breakfasts and making her house special hot chocolates for the few stragglers that came in, it was time for Molly to close up and head across the square to the main hotel kitchen to start her second job of the day.

* * *

As soon as she arrived at the hotel, Molly raced into the pantry, tying her apron strings behind her as she went. Pulling her long thick hair up into a topknot, she grabbed the roster to see she had been assigned a small sixtieth birthday celebration being held in the hotel's private dining room. She flicked her eyes down the list for allergies and got to work preparing a tasting menu. She decided on a ten-course degustation that would keep her so incredibly focused, she'd have no time to even think about the humiliation of the previous evening. The horrified expression on Levi's face. The ridiculous way he'd fled the room on finding her naked. It was making her blood boil just thinking about it. She felt such a fool.

Before she knew it, she'd taken her anger out on a whole basket of vegetables that were now so finely sliced and chopped she was ready to begin assembling. This was always the best part of molecular gastronomy.

Petra walked quickly over to her.

'Good news, Molly.'

Molly saw the supervisor was waving a roster. 'After the executive lunch you catered last week, there's been a request for you to chalet chef.'

'Thanks,' said Molly, 'but I'm happy staying here in the kitchen, out of harm's way.'

'Harm's way?' Petra blew out her cheeks. 'You didn't enjoy last night? That bad, huh?'

'Sorry, yes. No. Not really. Ignore me. I just mean I'm happy here, that's all. In the kitchen. Away from people.'

'Okay, well, I'm not sure you have much of a choice, seeing as this request came from one of the female members of the board. It was her husband's business lunch that you catered, and it was a huge success. They've asked specifically for you. They've got a family wedding coming up and I think they want to try you out.'

Like road-testing a second-hand car?

Molly groaned. 'It's not up at the Cigar Lounge, is it?'

'No. You couldn't be further away, in fact. Their lodge is over the pass on the opposite side of the resort. It's fairly remote, so you'd take a driver and van up with everything you need for the week.'

'A whole week? But I'd have to close the restaurant.'

'You've only been opening for breakfast, haven't you? The money you'd get for one week at the lodge will triple what you make in a month. It might be worth it. Give you a break?' Petra pointed to the mountain of vegetables she had chopped.

Molly considered it. The money would be great but the last thing she needed was an intensive week as a private chef, surrounded by a happy family. She imagined herself weeping miserably into the cookie dough while they sang French carols round the fire. 'I'm sorry. I'm not sure I'd be the right person for that.'

Petra looked disappointed. 'Please think about it.'

* * *

Later that afternoon, Molly walked around in a bit of a daze, wondering if shutting the restaurant and running away to the lodge might, in fact, be the right thing to do. Her attention was supposed to be on shopping at the bustling market for fresh produce, but as she swept her gaze around the colourful stalls overflowing with fruit and vegetables, stalls brimming with cheeses and the smell of freshly baked bread and cured meats filling the air, all she could think about was Levi's kind eyes, crinkled with laughter, his kissable lips curled at the corners. Did she really *never* want to see him again?

'It's you! Isn't it?'

Molly was jolted from her daydreaming. It took her a second to recognise who was talking to her in such a vexed Italian accent. It was the voluptuous redhead from the Cigar Lounge.

The woman regarded her coldly. 'It's difficult to place someone out of costume. You were the guest at the hen party, no?' She looked Molly up and down disapprovingly, eyeing her bulging bags of produce and her chef's apron peeking out from under her thickly padded coat. 'Ah. Not a guest. You work here?'

Molly froze.

'Where do you work?' she ordered. 'I want to speak with your superior.'

Molly took in her immaculate features. She was beautiful, but Molly found something hard and snobbish about her manner. She hated confrontation but she straightened, lifting her chin. 'Why?'

'To complain, of course.'

'I thought the camel had been taken care of.'

'That is not the point.'

'I think it is very much the point.'

'Waiting staff are not allowed to fraternise at these parties. You were clearly breaking the rules and I saw you with a phone. Taking pictures is strictly forbidden. Selling photos to newspapers is a sackable offence.'

Molly took immediate umbrage to her tone. 'I'm a chef, *actually*. Not that it has anything to do with you what job I do. And the photo was only of me, not any famous people. I couldn't care less what they get up to.'

'There's something about the hired help men simply can't resist,' the woman said in a laughing tone, her eyes quite serious. She drew her over-filled red lips into a sneer. 'The whore that broke the camel's back. That would be amusing if it wasn't so tragic.'

Molly raised her eyebrows, and the redhead continued as though she wasn't delivering a major insult.

'A word of caution. Angelo is way out of your league. You'll be nothing but a one-night stand to him.' She tilted her head to fix Molly a look of warning. 'Whereas he and I have something longer term. Do you understand me?'

Molly stiffened. The news was like ice freezing her veins. She'd never liked bullies or people who tried to manipulate others. But nor was she used to standing up to them. She lowered her gaze.

'There's nothing going on with me and the, erm, guest that you mentioned. And anyway.' Molly raised her eyes to meet the steely gaze of the woman in front of her, who seemed a lot less imposing with her breasts securely covered and that fire-engine-red hair stowed under her hat. She hoped that she wasn't about to tell tales to Petra and get her fired. 'What I do outside of work is really none of your business.'

'You're new here, so let me give you some advice—'

'Thanks, but I'm good. I'm also incredibly busy,' Molly interrupted, holding up her bags full of shopping with a forced smile.

'Don't say I didn't warn you.' The redhead scowled at her. 'And I *am* still going to complain about you. You work in a kitchen? I should have no problem tracking down your boss.'

Molly scurried away before the conversation could go any further. She might detest conflict but even the mere mention of Levi and wild emotion seemed to rip through her like a tornado. She felt the burning glare of the redhead on her back, unsure of what had just happened. Why should Molly care about what the redhead and Levi did or did not get up to?

Then it came to her. The reason she was doing all of this in the first place. She swivelled round and made her way back to the hotel kitchen. Petra was busy flying around the place yelling instructions to a team of twenty sous-chefs. She glanced up at Molly approaching.

'Is the chalet chef job at the lodge still going?'

Petra's face lit up. 'Yes, but you'll need to plan out the menus as soon as possible because you'll be leaving to go there in a few days.'

'A few days?'

'They're flying in from Geneva. Private jets of course.'

'And the place is remote?'

Petra nodded. 'It's a beautiful spot. The views alone are worth the trip. You'd get some time off to ski and relax. They have an excellent state-of-the-art spa up there.'

Molly yearned for some heat to relieve her sore, weary muscles. 'I'm not even sure I'd know *how* to relax, it's been so long.'

'How hard can cooking for one family be? It's nothing compared to what you've been doing. And if you're a success, it will open doors for you that you could only imagine, especially if they ask you to cater the wedding or future Christmas holiday dinners. They might endorse your restaurant. After all, they do own this place.' Petra swept her arm around the kitchen towards the window and beyond.

'It *would* be good for business...' Molly twirled a strand of her hair anxiously. Ava was the one who took all the risks. She had been the driving force behind their shared dream of owning a chain of Michelin-starred restaurants, glittering like fine-dining diamonds across the Alps. 'And I don't have any plans for Christmas Day, I suppose.' This wasn't true. Molly had planned to clean the restaurant from top to bottom and then spend the evening crying alone into some soup.

'What? You can always spend Christmas Day here with me, cooking for the four hundred covers we have booked in.' Petra laughed. 'Good job I have no children to go home to, isn't it?'

'Same. My parents booked a cruise the moment I told them I would be staying here to work.'

Petra shrugged. 'Then this will be perfect for you. Think of the Christmas tips you'll get.'

A guaranteed week of not bumping into Levi or Angelo or whatever he was calling himself (she'd done nothing but lie to him anyway) and avoiding both the angry redhead (she could do without the complaints procedure) and Keela (she'd fled without a word of explanation) seemed the perfect solution. The number of people she was dodging was really beginning to add up. Grateful for the escape and who knows, maybe even time to complete her bucket list, she agreed to take the job.

'Just a word of caution though,' Petra warned. 'Their standards are extremely high, so don't skimp. You have an unlimited budget. Take one of the porters with you and get everything you need from the market. I'll look forward to approving the menus. Do everything you can to impress them. It's not just your reputation on the line, it's mine too.'

8

'LIFE IS EITHER A DARING ADVENTURE OR NOTHING.' HELEN KELLER

Molly arrived at the lodge to find it decorated like a Christmas Hallmark movie set and was greeted by the uniformed chalet host who showed her to her accommodation.

'Wow. It's huge!' Molly exclaimed in delight. The contrast to her small attic-style bedroom in the eaves above the restaurant was unbelievable. 'Are you sure this is my room?' Molly crossed the bedroom to open the sliding glass doors. She would wake up every day to a spectacular view of the snow-capped mountains. She glanced at the small table and chairs for two on the spacious wooden balcony and spun round. 'All for me?'

The host laughed. 'You should see my room. I'm Toby by the way.'

'You're American?'

'From upstate New York.'

'I'm Molly, from England. This place is blowing my mind.'

'Yeah, it's pretty impressive. Wait until you check out the rest of it. This family sure know a thing or two about living in style. Can you believe they flew in the same Christmas planners who decorate The Plaza in New York to do the same with this lodge? Apparently, they've strung over fourteen thousand lights around the property. It's like Santa's Grotto on steroids.'

'It's magnificent.'

'And the French president stayed here last week. He's a friend of theirs!' Toby twittered on excitedly. 'You never know who will pop by. Anyway, I'll let you unpack, and then I'll give you the grand tour. In terms of staff, it's you in charge of the kitchen and me for everything else. Although, I'll shout if I need help with anything. We'll be kept busy, I can guarantee that much.'

So much for getting time to complete the bucket list.

As soon as he left, Molly stepped back out onto the wide wooden veranda to discover that it circled the entire lodge and was faced with a flurry of snowflakes and an icy blast of wind. Pulling her hat low, she ventured further out. Even through the falling flakes she could appreciate the breathtaking view. It was jaw-droppingly spectacular. The snow-covered mountains were incredibly imposing and loomed high above the lodge. The dense forest lying at the base of the mountain had a magical quality. It was like a postcard. She made for the other side of the veranda and took in a cold, sharp breath at the view before her. She saw the distant lights of Val D'Amore, the cable cars running up and down the slopes, the ski lifts and people mere dots of colour moving around. A huge church spire with a clock on it rose from a small town near the resort. And there, in the corner of the main square, the quirky, round, stone chimney of Le Petit Ange peeked above the snow-covered rooftops and the distant smoke billowing from chimneypots. Her home. Within minutes the cold began seeping into her bones. She scuttled back inside, grateful for the instant hit of warmth.

Molly sat on the edge of the sumptuous king-size bed marvelling at the opulence of her surroundings. She flopped backwards into the softest bedding she'd ever encountered. The whole room oozed Christmas, warmth, holiday spirit. Rich reds, golds and greens adorned the covers, the wall art, the thick luxurious carpet. After the bizarre few days she'd had, she would welcome some time to reflect, gather her thoughts and focus on work. A familiar melancholy swept over her as she imagined what Ava would have made of it all, as the adventurous one of the two. She was always the centre of attention while Molly happily faded into the background. Two halves of a perfect whole. It was almost as though Ava was here, pulling the strings to make sure Molly was plunged into a new and daring reality. It was all so bittersweet. With a small sigh, she pulled herself up and wandered into the bathroom to freshen up. She would unpack all the food produce, organise the cupboards and make sure all of the cooking utensils were where she needed them to be. She loved nothing more than to be meticulous in the kitchen. Toby had explained that the family wouldn't be arriving for a while, so she would have plenty of time to settle in, prepare a schedule and tick a few challenges off her bucket list.

* * *

Later that afternoon, exhausted from unpacking and painstakingly reorganising the kitchen, Molly bumped into Toby as she was crossing the main lounge towards the laundry room.

'By the way, I'm off to pick up the family from the airport in the people carrier. We'll stay overnight at the resort because there's heavy snow forecast for tonight so we won't be able to get up to the lodge. We'll be back tomorrow evening. I've left an itinerary on the bench. We should be back for dinner, but I'll call you first thing if that changes, okay? There'll be around five or six plus you and me. Unless they invite friends. You never really know with this family. Just be prepared for anything. I've highlighted all the food preferences and allergies.'

'How bad do you think the snowfall will be?'

'Only bad enough for you to stay in and use all of the spa facilities before we get back here.' Toby grinned. 'They are amazing. You should try them all out tonight while you can. They have a massage chair that is simply incredible. It does your head down to your toes. Oh, and the pool is heated, and the steam room and sauna rooms are permanently on, so knock yourself out. There'll be no peace once the family arrives.'

Thinking of everything she still had to achieve, Molly grinned. 'Excellent idea. Do you want me to make you something to eat before you go?'

Toby declined politely. 'Thanks but I'm heading

straight off now before it gets dark. See you tomorrow.'

Molly almost ran back to her room to grab her swimming costume, ignoring a flashback to the modest one that Levi had lent her. She picked up the bucket list and flicked her eyes down the catalogue of instructions.

For the love of all that is holy...

'Oh my God, Ava, why were you so obsessed with doing things naked?' she whispered to herself, only half laughing. 'Sauna, ten full minutes, Vitruvian Man, naked,' she read aloud. Molly shook her head, remembering how mischievous her friend had been. They were opposites in every way. At least she hadn't written 'in a sauna full of giant Dutch football players'. In the mood to get it over with and having made sure every door and window in the chalet was firmly locked, Molly made her way down to the spa area in the basement. She stood at the glass door and drank in the sight before her. It was better than any spa she had ever seen. It was an oasis of sparkles. Lights in the floor made everything shimmer and glitter. The floor was polished marble, the walls a creamy stone colour. The hot tub was sunk into the ground and had flickering candles round the outside. An unopened magnum of champagne stood in an ice bucket next to it along with a tray of crystal flutes. These billionaires never seemed to miss a trick when it came to occasions for champagne. She looked wistfully at the water bubbling away wondering if she'd ever get another chance to fulfil the first task on the list. Her gaze wandered around the barely lit room. The air was fragrant and soothing. There were massage tables with towels and rose petals on. Shelves stocked with essential oils and lotions lined the walls while discreet uplighting made the most of the artwork. The full-length pool, surrounded with ornately patterned tiles and edged with gold, twinkled invitingly. This place heightened every sense as she reached out to feel a butter-soft drape hanging over one of the loungers. She wandered around breathing in the flowery scent blooming from the many stone bowls of pot pourri dotted about and sighed with contentment. She had found her happy place.

She hurriedly undressed, leaving her clothes in a neat pile on the chaise longue outside the sauna door, and wrapped herself in one of the white fluffy towels that were piled up all over the place. Spotting the massage chair, she went over. The luxurious white leather padded seat with wide flat armrests looked inviting. It would certainly calm her nerves before the sauna challenge. She reclined backwards and pressed the button. It felt as though she was floating on a cloud and when the vibrations rumbled through her body, causing tingles from her head to her toes, she was thrown into a state of deep relaxation. A few minutes in, her traitorous mind wandered to Levi. Flashbacks of him gazing at her in the hot tub, with his dark mischievous eyes and his lazy smile. She allowed herself to imagine his hot mouth on hers and the feel of his touch. A moan escaped her lips as the chair worked its magic.

Once she'd had three goes on the chair and a variety of steamy daydreams all about Levi, she was suitably relaxed and horny enough to try the naked sauna. She took out her phone. How to evidence this? Molly stepped inside the sauna and regarded the glass door as she closed it behind her. Even though the lighting was very low, she was casting a rather defined shadow against the door. She hesitantly threw her towel onto the wooden bench and stood in the pose of the Vitruvian Man, arms and legs akimbo, as she took a photo of her silhouette. That would have to do. She set the timer to ten minutes and placed the phone on the towel. She would write a strongly worded entry into Ava's journal about this.

'Why spreadeagled? Why? Why do I have to be naked for *ten* whole minutes, Ava?' she asked the hissing clouds billowing from the hot coal bed as she poured a wooden ladleful of water over them. 'Why not seven minutes? Or four and a half?'

She assumed the pose.

Even alone, this felt too risqué.

Five minutes crawled by as she took deep calming breaths in, exhaling as slowly as possible, reassuring herself that all the doors and windows to the lodge were bolted shut. It's funny how quickly something bizarre can become quite normal. She kept her arms and legs stretched wide and let the heat relax her bones.

It wasn't as terrible as she had first imagined.

In fact, it was positively freeing.

Not that she'd ever become a naturist. She was too prudish for that. Too British. Although Molly was beginning to appreciate the Scandinavians and their lack of inhibitions where saunas were concerned. Maybe this *could* become a thing for her. She'd certainly never felt this relaxed in her life. It was sheer bliss. She would happily do this every day for the rest of her—

Suddenly the door to the sauna swung open.

She gasped in shock.

A man stood in the doorway.

Time stood still as realisation dawned.

It was him.

Levi was standing in front of her, wearing only a towel knotted at his waist. He looked her over with an alarmed expression as she stood, stark naked, arms and legs spread wide. He did a double take. 'Jesus Christ, not you again!' he moaned as she let out a piercing scream.

'Calm down. It's just me!' he barked after a few seconds of her screeching at an ear-splitting decibel.

Molly's scream trailed off. She blinked rapidly. What cruel twist of fate was this? Who had she harmed in a previous life? What bad karma was at play here?

Levi tightened the towel round his waist, his eyebrows knitted together. 'Mind telling me what you're doing? Is this some sort of bizarre Satanic ritual?'

'No!' Molly's hands whipped down to cover herself. Had anyone ever *actually* died of embarrassment? Because if not, she feared she may become the first.

'Are you breaking and entering?' he asked. He flicked his eyes over her naked body. 'You don't exactly look dressed for it. I hate to imagine where you've hidden the crowbar.'

Molly shook her head violently. 'Of course I'm not! I wouldn't have the first clue what to steal.'

Levi raised an eyebrow.

'Well, I would,' she said, nodding towards a solid-gold bust of Buddha with a ruby for a third eye, right next to where he was standing. 'But you're right, I shouldn't be here,' she said, panicking. 'Please don't tell anybody. I'm so sorry. You see, I—'

'It's not often you hear of thieves taking a quick wellness break before they steal the family jewels. Or is that a thing now? It's so hard to keep up,' he said drily. 'Good mental health is so important.'

Molly felt embarrassment surge through her, bringing her back to her senses. She grabbed her towel to cover up.

Levi remained disgruntled. 'Bit late for that, isn't it?'

She grimaced. *The mortification of it. My naked body no longer being of any surprise to him whatsoever. Shoot me now.*

'I heard moaning. I thought someone had had a fall.'

Moaning?

Oh my God. He'd heard her on the massage chair. Had she subconsciously manifested him a second time? Perhaps her brain was in urgent need of rewiring.

The timer alarm went off on her phone, causing them both to jump.

Levi screwed his eyes in confusion. 'Okay. Can you please tell me what you're doing?'

Did he mean why the Vitruvian Man pose or did he mean 'doing' in the wider sense?

'Never mind what *I'm* doing. What are *you* doing here?' she said, hurriedly wrapping the towel around herself. 'You have a guest room over at the Cigar Lounge.'

'And I also own this lodge.'

Have these billionaires never heard of renting?

'But you're on holiday. A holidaymaker. Here for the wedding.'

He frowned. 'I'm staying here with my family, but you knew that, didn't you?' In one tiny second, the atmosphere was charged with tension.

'No! I didn't. I came here to avoid you, not to be trapped in the same house.'

'Avoid me? I don't believe you.'

Molly tried to make sense of what was going on. She watched Levi sit down on the opposite bench as though it was the most completely normal thing to do when faced with a naked woman who has twice imposed herself on him and should by rights be hauled in front of some sort of civil liberties tribunal.

Levi screwed his eyes. 'Seriously. What is happening? Are you following me?'

'What? No! Of course not. I'm a chef!'

'Yeah, so you said. Winner of the British Bangers Weekly. That doesn't explain why I keep seeing you everywhere I go. Did Freda invite you? Are you and her friends?'

'Freda? Who's that? Your wife?'

OMG. Why would a thing like that come out of her mouth? It didn't even make sense. A man she barely knew should be able to mention any female name without her yelling 'Is that your wife?' like a jealous ex-girlfriend.

'Never mind,' he said simply, putting his hands on his hips. 'What are you doing here?'

'Petra hired me,' Molly wailed, not proud of the way she was throwing the hotel kitchen manager under the bus, but she was flailing big time. 'She said it was money for old rope. A few meals here and there and loads of time to myself to relax. And a huge Christmas bonus at the end for basically not doing anything.' What happened to her filter? Where was it? Had it evaporated with the heat?

Levi let out a low groan. 'You're the chalet chef?' He sounded incredibly disappointed. He rubbed his hands down his face. 'But you said you ran your own company.'

'Am I going to be fired?'

Levi didn't answer. 'How did you end up in this chalet?'

Good question.

Molly had no idea where to begin. How could she explain such a chain of events? That for eight years she had been too busy cooking happily behind the scenes to live an actual life, while Ava went out and dazzled clients? Or that when they had bought the failing restaurant from Ava's French great-aunt, they'd left the UK to embark on the adventure of a lifetime? Or that together they had turned the restaurant around and amassed a small fortune, but Molly couldn't access any of it because of some ridiculous legal oversight? And that now it was almost too late, and Molly was in danger of losing everything, and that was why she was standing spreadeagled, naked in his sauna? 'The family made a special request after I catered a business lunch.'

As though sensing the shift in energy, Levi cleared his throat. 'And where does my sauna fit in to all this?'

Molly felt her cheeks flame. Her words deserted her. She had no idea how to answer that. Should she reveal just how much of an emotional and financial mess she was in, or would he run screaming for the hills? She suspected her *baggage* might be too much, too soon.

'When you feel like being straight with me, I'm all ears.' He shifted in his seat. He was going nowhere.

She stroked the hair from her face, heat rising from her chest. 'Toby suggested this. Not the naked part, but he said that nobody would be around until tomorrow evening.'

'I'm not sure I believe you.'

'Well, it's true.'

Levi regarded her. 'Sit down.'

Molly did as he instructed. 'I assure you. After the other night, I have no interest in you. I'm just here to work. That's all.'

'So our meeting at the Cigar Lounge wasn't a coincidence?'

'Yes, it was. Absolutely.' Molly bit her lips together. 'However, there might have been some rogue manifesting involved.'

Levi didn't even try to hide a baffled look. 'Can you see why it's incredibly hard for me to believe a word you're saying now?'

Molly held up her hands. 'I know this looks bad. But to be fair, I thought you were here on holiday and *single*. Then that redhead you're seeing said that you couldn't resist the hired help.'

'She said *what*?' Levi said, astounded.

Molly's cheeks were on fire. 'I mean, what were you doing kissing *me* if you're not even available?'

'Who are you talking about? What redhead?' Levi asked, lines creasing his brow.

'The burlesque dancer. The one full of lip filler and collagen implants.' How many redheads was he familiar with, for goodness' sake? 'She warned me to stay away from you. She more or less implied that you and she are... that you, erm, you are, well, might be intimate with one another.' *Why? Why are you saying these things? Please stop saying these things.*

Levi shook his head. 'Don't concern yourself with her.'

'Why shouldn't it concern me?' Molly fiddled with her towel.

'It shouldn't concern you because none of what she said is true.'

'Well, good.' Molly was furious at herself for sounding so pleased.

Levi picked up on it immediately. His expression softened.

'She didn't seem like a nice lady anyway. Very gossipy. If that's your type.'

Levi tilted his head. 'You weren't jealous, were you?'

'Absolutely not. No way. Not in a million years.

Like I said, I have zero interest in you.' She was beginning to sound childish even to her own ears. She lifted her chin. 'I'm still very upset with you about what happened,' she blurted.

She had often wondered where this compulsion to blurt out her true feelings came from. It was quite an unappealing and decidedly unhelpful trait. Especially now. In this stifling hot sauna. Where, she supposed, she was baring everything, so why not her soul?

Levi raked a hand through his hair. 'Yeah, about that. I don't know what to say. Believe me, I've thought about nothing else since. I shouldn't have left you while you were so upset. Then you disappeared on me. I tried to find you but... of course I was searching for a guest, not a member of staff.'

Molly took a beat to study him. He'd tried to search for her?

'Apology not accepted. The way you behaved was very rude.' She lowered her voice. The memory of her begging him to give her a second chance and him rejecting her outright burned to her very core.

'Well, I didn't mean to be rude. And you looked in no state to be doing whatever it is you wanted to do with me in the hot tub, anyway.'

How to answer? The words clogged in her throat. Molly decided on the truth. 'I simply wanted to drink champagne with you while naked in the hot tub.' *Is that really too much to ask?*

'And?' Levi asked. 'I've never been naked in a hot tub and known it to stop there, have you?'

Did he have to give her such a visual? Molly felt a fluttering in her stomach. Any more of this talk and she would combust right in front of him. She stared down at her perfectly painted toes and wiggled them to check this was really happening. 'If I'm honest, I did hope for a little more.'

Gross understatement. She had been hoping for the sexual Olympics of her dreams. A wild night of passion so incredible it would carry her through the rest of her life because she was absolutely certain of one thing: she'd never ever meet anyone as charismatic and attractive as this man currently sharing a sauna with her. Not in a million lifetimes.

She glanced up to look him in the eye. 'But in hindsight, I can see why you might have had reservations about me. It wasn't my finest hour. I'm not usually that pushy or one to make such an exhibition of myself.' Practically begging him to put an end to her dry spell. 'And to be fair, I haven't drank in over a year. It may have exacerbated my tendency to catastrophise.'

Levi folded his arms, surprise etched on his face.

Contrary to what she was saying, he had just found her naked and spreadeagled, and if memory served her correctly, she was quaffing back the booze as though her throat was on fire.

'You're really selling yourself, aren't you?' He was biting his lip to refrain from laughing. 'It's refreshing. You're... very different to the women I'm usually introduced to, that's for sure.'

And just like that, Molly's pulse quickened. She fought the temptation to follow the rivulets of water meandering across his broad shoulders and down his toned arms with her finger. This was surely the height of unprofessional behaviour. Could she not be within two metres of the man without wanting to throw her legs open wide? She self-consciously scooped up her thick, long hair into a topknot and adjusted her towel to make it more secure.

Levi leaned back against the wood-panelled wall and casually swung his legs up to stretch them out along the bench. He continued to pin her to the seat with a penetrating gaze.

His long lean legs were tanned and muscular, his stomach taut, his biceps like small ripe watermelons, and his perfect symmetrical face with day-old stubble and eyes that were made for getting lost in seemed too good to be true. In short, he was a human designed to

make love. Pure and simple. He was the very defini-
tion of sex and sensuality. He raked his hand lazily
through his hair again before raising his eyebrows at
her. Molly cleared her throat timidly. She wanted him.
Her chest tightened, making it harder to speak in a
normal tone.

'So I guess we should formally introduce ourselves. As you know, I'm Molly Johnson, chalet chef
for the next week,' she said, keeping her eyes on his.
'And you are?'

Levi raised his eyebrows again in answer as
though it was a rhetorical question.

'After all, you could be any mass-murdering billionaire wandering in off the slopes for all I know,
with your many names. Is it Angelo or Levi?' Molly
rattled on.

He wasn't going to indulge her, so she could only
assume he was someone she shouldn't be mixing
with. She rubbed her throat with her hand. He was
overwhelmingly attractive. Knee-tremblingly gorgeous. Even the way beads of sweat trickled sensually
down his smooth chest, over his defined pecs and
down over his washboard stomach was like a piece of
priceless art. He was still making no attempt to tell her
who he was. The conversation was going nowhere.

'Well, that's quite long enough in the sauna for me.

Anyway, nice to have met you again. I know that staff and guests aren't supposed to fraternise.' She rose unsteadily to her feet. 'I'll try to stay out of your way.'

Silence.

Heavy silence.

Silence loaded with desperation to straddle him and avail herself of the pleasure she had ached to experience the very first time she'd met him. Molly gave herself a mental slap. He hadn't told her a thing. She didn't have the first clue who he was. She reached for the door.

'Wait,' he commanded, halting her with one word.

Oh my.

His gaze roamed the length of her body until their eyes collided. She could barely breathe. She wanted him. More than anything she'd ever wanted in her whole life. He'd been in her thoughts every second since the moment she'd first seen him. And now, here he was asking her to stay, his voice dripping with promise.

'Don't forget your phone.' He nodded to the bench.

She'd never been so disappointed in her life, and it must have shown on her face. A half-grin tugged at his mouth. 'I'm surprised you haven't tried to get me in the hot tub. Or didn't you notice it on your way in?'

Molly groaned. 'Please don't remind me. I'm already embarrassed enough.'

She waited a beat.

Was this him hinting?

Could the hot tub be an option? She was already naked under the towel. Practically halfway through the challenge already. 'Unless of course you'd like to share a hot tub with me? I'm game if you are.'

She met his fiery gaze.

And like lightning, he was in front of her. His face was hovering close to hers. The electricity flying between them was unmistakeable. 'Come with me.' He reached for her hand and yanked open the sauna door, pulling her with him.

This was happening.

It was finally happening.

Molly followed him over to the shower. *Yes, good idea*, she thought. *A hot, soapy shower together before doing the deed. Very spontaneous. Very romantic. Very hygienic.* As soon as they reached the mosaic-tiled open shower, overcome with excitement, she flung off her towel expecting him to do the same. How had she ever had a problem with nudity? She looped her arms around his neck, pressing her hot skin against him, and stood on her tiptoes ready for his hungry lips to meet hers.

There was a moment of confusion as she followed Levi's gaze to the huge wooden bucket above them. Before she had time to protest, he'd pulled the cord and drenched them both in icy water.

'Are you crazy? This is so not what I thought you had in mind,' she said, shivering, every nerve in her body tingling.

'We could both do with cooling off,' he said sternly, taking two new, huge fluffy white towels from the rack nearby and handing her one.

Molly took it from him and wrapped it quickly around herself as he did the same. He was still looking at her with an intensity she'd never experienced before. She bit her lip, thinking of what to do. What to say. Her mind was a complete blank. Slowly she came to her senses. 'So, about the hot tub. Are we... Does this mean... Do you...?'

As she tried and failed to form a coherent sentence, her teeth still chattering, Levi put his hands on her shoulders. 'Look, I don't want this to sound rude but...'

He was giving her the brush off. He was giving her the *brush off*! *He* was giving *her* the brush off! Her whole being drooped. 'Oh, you are way past rude, mister. Way past. You're doing it again, aren't you? OH. MY. GOD. What is wrong with me?' She stepped away from him, her eyes full of fire. 'How dare you! Can't I have just one magical bloody moment in an effing hot tub to treasure without you ruining it?'

'You work here. You're off limits. Okay? It's very simple.' He looked her dead in the eye.

His words felt like a slap.

They stood staring at one another, neither speaking.

A disturbing pattern was beginning to emerge. Had he forgotten he'd already humiliated her, leaving her naked in his other hot tub? And now here he was, doing it all over again.

9

HELL HATH NO FURY

Molly woke in a blaze of fury. She had not managed to sleep one wink, plagued by dreams of Levi. She was furious with him, but she was more furious with herself. She'd thrown herself at him yet again.

After showering and dressing, she thumped through to the kitchen to check the notes Toby had left and to see what time the family were expected to arrive. Outside every window there was a blanket of white sweeping over the land, enveloping the glittering boughs of the pine trees that completed the picture-perfect wintry scene. Snow had fallen heavily during the night and was still coming down very thickly. There was no sign of Levi, but the fire in the living room was roaring, giving off a delicious heat throughout the open-plan lounge. Levi must have lit it before he left. At the thought of him, her chest twanged with disappointment. She felt like a prize fool. A naïve, stupid, infatuated idiot. She reached out to take the notes stuck to the front of the fridge and studied them. Levi's name was first on the list, the rest of the family's names below. *Oh God.* He would be staying here the whole time. There would be no escaping him. He would be a constant reminder of how she had embarrassed herself.

Her phone pinged with a message. It was Toby announcing that they would be staying at the resort again tonight due to the inclement weather. He made no mention of Levi.

Molly decided it was time for a bit of googling. She typed Levi's name into the search engine, checking Toby's list to make sure she got the correct spelling of their French surname.

'Don't bother,' said Levi, coming up behind her. 'The Wi-Fi's been off all morning. Don't bother with mobile either. The 5G keeps dropping out.'

She spun round, whipping her phone away. Like a hawk, he put two and two together, eyeing her phone with suspicion.

'Googling me?'

Molly felt her cheeks blaze.

'No, of course not. No! Never. Absolutely prepos-
terous. How very dare you!' *Stop now, for the love of
everything good, stop now.*

'Fine. Whatever.'

Molly studied him. He didn't have the air of a man
who had been wracked with guilt over facing the
woman he'd so rudely rejected the previous evening.
He had the face of a man irritated by the loss of Wi-
Fi.

'Since I can't get any work done, I might as well
have breakfast,' he continued. 'I'll have the eggs Florentine.'

'Pardon me?' she asked.

'With steamed spinach and toasted flax seeds. It's
on the menu.'

Molly stared at him, her mouth agape.

'You know. The menu? I assume you wrote it. This
shouldn't be breaking news.'

Rude. Arrogant. Annoyingly correct.

'You treat me like... like... well, erm... and then you
expect me to *cook* for you?'

Levi arched an eyebrow.

'Well, if you think for a second that you can just...
just... and then...' Molly was becoming increasingly
flustered.

'Fine,' he said, rolling his eyes. 'This is exactly

what I was talking about. If you're not going to do the job I'm paying you to do, I'll just make them myself.'

Molly followed him across the kitchen to the pantry. Her meticulously ordered pantry. He swung open the door and marched in, with her following too closely behind.

'I think you'll find the Val D'Amore resort *owners* pay my wages, thank you very much. And for your information, they don't pay me enough to put up with rude, arrogant, hot-blooded holidaymakers who feel they can lead a poor innocent woman on and then dispense with her at their convenience, without so much as a reasonable apology!'

Molly's lungs were billowing in her chest, indignation seething out of her. Levi towered over her. His close proximity, in the now not so spacious cupboard, was immediately unnerving.

'I'm the boss,' he said coolly, as though she must already know.

Molly let this piece of information land.

'You can't possibly be.'

'On what basis?'

This was a very reasonable question. It deserved a reasonable answer.

'On the basis of...' Molly racked her brains before giving in to defeat. Lack of sleep was playing havoc with her judgement. Petra could have warned her that the woman on the board was also the mother of the man in charge. 'On the basis of you should have mentioned it when we first met...' She trailed off.

'Okay, well, I'm sorry to be the bearer of bad news, but I own the whole Val D'Amore resort, this lodge, everything in it, all the land around it, the mountains you see outside, the roads you drove in on. The ski lifts, the runs, the clubs and restaurants, all mine.'

'Everything?' she gasped. How was that even possible?

Levi sighed impatiently. 'Everything. Although, if we're going to split hairs then I own everything *except* one last tiny little food hut in the corner of the square that will soon be added to the portfolio. Happy now? No need to google me. I'm telling you, I pay you. And now apparently, I am also paying you to watch me cook for myself.'

Molly's jaw dropped open. He might be rich, but he was still very rude. She returned his cold stare.

'How was I supposed to know you owned everything? Correction. Nearly everything.'

How dare he refer to her restaurant as a tiny little food hut?

Levi frowned quizzically. 'Didn't you find out before your interview? Did you do any due diligence before you decided to leave your homeland and trek all the way across Europe to work as a chalet chef?'

He was once again making a valid point. Her face fell. 'That still doesn't excuse the way you've behaved towards me. Being super rich doesn't give you the right to—'

'It doesn't. You're right,' he huffed. 'But I find it very difficult to believe that you haven't planned all of this. It wouldn't be the first time a woman has gone out of her way to "befriend" me. In the cold light of day, you being here at my lodge is too coincidental. I won't be made a fool of, Molly.'

Molly choked. What was he accusing her of? Being a gold digger?

'Okay, I see. Well, apart from none of that being remotely true, let's pretend the last few days simply did not exist, shall we? I'll be your chalet chef, you be you, rude and arrogant, enjoying your luxury winter break, and no harm done.' She heard her voice catching. 'After all, it clearly meant nothing to you anyway.'

Molly, with tears pooling in her eyes, swivelled around so that he couldn't see her. She had some pride left; not much, but some.

'That's not true, I just meant—'

'It's fine. I don't want to talk about it. It's humiliating enough. Let's just try to avoid each other as much as possible, with the exception of you *paying me* to prepare your breakfast, lunch, afternoon snack, pre-dinner aperitifs and five-course, haute-cuisine fecking dinner, until this whole nightmare is over.'

She heard him tut behind her as she slammed the door shut. She leaned against it to calm herself. He really was infuriating. She heard him do a loud 'Ahem.'

Shit! She gingerly opened it again. He was standing in the darkness with a thunderous expression on his face.

'Do you still need me to make the eggs Florentine?' she asked through tight lips.

Levi put his hands on his hips. 'Don't bother. I'll sort myself out.' He eyed the neatly stacked shelves. 'How hard can it be?'

Molly bristled. He could be incredibly dismissive.

'I appreciate this is all uncomfortable for you. You can begin duties once my family gets here.' At least his voice had softened when he spoke to her. Maybe he did have *one* remorseful bone in his body after all. 'And I'd appreciate your discretion. I need you to keep these emotional outbursts, this infatuation or crush or whatever it is, in check. I don't like people to know my private business, not even my family.'

He was ashamed of her! Molly's eyes ballooned. Could this get any worse? She felt an inch high.

'Fine!' she yelled, slamming the door shut again.

She felt like screaming at him. It was far from fine. As far from fine as it was possible to get. He was so annoying and arrogant. She would not sleep with him now if her life depended on it. And as for her eggs bloody Florentine. She would show him. How dare he dismiss her so easily. He was paying her to cook so she would bloody well show him what an amazing cook she was. She hadn't designed the menu to go all out to impress for nothing.

A few minutes later, Levi emerged from the pantry with an armful of supplies and clearly no idea what to do with them. This cheered Molly as she ignored his many attempts to find a saucepan, searching high and low in the cupboards, and began clarifying her butter and whisking in the ingredients for a smooth and rich Hollandaise sauce.

'Where are all the pans? I've tried every cupboard,' he asked in an exasperated voice. Molly shrugged her shoulders. She knew exactly where every single pan was. She had reorganised the entire kitchen the moment she arrived. If she was anything at all, it was unnervingly meticulous in the kitchen.

'Fine, if you want to be childish about it,' Levi said, dumping all his ingredients on the bench.

She did indeed want to be childish about it. She leaned across, ignoring him, to retrieve the bagels that had just popped up in the toaster, and carried on whisking, blanching the spinach, and in a whirl, she laid out a plate, tossed on the bagels, buttered them lightly, took out the poached eggs, laid them carefully on top, drizzled the sauce, seasoned them with black pepper and garnished them with shavings of parmesan, a sprinkle of toasted flax seeds and a pinch of the French-farmed sea salt she never went anywhere without. It was her secret weapon. The eggs smelled and looked amazing. The spinach, twirled into a nest underneath, added colour and texture. It had taken her under five minutes. Levi glared at her, his bread now burning in the toaster and his box of eggs yet to be cracked.

'Shame you were in such a hurry to dismiss me,' she said brightly as she carried them away. 'I mean, how hard can it be, right?'

* * *

Stomping back to her room, Molly scraped the eggs into the bin. Stubbornness had made her not give them to Levi, but anger had stolen her appetite. Now that the rest of the family were no longer going to arrive today, she suddenly had an entire day to fill. Plopping down on her bed, she took out Ava's bucket list journal. There was no way that Levi was getting his hands on her restaurant. She had to find a way to save Le Petit Ange or Ava would come back from the grave and haunt her forever. She stroked the smooth cover and with a wistful sigh flicked through the pages of Ava's writing, the photos of her walking on stilts, petting an elephant in Thailand, dancing in the rain during a typhoon. Molly picked up a pen and began filling in the blank pages with dates, times and her thoughts on the three challenges she had been able to tick off. The priceless camel, the wedding, the naked sauna. *Excruciating.* Nine more left and five days to complete them.

After she made sure that Levi was not hovering around, Molly made her way back into the open-plan, state-of-the-art kitchen to prep for the meals for the following few days. She was not prepared for the mess that awaited her. To all intents and purposes, it looked as though a gang of youths had broken in and had a food fight. The benches were cluttered with tubs of butter and jars of peanut butter and jam with the lids left off. Broken eggshells and bags of open flour spilled across chopping boards, abandoned utensils lay next to three frying pans, each with charred scrambled eggs in, lying discarded on the hob. A carton of milk and a split bag of spinach were propped up against the toaster, which still had burnt bagels in it. Lord knows what he had eventually managed to eat. Molly rubbed at her tired eyes. Levi clearly had no idea how to cook. There was a pack of bacon open on the countertop. It was from America. Out of curiosity she opened the fridge to return it and found a selection of drinks and foods, also from America, that must have been shipped in. How the other half lives! She got to work cleaning the surfaces and loading all the plates and dishes into the dishwasher. Levi must expect his staff to run around after him. Cleaning up was obviously beneath him. She wondered if he had been born into such privilege. Did he have staff to do everything for him? Luckily for her, she liked the therapeutic nature of cleaning. Her kitchen at home was always spotless. As a chef it was second nature to tidy up after herself.

She might as well keep busy and show him how professional she was capable of being because, as much as she hated to admit it to herself, he had seen a very unprofessional side to her so far. A side to her that until she'd set eyes on him at the Cigar Lounge, she'd not even known existed. She took a moment to let the events of the last few days percolate. While she was still furious with Levi and how unfeeling he was capable of being, there was no denying that the sexual chemistry they shared was off the charts. She'd never imagined kissing someone could feel like that.

'What are you smiling about?'

Molly jumped, dropping the carton of cherry tomatoes she was holding. She watched them scatter everywhere. *Typical.* She swooped down to retrieve them.

'Sorry,' said Levi, bending to help her. 'I didn't mean to startle you. I came to clean up the mess I left behind.'

Me, or the mess on the bench? she thought.

Molly continued picking the tomatoes up as he crouched right beside her. What did he not understand about avoiding each other for the week? This was practically the opposite of what they'd agreed. She sneaked a look at him, instantly regretting it when their eyes collided and her heart leapt traitorously. She hastily fished up the remaining cherry tomatoes. She couldn't think straight with him around. New rules would have to be brought in.

'So, what were you smiling about?' he asked again.

Molly's cheeks burned. *You. I was thinking about you.*

'Nothing. No one. Not a thing,' she yelped in a high-pitched voice, standing up, ramrod straight.

'Okay, weird. Well, sorry about the mess I left behind me,' Levi said, indicating the dishes and pans and trail of food littering the workspace. 'You were right about the eggs. I apologise.'

Molly ignored him. *I should think so.*

'And I think it might be better if I just let you cook for me instead.'

Presumptuous.

'I'm very busy.' Levi pointed to his laptop. 'I don't have time for cooking, so it's probably for the best.'

Arrogant.

'Are you still in a mood with me? Because, in all honesty, I need you to be more professional about it. About what happened between us. Or rather what didn't happen between us.'

The cheek of him to rub it in like that!

'Let me guess,' she said. 'You dated someone who worked for you, and it went sour?'

'Something like that but throw in destroying family relationships and an ugly lawsuit and you're almost there. Everyone wants something from me. And it's usually money. I tend never to trust anyone.'

'I would *never* ever do anything like that! *Never!* How dare you!'

'I didn't say that.'

'You didn't have to!' She threw the poor cherry tomatoes rather violently into the sink to wash later.

'Can you at least look at me while I'm talking to you?' he commanded, his voice rising. She heard the annoyance in his tone. She was really getting under his skin.

Excellent.

'Molly, look at me. I'm trying to apologise. I'm sorry, okay? Where are you going? Come back here. Don't walk away from me while I'm...'

10

REVENGE, A DISH BEST SERVED BOLD

Molly slammed her bedroom door and sagged against it, inhaling deeply. If that man thought a simple, half-hearted apology would cut it then he was sorely mistaken. She would prepare his meals and leave them out for him as she was being paid to do but anything else, any further interaction, was out of the question. She was not a woman to be toyed with. He had been very rude, leaving her spreadeagled begging for sex. Not once but twice! And to basically accuse her of having an ulterior motive for seducing him. She quickly dismissed the notion that she had, in fact, originally tried to seduce him to tick off her list. They'd moved past that with his incessant rejections. This was about dignity and pride. He might be rich, with an excellent portfolio of land and property and an expert command of how business worked, but he clearly had no idea how women worked.

Miraculously, Molly managed to keep busy the whole day and more crucially, kept her clothes *on* and her eyes *off* Levi, who had, rather distractingly, decided to work on his laptop from the lounge, in front of the roaring fire, while she prepared vegetables and starters for their evening meal across from him in the open-plan kitchen. Toby had messaged again to confirm that they would definitely *not* be arriving tonight as originally planned. She flicked her eyes over to Levi. He was deep in thought. The 5G signal had been off and on all afternoon, causing him no end of frustration. Disappointingly, she found herself yearning to take his mind off his troubles as she deftly chopped, poached and steamed her way through the afternoon, every nerve ending aware of him until she could bear it no longer. She would need to have another word with herself. Levi was forbidden fruit in every sense, and he was right about her having a crush on him. She must find a way to quash it. Besides, she was still furious with him. Her brain just needed to keep reminding her heart.

As though catching her thoughts, he put his

laptop aside and strolled over. 'I can't concentrate with you constantly ogling me,' he said wryly.

'I'm not ogling,' Molly retorted. He really was an insufferable big head.

She stiffened as he stood next to her. All the hairs on her arms prickled. The electricity between them was palpable.

'Is that so?' Levi scratched his chin playfully.

'You seem to be having an about-turn on our agreement to stay away from each other. Well, it won't work.'

'You're still annoyed with me because I wouldn't have sex with you?'

'No. And... yes. But it was more the way you rejected me.' Molly would have to be the grown-up here. 'I'm disappointed with the lack of empathy and the accusations surrounding my intent, which by the way was completely innocent. And furthermore, you have no reason to be concerned because those feelings are very much non-existent now. There will be no repeat of the... unwanted advances. You are quite safe.'

Why did she sound as though she was standing trial in a small claims court? Any second now she'd be calling him M'Lud.

'That's good to know. I'm sorry for any offence taken.'

Molly felt slighted at his lack of contrition. 'I'm sure you are,' she said tightly.

'Okay. Point taken. I guess I need to go big with the apology.'

'No need. I'm quite indifferent to you now.' Molly continued chopping her vegetables.

'So it would seem. I have to say, you have a remarkable ability to turn yourself on and off like a tap.'

She went to the sink to retrieve her tomatoes to put a little distance between them. 'I will be keeping myself to myself.'

'Glad to hear it.'

He didn't have to sound so pleased about it.

'Especially as it's our last night alone together.'

His words danced around in the air as she returned to the bench. He was leaning casually against it, causing her stomach to flutter.

Was his voice loaded with sexual ambiguity? Molly couldn't tell as she gazed into his eyes. They twinkled with mischief.

'Meaning?' She really shouldn't be encouraging him.

'I feel partly to blame for this... this falling out. Let me make it up to you tonight. I don't want to spend the entire week with you mad at me.' He gave her a sheepish grin. 'Have dinner with me.'

She raised an eyebrow. 'Don't you mean "cook dinner for me and stop sulking while you're at it"?'

A small puff of laughter escaped Levi's lips. 'Yes. Please. And I promise I'll be the most charming and attentive companion. I'll even help you cook it.' He blinked slowly, waiting for her to answer. He was like a magnet drawing her in. 'It could be fun.'

'If this is a pathetic attempt to flirt with me then you had your chance. Two chances, in fact,' Molly said, tilting her chin defiantly. 'Just because the Wi-Fi keeps dropping out, and you're trapped in the house because of the weather, and your family aren't arriving until tomorrow, doesn't mean I'll be your plaything, your entertainment for the evening.'

She was *so* up for being his plaything that it was unnerving, and felt like a slight against all women everywhere. She really must put up a modicum of resistance. She stepped away from him.

'What if I'm not playing?' he said in a more serious tone.

Lies. All lies.

'I find your attempts at sincerity incredibly off-putting and counterproductive.'

Levi took a step towards her, looking her up and down. Luckily, she had gone all out to cover up. 'Funny, because I find those gigantic sweatpants you're wearing enormously off-putting and counterproductive. Ditto the scarf and three cardigans. Are you sure you're warm enough?'

And just like that, Molly was thrown back to the night he came to her rescue at the Cigar Lounge, him taking off his jacket and wrapping it around her. Their heated kiss in the lift. His hands wandering over her stockings, tugging at the bodice, the top of her breasts spilling out of the tight-fitting corset.

Levi seemed trapped in the same moment, his pupils dilating. 'That was some outfit you were wearing the first time I saw you.'

Oh.

He was a very difficult man to stay angry with. That chemistry, that spark between them, that energy that seemed to ignite whenever they were within an inch of one another, exploded into the air. Molly threw a mushroom at him. 'Why are you flirting with me when you have no intention of seeing it through? You blow hot and cold with the wind.'

Truthfully, they were as bad as each other.

Levi placed his hand on his heart, smiling. 'Can't a man get to know a woman without her always thinking it has to end in sex? If only there had been a global movement to shift the balance between the sexes.'

Away from his laptop, she had to admit, he was very amusing. 'Okay. I'll have dinner with you. Happy?'

'And I promise *not* to flirt with you. I'd hate for you to be in a permanent state of arousal. Anything could happen.' Levi leaned across the counter towards her. Traces of vanilla and spiced bergamot filled her nostrils.

Suddenly an idea came to her. She pulled away. He needed to be taken down a peg or two. She needed to let him know who the boss was. 'Meet me back here in half an hour.'

* * *

A short but hectic while later, she had wrestled herself back into the burlesque costume and was sauntering seductively, just like she'd seen the women in the Cigar Lounge do it, into the kitchen area. Levi's eyes were out on stalks.

His eyes swept over her long legs sheathed in stockings. She fingered the little red bows teasingly at the top of each stocking before drawing his eyes to the frilly skirt, no longer than crotch-level. She saw his excited gaze follow her hands as she put them to her waist. It looked tiny, pulled in tight, the red corset doing a sterling job of creating delicious womanly curves that accentuated her breasts to perfection. Two generous mounds of sumptuous bosom peeking over the top of the corset, half hidden by the thick mane of hair tumbling down her bare shoulders. Levi stared at her cleavage, his mouth falling slightly open. She'd just had time to give her lips a slick of red gloss. She batted her eyes slowly at him. She was in the mood to teach him a lesson. She'd have him begging for her by the end of the night and she would reject him, like he'd done to her.

'What would you like me to do first?'

I'd like you to whip your top off and flex those spectacular muscles at me.

'Right, right.' She tried to think of something sensible to say. 'You can stand over there, far away from me, and erm, chop this up.'

Levi looked down at the vegetable she was holding out. It was very suggestive as far as carrots go. He took the carrot from her hand, his fingers grazing hers. The whole exchange was loaded with sexual euphemism. Molly found that she was rooted to the spot, watching as though in a trance as he trailed the carrot slowly across the palm of his hand before pointing it at her.

'Nice carrot,' he said. She held her breath, unsure of what was coming next. He was wild and unpredictable and thrilling, and he had her nerves on end. He took a step around the counter towards her. 'What do you want me to do with it?'

She could barely look him in the eye. 'What would *you* like to do with it?' She was all for empowering people in the workplace.

His eyes flashed, a dangerous twinkle lighting up his whole face.

She barely managed to squeak, 'Because I was thinking, shave it into neat ribbons.'

'Okay, you're the boss. I'll shave it into neat ribbons. Anything else I can do for you?' He was making it sound filthy.

'In what way is this not flirting?' Molly said huskily, stepping towards him. She looked slowly up at him.

'In what way is wearing this outfit not flirting?'

Touché.

Perhaps it was time to be more assertive. 'Take off your top,' she ordered.

Oh God. Was she really going to do this?

'Things are about to get messy.' She cleared her throat nervously. 'We're making a panna cotta slippery nipple for dessert.'

Levi rolled his eyes playfully and did as he was told. 'Sounds delicious.'

As he lifted the hem of his T-shirt and slid it over his head, she took a deep breath in, sure that she was *almost* completely in charge of this game she was playing. She would show him all right.

He stood in front of her, the soft fabric of his jogging pants clinging to every muscle. She saw the excitement she was causing and felt instantly empowered. She would soon have him grovelling for mercy.

'Hold this,' she instructed, taking a clip from her hair to release the theatrical feather fascinator. He took the clip while she trailed the feather teasingly down his torso, slowly down to his crotch. His erection sprang to attention. She was going to enjoy torturing him. He would have no idea that it would all come to nothing. She would be cruel in her revenge. And serve it cold. Just like he had been cruel towards her.

Instinctively he reached out to touch her. She slapped him away with a long, black, satin-gloved hand. He stood back, realisation dawning as to the punishment ahead. Levi regarded her for a moment. 'Before you go any further,' he said firmly, 'I'm not into playing games. So whatever revenge fantasy you've cooked up in your head, it won't work.'

For fuck's sake.

Molly's eyes widened. He had hit the nail on the

head. She was only seconds into the powerplay, and he'd trumped her already.

'You really have zero skills when it comes to lying. You'd make a terrible poker player.'

She put her hands on her hips.

'I'm right, aren't I?' He was straining to keep from chuckling. 'You wanted me to suffer. To tease me and then walk away, leaving me begging and humiliated.'

'You are so incredibly annoying!' she yelled, twisting away, flustered.

The game was up.

Molly grabbed her apron and swiftly tied the strings around her waist. 'Chop these onions. I hope they sting your eyes.' She heard him sniggering. This was going to be a long night. 'And then you can shell this mountain of prawns. And then I'll think of something else hideous you can do.'

He looked incredibly sexy standing there bare chested. She tilted her head. 'What? Why are you looking at me like that?'

Levi put his knife down and stepped towards her. 'You wear your feelings on your face. Trust me. You don't want someone like me.' His hand trailed lightly down her arm, causing her to shiver with anticipation. Mesmerised by his words, the way they lazily tumbled from his lips. Those inviting, warm lips that he used with extraordinary skill.

She blinked slowly.

He was doing it again, drawing her in.

Molly leaned in towards him, her lips hovering over his mouth. 'But what if I do?' Where was her pride when she needed it? She pressed her lips lightly to his, teasing him before Levi surrendered. A low groan escaped from his throat as he tangled his hands in her hair, kissing her neck, instinctively going for the spot that rendered her a helpless mush. He dragged her lips back towards his, hungry for her. They kissed in a frenzy of excitement until she could bear it no longer. Levi hauled her up in one fluid movement to sit on the bench. His mouth moved down her throat to her cleavage, causing her to moan aloud.

'Christ,' he mumbled, tugging her corset down. Her breasts sprang free. He took her nipple between his lips, gently roaming his tongue over it, then the other.

Revenge was indeed sweet. Molly would happily stay lost in this moment forever.

It was then that they heard the front door slam.

11

PLAN A BACKFIRES

Molly yanked up her corset just in time. A man walked round the corner. He was tall. He was wearing a ski mask. He was entirely covered in snow. 'I'm not sure the weather will...' He lifted his goggles and stopped talking instantly.

Levi sprang away from her just as he had the other evening when they'd been caught. 'It's not what you think,' he blurted.

The man burst out laughing. 'I beg to differ.' He looked at Molly splayed out on the bench. 'Am I in the right place?' He swivelled around, checking his surroundings. 'Or have I wandered into the French version of Hooters by mistake?'

Oh. My. God.

It was Levi's brother. She recognised the broad frame, the crop of blond hair and the delighted expression instantly. 'Hello again.'

'We were—' began Levi.

'Chopping onions,' Molly shrilled.

'Discussing the menu,' Levi said loudly at the same time, which made his brother laugh even harder.

'Molly is making dinner,' added Levi, his tone suddenly formal. 'Molly is our... chef.'

'I am,' she said, sliding down from the bench. 'I'm the chef.'

'And will you be wearing that chef's uniform to cook in for the whole time?' said Levi's brother. 'Because if so, I think I'm going to enjoy this holiday much more than the last one.'

'Molly, this is my brother, Lucca,' Levi said sharply. 'Ignore him whenever possible.' Levi walked over to his brother and gave him the world's clumsiest hug. 'But if you'll excuse us, we'll let you get on with cooking while we catch up.' He turned his back on her. 'I wasn't expecting you today. Are the others on their way?' he asked Lucca stiffly, leading him towards the bedrooms. Over his shoulder he called to Molly, 'Perhaps a change of clothes might be in order.'

Molly couldn't believe that Levi was dismissing

her. And in such an offhand way. As though she was no one. As though his tongue hadn't just been flicking her nipples. Words failed her as she stomped back to her room very much bemoaning her impulsiveness. She deeply regretted the fact that she had gone all out to win a game she had no chance of winning, but most of all, she regretted this ridiculous costume and the six-inch heels that went with it.

As soon as she reached her room she changed back into her jogging bottoms and sweatshirt, tied her hair up and wiped away the lip gloss. She splashed her face with cold water and studied her reflection. *Foolish woman. Do what he's paying you to do and put all fantasies of bedding him out of your mind. Focus on what matters.*

She needed to fill in the blank pages of Ava's journal, with dates, times, photos and memories as evidence of having completed the bucket list, otherwise on Christmas Eve, she'd lose everything she and Ava had worked so hard for.

Molly let out a frustrated cry. She was so mad at herself. She belonged in her comfort zone where life was boring and busy but safe at least, and where she was always fully clothed. The sooner she completed what she needed to do, the sooner she could stop working for Levi, secure the deeds to the restaurant and get her business back up and running. Properly. Le Petit Ange deserved to be the successful Michelin-starred restaurant she and Ava had envisioned.

She made her way back to the kitchen. There was no sign of either of the brothers, so she put the radio on and busied herself with creating that evening's meal. Unsure exactly why, she wanted it to be mouth-wateringly spectacular. She felt as though her reputa-tion depended on it. While she was busy rubbing herbs into a joint of lamb, Toby messaged again to say that he would arrive with the rest of the family in time for lunch the following day, by helicopter. Molly shiv-ered. She would make sure to stay inside. Something about those massive rotating blades unnerved her. There was no mention of rogue brothers arriving early. She took out the bucket list and scanned the challenges left to tick off.

Fall madly in love
Spend the day blindfolded
Make your own face out of sausage meat
Publicly eat vanilla pudding out of a mayo jar
(with gusto)

How could she fall madly in love in just a few days? Was that even possible? She was definitely in lust, she knew that for sure. But Levi would be keeping a professional distance now that his family had started to arrive, so she had very little chance of getting to know him properly. She turned back to the list. There were at least two or three that she might get out of the way tonight, before everyone descended tomorrow. She whipped up some vanilla pudding and filled an empty mayonnaise jar, putting it in the fridge to set. She popped trays of delicious seasoned vegetables into the small oven ready for roasting. She set the huge rack of lamb rubbed with garlic and rosemary into the oven to slow roast. She would throw the hors d'oeuvres together later.

She slipped on a hair net and checked for signs of life nearby. She padded to the top of the stairs that led down to the spa area and heard Levi and Lucca chatting. It sounded like they would be down there a while. Molly wondered which task to complete next. She chose the quickest and easiest. She opened the fridge and pulled out what she needed – a giant pack of sausage meat. It was trickier than she first thought. She would have to lie down to do it. She cut out a face shape with eye holes and a slit for the mouth from a sheet of rice paper, dipped it in water for two minutes and draped the soft wrap over her face. She worked deftly, working the sausage meat across her face.

Making sure to mould it to her features. She whipped out her phone to take a selfie. She would take another one once it was cooked and decorated to look like her.

It took an age and several bouts of cursing her friend before the task was complete. Honestly, what was the point?

As Molly lay on the couch while the meat mask rested, she was reminded of when Ava decided they must learn how to make their own sausage, arguing that there would be a market for corporate BBQs and quirky-flavoured meats. The more bizarre and alcoholic-sounding the combination, the more popular they had become. As she lay, eyes closed, Molly revelled in the memories, the days spent laughing together, creating recipes with outlandish names. The What Happens in Vegas sausage with its shot of tequila and lime running through it had them tipsy by the end but was by far their most sought after. The Date Night steak, Manchego and red wine sausage had been another messy night, ending in a sausage that was 10 per cent proof but hugely popular. Sex on the Sausage was a turkey, vodka and cranberry-infused creation that graced every buffet they catered. No wonder they had won an award for their ingenuity.

Molly reached for the baking tray at her side and, with gloved hands, she gently peeled the meat mask from her face. She wondered how running the restaurant without her best friend at her side was ever going to work, let alone be any fun. Shaking away the heaviness, she added the final touches and placed her sausage-meat face in the small oven above the slow-roast lamb cooking in the main oven. She took a photo of it going in and breathed in the aromas. Blooms of garlic-infused herbs filled the kitchen.

'Something smells nice.'

Molly jumped, slamming the oven door shut.

'Sorry. I didn't mean to startle you,' said Lucca. 'I just wanted to apologise for walking in earlier and... erm' – he was trying not to sound amused while he explained – 'disturbing you. But here I am, doing it again.' He gave Molly a self-deprecating grin.

'No worries. You weren't disturbing anything.' Molly straightened, wiping her hands on her apron.

'Yes, that's what my brother said,' Lucca stated, sounding bemused. 'Is there anything occurring I should know about?'

Molly wondered how to answer this. Even a fool could see there was clearly something going on. Lucca had caught them in compromising positions twice now.

'What did Levi say?'

'My brother remained tight lipped as usual.'

'Did he now?'

'He never mixes business with pleasure so it's no surprise. He's hardly what you'd call a diagnosed people pleaser, unlike myself. And he's been professionally trained to deny everything.' Lucca was smiling at her in a friendly way. 'Are you sure nothing romantic is blossoming between you?'

'Why do you need to know?' she asked him, picking the jar of vanilla pudding from the fridge and spooning some into her mouth to give her some time to think. Why was she protecting Levi when he was trying to hide the truth? Molly wasn't sure, but it felt like the right thing to do. At least until she could establish what sort of brotherly relationship they had. She needed to bring this conversation to an end. Her chest burned at the thought of having to be untruthful. She took another spoonful of the cool pudding, grateful as it slid down her throat.

'No reason,' Lucca said. 'Wait. Are you eating mayonnaise?' he asked, his mouth open as he squinted at the label.

She put the jar down with a clack. 'Yes. Yes, I am.' She offered him some.

'Mayonnaise? Out of a jar?' he repeated. 'I always imagined gourmet chefs would have a hard time choosing what to eat. Normal food would taste too simple, too run-of-the-mill.'

She hoped he wasn't going to make a big deal out of it. Otherwise, she'd have to admit it was vanilla pudding. 'I'm sure you have some weird kinks of your own.' She busied herself wiping down the bench, pulling out salad from the box and rinsing it. 'I have a lot to do. Did you want something in particular?'

'No. I just thought I'd find out a bit more about you.'

Molly inwardly groaned. That was all she needed. 'Sorry. Nothing to tell.'

Lucca grinned as though he didn't believe her. 'Well, I'll look forward to getting to know you better. I'll be here for the whole week. Who knows what could happen?'

Wow. Molly's eyes widened. Lucca was clearly coming on to her. He'd only been in the house an hour.

Lucca seemed to hang around, waiting for a response. Molly stopped what she was doing to face him. 'Me. *I* know what will happen. Nothing.'

He laughed. 'Funny.'

'Not particularly.'

'We'll see.'

'No, we won't,' Molly said firmly. He may be as

handsome as his brother, but Lucca was already beginning to get on her nerves. Out of her peripheral vision she saw Levi crossing the lounge towards them.

'Lucca!' he barked. 'Leave her alone.'

Lucca threw his head back and laughed. 'I'm not doing anything. You've both said *nothing* is going on between you. We're all adults. I'm just being friendly.' He winked at Molly.

'Well, be *friendly* with someone else,' said Levi through gritted teeth. 'Molly is an employee of mine. Show some respect.'

Molly thought that that was a bit rich all things considered, but it was Lucca who was quick to take him down. 'The kind of respect you've been showing her?'

Touché.

'That's enough. I don't want to argue.' Levi regarded his brother. Both men were the same height but there was something about his confident air that gave Levi the edge.

'We wouldn't know how else to talk to each other,' Lucca replied cockily. 'Molly, apologies if I overstepped. I will leave you two to *pretending* that nothing is going on between you.'

As he sauntered off, Levi and Molly stood in uneasy silence.

'Sorry about him,' Levi said.

'From what I've seen, you're both as bad as each other.' Molly was still irked at the way Levi had so casually dismissed her earlier.

'Meaning?'

'One minute you're all over me, and the next you're treating me like I'm the hired help.'

'You literally *are* the hired help.'

Molly was finding his regular and maddeningly accurate observations increasingly annoying. 'Yes. How could I forget? Now, if you'll excuse me, I have meals to prepare.'

Levi stiffened. 'Don't feel you have to join us for dinner.'

'Happy not to.'

'We'll just help ourselves.'

'Isn't that what you usually do?'

Levi raised his eyebrows, but Molly was already slamming kitchen cupboard doors and drawers. She heard him say something like 'try not to be so puerile' before he left.

* * *

Hours later, Molly risked going back to the kitchen to fix herself some supper. She'd left everything warming in the ovens and hoped that the two men had left her something to eat. She opened the oven door to find a full rack of roasted lamb and vegetables. But... if they hadn't eaten that... Molly quickly checked the smaller oven to see that her meat face was gone.

'I'd heard that the resort had an innovative new chef, but that was quite something,' said Lucca, standing in front of her with an empty plate. 'And while I appreciated the irony of you quite literally serving yourself up on a platter, I'm not sure my brother did. Although, to be fair it did look remarkably like you.'

Oh, dear. There you go, Levi, you handsome bugger. Resentment on a plate. Enjoy!

Molly tried to picture Levi tucking in as he stared down at her image, made entirely of squashed sausage.

'By the way, great idea to use red pepper for the lips and sprouts for your hazel eyes. Very tasty. Quite delicious.'

'That was not meant for you.' She grabbed some oven gloves and bent down to retrieve the slow-roasted lamb. She put the heavy dish on the bench. The aromas filled the kitchen. She placed the rack of roasted vegetables beside it. '*This* was what was on the menu. Did you at least find the dessert I left for you?'

Lucca shook his head.

This was on her. She should have risen above it and served dinner properly. 'Apologies. I wouldn't normally abandon my post. Can I get you some dessert now? If it's not too late?'

Lucca's face lit up. 'Absolutely. I'll get some wine from the cellar. What dessert is it?'

'It's a kind of layered caramel turtle cheesecake with pistachio and kunafa.' Unsurprisingly, she'd gone off the idea of making the panna cotta slippery nipple.

'Wow. Sounds great. I'll be back in a minute. You dish up. Get two glasses. I know just the wine to go with it.'

Lucca dashed off, leaving Molly in a bit of a flap. Did this mean Lucca and Levi would be eating dessert, and she would be serving them? She grabbed her apron and quickly got the cream from the fridge to whisk up. She would grate a vanilla pod lightly into it. She needed to quickly make some caramel crunch for decoration. Like lightning, she added brown sugar to a pan of melting butter.

'Found it!' Lucca said, brandishing a dusty bottle.

'Whoa, that smells delicious. I'll get the bowls, shall I?'

'That's okay. This will only take two minutes then I can set the table for you both.'

'Both?'

'You and Levi?'

When Lucca didn't reply, Molly swivelled round to find him opening the wine. He poured two glasses and offered her one. 'I thought we'd have dessert together. Get to know one another. Cheers.'

Molly felt rude not taking the glass and clinked it to his. 'Oh, erm, thanks. That's kind of you. I think.'

Lucca laughed. 'We don't all treat our staff like second-class citizens in this family. Unlike my brother, I've never been one to judge a book by its cover. I knew that behind that fabulously sexy burlesque costume there was a dowdy chef just screaming to be let out.'

Molly glanced down at her meat-stained apron and baggy sweatpants and let out a huff of laughter as she took a sip. She felt her tastebuds instantly zing.

'Nice, isn't it?' Lucca said, turning the bottle over in his hand. 'I've been dying to try this one. Come and sit down. Let's finish the bottle.'

Alarm bells started ringing in her head. The last

thing she needed was to get caught drunk on the job. 'I'll bring the cheesecake over.'

She finished whisking the cream and piped out the cooling caramel onto baking paper. She placed two generous slabs of sumptuous cheesecake onto plates and arranged the caramel crisps, dollops of cream and drizzled caramel, crisscrossing it carefully over the plate.

'This looks very decadent,' Lucca said as she placed the two plates down on the large table. He had increased the flames in the fire, lowered the lights and suddenly, she became aware of music softly playing. It was all very unnecessary. 'Sit,' he instructed.

Molly perched reluctantly on the chair opposite.

'This is incredible,' he said, spooning the creamy filling into his mouth. 'The best thing I've ever had in my mouth. And that's quite the compliment I assure you.' He winked at her.

Molly had no words. She rose from her seat.

Lucca put his spoon down. 'Sorry. I should have warned you. I'm a notorious flirt.'

'So I see,' Molly said, hovering by the table. 'Is there any point in telling you you're wasting your time? Or would you just carry on regardless?'

Lucca laughed good naturedly, holding up his

hands in defeat. 'Sit back down and tell me all about yourself,' he said, his eyes twinkling.

Molly marvelled at how alike the brothers were. Very smooth. Very confident. Insanely handsome.

'Thank you but I'd rather leave you and Levi to enjoy your dessert together.' She swigged back the wine and placed the empty glass on the table.

'I told you, he's not coming.' Lucca refilled the glass. 'How long have you been in the employ of my emotionally repressed brother?'

She gingerly sat down. 'I assume you're the black sheep of the family?'

Lucca raised his glass. 'Absolutely. How could you tell?'

They were interrupted by Levi walking towards them. It was hard to tell what he was thinking. He appeared void of emotion. 'You two seem to be having a lovely evening,' he said, a slight edge to his voice. He picked up the dusty wine bottle. 'I'm so glad you found something worth celebrating.' He put it down with a thump.

'We're celebrating this delicious melt-in-your-mouth slice of paradise,' Lucca said, keeping his eyes trained on Molly. 'Besides, wine is to be drunk, not collected. Would you like a glass?'

Something was clearly going on between the two

brothers, yet Molly couldn't help the feeling that she was going to come out worst.

Levi bristled. 'No thanks. Enjoy your evening.'

Molly watched him walk away.

'Ignore him,' Lucca said. 'He's just pissed off that I opened the wine he was saving for Christmas Day to toast my sister's impending nuptials.'

'Don't you have another bottle of it?'

Lucca burst out laughing. 'Unfortunately not, no. It's the last of its kind. It cost over seventy grand. Drink up.'

Molly stared at her glass and immediately lost her appetite.

12

FOUR DAYS TO GO… PANIC STATIONS

The following morning, determined to be nothing but professional, Molly woke early and began preparing breakfast for the brothers. She had been mortified at the thought of Levi catching her quaffing his most expensive bottle of wine and him eating her sausage face, thinking she'd done it out of spite. To be fair, she would have made something much worse than her face if she'd had the idea first. But the expensive wine, never. She would never have accepted a glass if she'd known.

Her phone pinged. It was a message from Toby to ensure the house was extra warm, the rooms were ready, the spa prepped, and could she let him know of any last-minute foodstuffs they might need for the

week-long stay? Molly pinged back a long list of ingredients. She needed to severely up her game. She
wouldn't give Levi the satisfaction of thinking she was
childish and unprofessional. She would give the
whole family a culinary experience second to none,
and she would win the contract for catering this
mega-wedding they were planning. Rich people
tended to pay a lot of money for things like weddings.
And, of course, there was the bizarre matter of Levi
mentioning that he was interested in her company.
She needed to secure more business to avoid having to
sell. Although Molly was sure that once he found out
she was behind it, he'd feel differently about buying it.

'I think you should leave.'

Molly's head jerked up. Levi was standing in front
of her, casually dressed in jogging bottoms and a soft
T-shirt. His hair was ruffled, and he still seemed half
asleep. She'd never seen anyone look more attractive.
She closed her eyes, his words sinking in.

This was about the sausage face. And the overpriced wine.

'I didn't know about the wine. I swear. I couldn't
even finish it once I realised.'

His mouth formed a tight line. 'It's not about the
wine.'

'Well, then, if it's about the sausage—' she began.

'It isn't.'

'Honestly, that was not meant for you. I'd never serve my face for dinner. Or for any meal.'

'It's not about the meat management involving your face. Not that one anyway.'

Molly frowned. 'Sorry? I don't understand.'

Levi shuffled his feet, staring down as though his speech was written on his white sliders. 'It's you. It's the way we are when we're together.' He stepped towards her. 'It can't happen. It'll just get messy.'

He was right. It was already messy.

'And I don't want to hurt you.' His voice was low and faint. 'Besides, my family will be here soon. Lucca will tell them all. It'll just be embarrassing. It's better if you leave now, and we'll avoid the whole scenario.'

He was doing it again.

'You're embarrassed? I embarrass you?'

'That's not what I said.'

'I think it's exactly what you said.'

'See? You're getting all emotional and annoyed with me. I just want to see my family, get on with my work and not have any of this... this hassle.'

'So I'm a hassle now, am I?'

The words hung in the air. Molly had never felt so rejected. 'Fine. I'll go. But just to be clear' – she heard the tremble in her voice – 'what happened between us was not all one-sided. You wanted it just as much as me.'

Levi's face softened. 'Yes. And I'm sorry I let it get that far. I'm your boss. I should have known better.'

Molly bit her lip to stop it from wobbling, turning away so that he couldn't see her eyes fill.

'I'm sorry if I've upset you.' Levi tried to turn her back around, but she refused to budge. 'I'll arrange for you to go back on the minibus. Toby can drive you back to the hotel when he arrives with all the luggage.'

Molly still didn't trust herself to speak. She was gutted on so many levels. The news of returning to the resort should have been welcome, but the realisation that she'd probably never see Levi again, *ever*, tore at her unexpectedly. He was right. She'd caught feelings for him. Big time. But they were obviously not reciprocated.

'Molly. Can you at least look at me?' Levi said, his voice tender. 'I'm sorry. Okay?'

Molly saw a hurt expression cross his face.

'It's for the best.'

'I'm sure it is.' Molly felt her heart shredding into a thousand pieces.

* * *

An hour later, Molly was packed and ready to go. Instead of looking amazing, to show Levi exactly what he would be missing, she had a bright red face and puffy eyes. She'd done everything she could *not* to open the floodgates, but for some reason as she packed the ridiculous burlesque costume into her suitcase, tears started flowing and didn't stop. She had cried a river over Ava. She couldn't understand where these new tears were coming from. Surely she should be as dry as the Sahara by now.

An awful sound of whirring blades alerted her to the arrival of the family in the helicopter. Molly thought it best to avoid them and instead texted Toby to say she'd wait around the back of the lodge until the family were inside. It appeared Toby had been fully briefed. When she heard the crunching of boots on the snow outside the rear veranda, he did not look surprised to see her standing there with her suitcases.

He patted her gently on the arm. 'Didn't work out, huh?'

She shook her head.

'I've heard he can be incredibly hard to please these days.' He smiled sympathetically. 'Come on then. Let's get you back to where you belong, miserably slaving away in the hotel kitchen.' He elbowed her jovially. 'At least you got a couple of days of free-dom. And I hope you got a chance to try the spa. That heated pool. That sauna. That massage chair!'

Molly doubted that she'd ever experience a spa quite like that again, in her entire life.

'I know Petra will be pleased to have you back. Ap-parently, there's a waiting list of people who want to book you to cater their Christmas and New Year events. I'm gutted that I'll not get to sample your cooking while I'm here. You have quite the reputa-tion.' Toby took one of the suitcases from her.

At the thought of Levi sacking her, Molly blinked away hot tears, shivering as a cold wind swept around them. As if reflecting her mood, clouds appeared to block out the late-morning sunshine. Toby quickened his pace. He took Molly's hand to help her down the icy steps of the lodge. 'We'd better go. That doesn't look too good to me. Might be another storm heading this way.'

The sky grew dark and menacing. 'If you think you won't get to the resort and back before the storm hits, then I could take a snowmobile and go by my-self,' she said.

Toby considered it. 'There's the replacement chef waiting for me to pick them up. But then again, I'd hate to go and leave the family with no staff. They're expecting me to unpack all their things and run around after them.'

'That's settled then,' Molly said. 'Go back in and grab the snowmobile keys. I've prepared everything you need to serve dinner, just in case the other chef doesn't make it up here tonight. There's a range of desserts, starters and even breakfast pastries all prepped and ready to stick in the oven for tomorrow. Just ring me and I'll walk you through it.'

'Okay. Sounds like a plan.' Toby trudged quickly through the snow into the lodge while Molly dragged her cases over to the snowmobile to secure them onto the trailer. The snow fell heavily as a distant rumble of thunder sounded behind the mountains. It felt like an omen. A sign to leave this place. She'd come here to escape Levi and complete her bucket list tasks, and at least she had achieved a few of them. But if she stayed stuck in the hotel kitchen for the next week and couldn't finish the bucket list by the deadline, she'd lose her restaurant. Then what would be the point of staying in France at all? She might as well leave the restaurant closed, fly to Paris and speak to the solicitor face to face about what to do and how quickly she could do it. She wasn't giving up her dream without a fight, and time was running out.

Before she changed her mind, Molly took out her phone and texted Petra to say that Levi had dismissed her and that she would be terminating their contract as soon as she got back to the resort. She apologised for any inconvenience. At least she wouldn't have any explaining to do and could simply go straight to her lovely cupboard-sized room and pack up the rest of her belongings, which would take all of five minutes, and make her way to the airport. Who knows, depending on how it went with the solicitor, by nightfall she could be flying back to England, to stay in the safety of her parents' home, far away from this place. Back where she started. She'd swap snowmobiles, hot tubs and Levi's hot tongue flicking her nipples into a frenzy of desire for looking out onto a row of council houses while figuring out how to complete the remaining tasks. Alone for Christmas while her mum and dad enjoyed their cruise. How lovely.

Molly took a final look at the lodge, the many, many twinkling lights strung around it already lit even though it wasn't yet midday. Heartbreak aside, the last few days had been the most adventurous of her life. 'No regrets,' she whispered to the cold air, her breath instantly freezing.

Toby trudged back over, his boots crunching on the snow. 'Here are the keys, your walkie-talkie transceiver, which I've switched on, and a spare beacon. The mobile signal is very weak here so use it to let me know you've got to base, okay? Jeez, those clouds don't look good. You'd best hurry.'

Molly thanked him. 'Good luck with the family.'

Toby laughed. 'I'll need it. They're already complaining about the Wi-Fi and bickering over bedrooms.'

'Just as well I'm leaving.'

'Shame. We would have had fun,' said Toby. 'I'll call you when I'm done here. We can hang out.'

'Sure,' Molly said, turning the walkie-talkie over in her hand. She absolutely hated lying. 'Maybe, yes.'

Toby held his transceiver up to his lips. He pressed the talk button. 'Molly. Do you copy? Over.'

Molly pressed the button on her unit. 'Copy that. Over.'

Toby frowned. 'Damn it. You're quitting, aren't you? Over.'

'Afraid so. Over,' Molly admitted gloomily.

He let out a puff of air, immediately visible in the cold. 'Well, take good care, Molly Johnson.' Toby shoved the walkie-talkie in his ski trouser pocket and gave her a brief hug. 'Good luck with everything. Hope it all works out.'

Molly swung her leg over the snowmobile and gunned the engine. The soft snow sprayed out to the sides like a pair of giant wings and the snowmobile slid a couple of times before she could get full control of it. With a final glance, she saw Toby standing waving her off and, out of the corner of her eye, she saw Levi watching her from the doorway, his hands in his pockets, a serious expression on his face. A heaviness swept through her as she revved the machine harder and drove away along the icy track. If she couldn't get the restaurant back, then maybe it was fate telling her it was time to give up this fantasy life and return to the real world. The biggest hurdle would be trying to forget all about Levi LeRoux. Molly wasn't sure it would even be possible.

Snow sprayed onto her goggles and with the natural light fading, it was difficult to see the track clearly. Up ahead loomed a forested area which, on arrival, had seemed magical and wondrous in the morning light, and now looked dark and threatening. Molly sped up. She did not want to get lost or stuck among those trees. She braced herself against the snowstorm and continued in what she hoped was the right direction.

She slowed at the entrance to the forest. Something didn't feel right. It was then that she heard a loud cracking sound. Instinctively she knew it was not thunder. She stopped the snowmobile and twisted round in her seat. She recognised the distinctive ridge of snow collapsing and sliding away from the top of the nearby mountain. Remembering her avalanche training, she yanked the transceiver from her pocket, pressed the button and yelled, 'Avalanche! Mayday! Avalanche! Toby, do you copy? Over.'

She felt immediately overwhelmed with a sensation of dread as the avalanche took hold, growing in size and pace with each second. The rumbling sound was equally terrifying. And it looked as though it was heading towards the lodge. The transceiver crackled. She tried again. 'Mayday. Mayday! Toby, come in. Do you copy? Over.'

A distant voice replied. 'Please repeat. Over.'

'Avalanche!' she yelled. 'There's an avalanche heading for the lodge! Over.'

'Copy that. Molly...' The device crackled. She lost signal and couldn't catch what Toby was saying.

'Molly. What's your precise location? Over.'

Feeling dizzy at the sight before her, panic seized her ability to think straight. 'I'm not sure. There's snow everywhere. The avalanche is getting bigger and bigger. I don't know what to do! Over.'

'Molly. Stay calm. What do you see? Over.' It was Levi.

The air was filling with snow dust, clogging her throat. She wiped her goggles. 'I'm at the edge of the forest. Over.'

Adrenaline was shooting through her system, causing her to fixate on the worst-case scenario.

'Are you in the direct path? Over.'

Her eyes darted to the snow cascading downwards. 'Yes. I think so. Over.'

'Listen carefully. If you can, turn the snowmobile round and move to the side of the avalanche. The side of it. Over.' Levi was barking down the walkie-talkie. 'Can you make it back here to the lodge? Do you copy? Over.'

'I'll try. Over.' Molly gunned the engine so hard that it dug in deeper. Powdered snow billowed from the back and out to the sides, creating a pit. Another loud cracking sound alerted her to yet more snow dislodging higher up the mountain. She needed to move, and fast. With all her might she tried the engine one more time only to find that it made things worse.

'I'm stuck! The snowmobile is stuck! Over.'

The transceiver crackled but no response came. She tried again but it made no sound. She gulped in the freezing cold air trying not to hyperventilate.

Think, think. What do you do in this situation? It was getting too dark to set off on foot. There was no way she could outrun the avalanche, and she'd freeze before she even made it back to the lodge. Her only option was to get the snowmobile moving. She leapt off the machine. She could barely see for the snow coming down thick and harsh. She uncoupled the trailer. A few steps in and she was trudging through snow up to her knees. She climbed onto the snowmobile and restarted the engine. It refused to move against the snow drift that was rapidly accumulating.

Molly leapt back off and retraced her steps, her long hair whipping against her face, her fingers frozen despite her gloves, her body rapidly becoming a block of ice.

Think. Think.

She yanked her heavy suitcases from the back of the trailer. She threw one of them under the back of the machine, kicking at it until it wedged underneath. She grabbed the handles and yanked the machine from side to side. The deafening roar of the avalanche sounded ever closer. She was running out of time. Once the machine was loose and the front facing slightly upward, Molly risked leaping back on and tried again, this time much more slowly.

'Don't panic,' she repeated over and over. She tried

to use the motor's momentum to push off the ground. The machine bucked and, on the third try, jolted free of the pit. With seconds to spare, Molly swung the snowmobile around and away from the avalanche hurtling towards her.

13

I FACE MY FEARS WITH COURAGE AND CONFIDENCE (EXCEPT WHILE BEING BURIED ALIVE)

Toby was already tearing through the snow towards her as the lodge came into view. She could just make out the lights of his snowmobile up ahead, still quite some distance away. Toby swung his machine around in front of her, waving his arm for her to follow him. He veered off the track through a small copse of pines. Molly followed, weaving in and out of the trees for what seemed like only seconds before he swerved to a stop in front of a wooden hut. Molly did the same. Toby leapt from his snowmobile and ran to her, grabbing her hand. She couldn't hear what he was yelling for the snow whipping around them. They raced into the hut, and he slammed the door shut behind them, plunging them into darkness. A horrifying roar shook the ground as the hut became enveloped in snow, whacking off the walls, making the whole thing shudder.

Molly stood still, petrified.

Time seemed to slow. Her breathing came quick and shallow. As the blood rushed to her head, she pulled off her goggles and helmet. She needed air. It was so thin. She couldn't get enough into her lungs. Spots appeared before her eyes. Toby rushed towards her. He grabbed hold of her just in time. She hadn't even realised she was falling.

He laid her down gently, kneeling beside her.

Molly breathed rapidly, trying to prevent herself from fainting. The roaring sound outside was beginning to fade.

'Molly. You're okay. We'll be safe here.'

That voice. That unmistakable accent. The one that had floored her the moment he first spoke. He yanked off his ski goggles.

She squinted in the dim light poking through the cracks of the skylight. 'Levi?' His face came into focus.

'Are you hurt?' he asked.

Molly shook her head and saw him visibly relax.

'Thank God.' Levi hunched his shoulders, unfolded his legs and sagged down on the floor beside her. He lifted the walkie-talkie to his lips. 'This is Levi. Do you copy? Over.'

It crackled to life. Toby's concerned voice was faint. 'Copy that. Are you both safe? Over.'

'Yes. We're at the hunting lodge. Everyone in the main house okay? Over.'

'Shutters down. Everyone safe. Thanks to Molly's warning. Over.'

'Resort notified? Over.'

'All protocols in place, boss. But it seems like it headed away from the resort. Over.'

'Thanks, Toby. Give us a minute to assess the situation. I'll be in touch. Over and out.'

Levi slumped to a lying position. 'Oh man. That was way too close.'

Molly was struggling to speak, her mouth dry. 'Thank you for coming to get me.'

'It was my stupid fault you were out there in the first place. Thanks to you everyone is safe.'

Oh.

A myriad of emotions swirled around, jumbling her thoughts as they lay staring at the high wooden ceiling, the skylight illuminating the one light fixture swinging above them. Molly watched it swing until the rumbling sound outside faded. The lodge stopped shuddering, and the lightshade eventually stopped swinging. The avalanche had subsided. She heard Levi let out a loud breath as he lay next to her on the wooden floor. They lay side by side until their breathing had regulated.

She had almost died today. Her life flashed before her eyes. Such a short and uneventful life. Most of it spent in a kitchen washing up pots and pans.

Levi stood up, the snow melting on his ski jacket. He held out a hand to help her. Molly took it as he pulled her easily up. They began to speak at the same time.

'I'm sorry I've been acting so crazy,' said Molly.

'I'm sorry I asked you to leave,' said Levi over her.

She regarded him for a moment and waited for him to explain. Levi seemed unsure of what to say, mixed feelings running across his face.

'Why did you fire me?'

'I didn't fire you. I just wanted to avoid a... situation from happening.' Levi took off his wet coat. Molly noticed his hair, T-shirt and jogging pants were soaked through. He'd obviously just grabbed a jacket and raced out to rescue her. He strode over to the moose antlers hanging on the wall and hung his jacket up. It dripped into a bucket lying underneath on the wooden floor. He reached over to flick on a light switch and all the lamps lit up at once. 'There's no boot room here for kit. Just this drip bucket and clothes horse.'

Molly gazed around the room. 'Wow, this place really is stunning.'

Levi was kneeling on the rug, twisting knobs by the huge stone fireplace which made it roar to life. She watched him hunch in front of the fire, rubbing his hands for warmth. Molly was glad of the heat. She was sure her lips must be blue. Levi guided her to the sole armchair in the centre of the room, instantly dropping to his knees. He pulled off her boots.

'We need to get you warmed up before hypothermia sets in. You're shivering.'

It wasn't the snow that was making her shiver. She pulled her scarf off in a daze. Would every encounter with Levi render her a big mess of jelly? He helped unzip her coat and neatly put it on the peg next to his, likewise tucking her boots into the designated boxes. He was a neat freak like her.

Impressive.

She tried to remove her salopettes without falling over. Why was skiwear so unnecessarily uncooperative?

He walked back over to give her a hand, bending to hold the salopettes as she stepped out of them.

Those dark eyes of his, framed with thick lashes, caused butterflies to flutter in her stomach.

For no reason she could understand, neither of them spoke. 'It's like we've forgotten how to have a conversation with our clothes on,' he said matter-of-factly, straightening up.

Genuine laughter danced from her lips. A sound she hadn't heard for a long, long time. 'I know. None of this came up in the interview,' Molly said, choking back a flurry of giggles to get the words out. 'In fact, I'm surprised with me *not* being naked, you bothered rescuing me at all.'

Levi threw back his head and laughed. It was instantly infectious. And before she knew it, there were tears of laughter rolling down her cheeks. It was a while before they both caught their breath.

'I haven't laughed like that in forever,' Molly said, wiping her cheeks with the back of her hand.

'Me neither. It feels good. It's probably delayed shock.' After a moment, Levi stood up. He grabbed a remote on the large oak mantelpiece above the fire and within seconds, flames roared brighter. The blast of heat was instant. Levi pulled her from the chair, gently down to the rug. 'Are you sure you're okay?'

Molly held her hands out to warm them as she sat cross-legged and leaned forward. Levi rested on his knees beside her, dark patches growing where his clothes were damp.

He followed her gaze.

She felt a fluttering in her stomach. She had been so furious at him, but now their fallout had been well and truly put into perspective. 'Maybe we should get you out of those wet things.' Molly tried to keep a straight face.

Levi shook his head slowly. 'I knew it. This avalanche was probably all your doing.' He began laughing again, the tension draining from his face.

Molly chuckled. It was a relief to feel her heartbeat return to normal.

Levi's face dropped slightly. 'I'd probably deserve it. I'm sorry for the way I acted.'

Molly took a deep breath in. 'Me too. I probably shouldn't have... you know. But...'

Levi reached out to put a hand gently on her arm. 'You do *not* need to apologise. This was all on me.'

She swept her gaze around the room. The light brown worn-leather armchair was draped in richly coloured, warm woollen throws. The coffee table was strewn with magazines, opened books and financial periodicals lying face down. Lamps, cushions, neat stacks of books and large vases of dried flowers gave the place a homely ambiance. Molly breathed in the woody floral scent. 'Do you stay here?'

'When I need time alone to escape my family and to think, yes.'

Molly was having trouble concentrating. Levi's T-shirt was sticking to his torso. His jogging pants were hanging low, revealing a glimpse of that taut stomach. A fine line of hair snaked its way down to...

'I like the solitude. It clears my mind. Allows me to think and plan. I practise Hansei. A mindful Japanese approach to business.'

Molly was only vaguely aware of what he was saying. Levi had grabbed a towel. He was lifting his wet T-shirt to pat down his stomach and his arms. She became mesmerised by his forearms, so strong with a light sprinkling of dark hair. Her pulse raced, causing her to become lightheaded, his voice drifting away.

Levi cleared his throat.

Molly snapped to attention. She hadn't been listening to a single word. 'Yes. That's right. Me too. To all of those things.'

But it was too late. She saw her own lustful thoughts mirrored in the dark eyes staring back at her.

'I doubt you could repeat a word of what I just said.'

'It's the avalanche,' she said, her breath quickening. 'It has affected my ability to concentrate.' The electricity crackled between them. She was acutely aware of her chest rising and falling.

Levi, looking unravelled, shook his hair, drops of wet snow showering her. 'Yes. The trauma of a near-miss. It elevates the... erm, the...' He closed his mouth and opened it again. 'You're right. We should get out of these clothes.' Levi seemed alarmed at his own words. 'I mean separately. Not together.' He hurried across the room to a big wooden door, as though to put a safe distance between them.

Her mind flew to the last text message she sent to Petra, her line manager. Levi was no longer her boss. And her thoughts about him were anything but professional. 'I can stay in these. They're not that wet. Both my cases are back at the forest. Hopefully not under a mountain of snow.' While Levi disappeared into the bedroom, Molly walked over to the large picture window and pulled the cord next to it to lift the shutter, snow falling heavily onto the sill. As soon as it stopped, she would get going before it got really dark. Ava's precious journal was in one of those cases and she needed to get it back. Besides, it wasn't fair on either of them to play these games. She would be the one to get hurt. Plus, she was a woman on a mission to save her business. She needed to stay focused.

Within seconds he'd emerged from the bedroom wearing dry clothes. He was rubbing a towel on his hair, making it stick out in all directions. Molly marvelled at how he could look effortlessly good no matter what the angle or circumstance.

'It's all yours. The bathroom is off the bedroom. If you do want to change, the drawers are full of stuff. Just pick something warm and comfortable until I work out how long we'll be stuck here. I have a ton of calls to make while I try and get the heating to work.'

As soon as she walked into the bathroom, the blooms of expensive-smelling spicy and exotic aromas hit her. It was like walking into a lavish five-star hotel ensuite. The bedroom was noticeably more authentic and olde-worlde looking. It had an inviting, sumptuous queen-size bed with a huge old oak bed frame, with layers and layers of elaborately quilted blankets, cushions and plush plump pillows. Molly wished she could collapse onto it. She suddenly felt drained of energy now the adrenaline rush was deserting her.

Her clothes now felt uncomfortably damp. She pulled open the first heavy drawer to find a plethora of neatly folded sweatshirts and jumpers. The second drawer had lots of jogging pants and jeans. She pulled out a pair of joggers and a sweatshirt and hastily put them on before wandering back through to the main room and the roaring log fire. Her eyes darted about. There was an open door to her left which must lead to a kitchen, but apart from that and the bedroom, this was all there was to the lodge. It was picture perfect. She could see why Levi would stay here. It oozed peace and tranquillity. Molly plonked herself down on the chair and sank into the cushions. She dragged a blanket over her for comfort.

'Well, I'm afraid it doesn't look like we're getting out of here anytime soon. I can't even get a mobile signal for more than a few seconds. Could be days at this rate.'

Molly almost choked. 'Without Wi-Fi?' She gasped. 'However will you manage?'

Levi chuckled. 'Contrary to popular belief, I'm not a complete workaholic. I'm sure we'll find something to keep us entertained.'

While Levi was being borderline delusional – he'd been glued to his laptop *and* spare laptop (who has a spare laptop?) and phone since the second she'd met him – there was only *one* thing on Molly's mind at this moment. She was running out of time. How was she going to complete the bucket list without him finding out about it?

Levi stopped peering out of the window and turned to her. Oh dear, she could lose herself for days in that gorgeous face of his. She fancied him. With every fibre of her being. She would need the self-control and discipline of a Tibetan monk to hide her true feelings for him while they were stuck here together. She picked up one of the French magazines for something to distract her while Levi paced up and down the room like a panther. She listened as he rapidly gave out instructions to his staff on the phone every chance the patchy mobile signal allowed. He switched between four languages with ease. He sounded important and incredibly intelligent. He sounded kind and generous. Christ Almighty, she wasn't sure she could last a few hours here, never mind a few days. Then a thought struck her. Make that *two* things on Molly's mind.

There was only one bed.

* * *

As the sky grew ever darker, Levi increased the heating and switched on the remaining lamps. They threw comforting shapes across the small room. It was cosy and homely. A large bookcase housed several well-thumbed fiction and non-fiction titles in French, Italian and English, board games and puzzles. It reminded Molly of her childhood.

'Well, if we're going to be stuck with each other then I suggest some board gaming,' Molly said. She needed a distraction because just being near Levi was sending her pulse sky high. She fiddled with an antique radio and found a French station playing old-fashioned music. After pulling out a few board games, she settled on a French version of Cluedo.

'Thank goodness one of us doesn't have a multi-million-dollar global empire to run,' Levi quipped, walking over to the kitchenette to pick up a bottle of wine. He inspected the label, opened it, poured two glasses and brought them over. 'It's not quite what you were drinking last night with my brother, but it might do.'

'There's no way I would have accepted a glass from him had I known what it was. I thought he was setting the table for you, not me.'

Levi didn't make eye contact with her as he set the glass down on the coffee table next to the Cluedo board. 'He'll have done it on purpose to rile me. It's his way of getting my attention.'

'Opening your expensive bottles of wine? Why doesn't he just WhatsApp you annoying memes or send you videos of cats line dancing, like normal people?'

'I guess I'm not always available.'

Oh.

'I've been busy working.'

'I know what that's like,' Molly said sympathetically. 'But it's never too late to change, as they say.'

Levi's lip quirked. 'Forgive me but you don't strike me as the workaholic type.'

If only he knew.

'What changed for you?' he probed.

Where to start? My best friend died? I let all my staff go? I failed to keep the restaurant going?

Molly shrugged. 'Things beyond my control.'

Levi remained silent. His dark eyes pierced hers. She felt as though he was staring right into her soul. As though he understood that sadness consumed it, and she wasn't yet ready to let go of it.

'Le Colonel Moutarde?' Levi asked, flicking through the Cluedo cards and fanning them out for her to choose.

'Not sure I'd suit the moustache. What do they call Miss Scarlett?'

'Mademoiselle Rose.'

'How many languages do you speak?'

'Only three fluently but I can generally get by in German and Spanish too, as they're so similar to the others. What about you?'

'*Je m'appelle* Molly. *J'aime faire du shopping. Je suis de l'Angleterre.*'

'Also fluent in French.' Levi chuckled. 'Please help yourself to my extensive collection of French periodicals on the global economy.'

'I thought you'd never ask.'

After rejecting another offer to take the armchair, Levi settled on the rug ready to play. The evening passed quickly with the roaring fire, the snow coming down and Levi sprawled in front of her while she embarked on some good-natured cheating much to his amusement. She was unused to drinking, and the delicious wine was going straight to her head. It was making her bold and nosy. 'Your family. Do you see them often?'

Levi shrugged. 'They're all a little needy and no, I don't see them much. Once a year, during the holidays.'

'So you're missing your one and only chance to see them?' Molly shook the dice and moved her token. Neither of them had been in a particular rush to win the game.

Levi shrugged. His phone bleeped. And kept bleeping.

'Is everything okay at the resort?' Molly asked.

Levi exhaled noisily. 'Yes, everything at the resort

is fine. It's just us that have been cut off by the avalanche, but that's not who's messaging.' He shook his
head scrolling through the texts. 'It's my mother and
this ridiculous week-long mega-wedding she's planning for my sister. I doubt she even wants one that
big.'

'Are they Indian?'

'Hah. No. My mother is American, old money. My
father is a French hothead. Used to be an art dealer,
even older money. They have been married forever.
Rock solid. My sister is a typical millennial, wants
everything given to her on a plate, and my brother,
well, you've met him. He's a real womaniser, a loose
cannon. Parties round the globe full-time.'

'Every family should have at least one loose cannon,' Molly insisted, pouring more wine into their
glasses. 'Tell me about you,' she demanded. 'What's it
like?'

Levi scoffed. 'Being a successful billionaire?'

'Yes. Is it as tiring as it sounds?'

He treated her to a husky chuckle. 'It has its
moments.'

'You don't like to give much away, do you?'

'That would be my years spent at Harvard Law
School. I'm economical with the truth.'

'And this resort – Val D'Amore. Did you build it or inherit it or buy it over time or what?'

Levi regarded her. 'And this nosiness of yours, did you inherit it, or have you developed it over time, or what?'

Molly chuckled, unfolding her legs. 'Fair enough.' She picked up a heavy glass paperweight from the coffee table that said 'Levi LeRoux' on it. 'Do you put your name on everything you own? Are you like a male version of Oprah? Should I be stealing this?'

Levi regarded the glass object. 'You know, you always think nothing will top making your first fifty million or buying your second island, but that's nothing compared to being recognised with a sit-down dinner in a room full of strangers, while they give you an oddly shaped award made of glass with your name scratched onto it.'

Molly giggled, getting up. 'I felt the same way at the Annual Sausage Awards.'

Levi burst out laughing and Molly felt an instant bloom of joy at the sound. 'I can certainly make you a sit-down snack for your heroic efforts in saving my life today but don't expect an award to go with it. Are you hungry?'

She held out her hand to pull him up. As soon as he took it, she wished she hadn't. She turned to immediate mush. She dropped his hand. It was the wine. It was making her feel things she shouldn't.

Levi followed her to the kitchenette, watching her as she clattered about, grating cheese, chopping herbs, whisking eggs, toasting big slabs of frozen homemade bread. She cut strips of bacon and left them sizzling while she searched for plates.

'A cheese toastie?' Levi smirked.

'A Molly cheese toastie special. Where are the fresh figs and the rounds of camembert?'

'No idea. I usually have food delivered, and the fresh stuff is only for emergencies like this one.'

'Thank goodness I'm so creative.'

Levi watched, mesmerised as Molly improvised, flitting around the small space, deftly stirring, poking, toasting, and as the smells increased in intensity, she heard his stomach growl.

'You take the chair this time,' said Molly as they walked back to the fireplace. She sat cross-legged in front of him and watched as he took his first bite of the toastie. When his eyes lit up, she ate her own.

'That was fantastic. They do say the way to a man's heart is—' Levi stopped talking and reached for his wine, taking a huge slug.

Her skin prickled. She had caused this with her relentless pursuit of him. 'I'm sorry.'

'Sorry for what?'

'Sorry I came on to you so strong. Sorry I made such a fool of myself. Sorry you have to watch everything you do and say around me. The list is endless.'

'Don't apologise.' His eyes were twinkling with mischief. 'I got used to it with alarming speed.'

Molly laughed.

'But if it's any consolation, you have been the hardest to resist.'

Molly blinked slowly at him. 'And if I wasn't technically your employee?'

He stalled before answering her. 'But you are. Case closed.'

* * *

After they had cleared the plates, there was the awkward issue of the bed to consider. 'You take it,' said Levi. 'I insist.'

'No. I insist. It's your hut. Your bed.' Molly was scoring a silent point for when he had called her beautiful, quaint restaurant a *food hut*. She felt inwardly smug.

'That's very kind but it's a hunting lodge not a *hut*, and I'm giving you the bed for the night. I'll sleep here in the chair. That's final.'

'You're too big for the chair. You take the bed. I'll be fine here.'

'Christ. Are you always this stubborn?'

'Yes. Are you?'

Levi stopped unpacking blankets from a drawer in the bedroom. 'This is silly. I'm sure we can spend one night in the bed together and keep our hands to ourselves.'

Molly held her hands up. 'Mine want nothing to do with you, so you're quite safe.'

'Are you sure?'

'Absolutely. You've rejected me three times now. I'm not going in for a fourth.'

'I wouldn't call it rejection. That was me being a good boss and not letting things go too far.'

Too far? Molly had a searing flashback to Levi's tongue flicking her nipples while overwhelming desire ripped through her entire body. 'Yeah. Whatever.'

Levi turned down the many covers on the bed. 'We'll sleep with our clothes on. I'll make a wall with these.'

Molly watched him roll up quilts and blankets and line them up down the middle of the mattress. Her soul drooped. He really didn't want to run the risk of her accidentally touching him during the night.

'I have spare toothbrushes in the bathroom. And T-shirts if you get hot in that sweater.'

Spare toothbrushes? How many visitors did he entertain here?

Molly fought off a pang of jealousy. 'That's very kind.'

They climbed into bed, each trying not to touch the other as they politely swapped pillows and shuffled under the numerous plush quilts. They were warm and cosy, the sheets silky as butter and freshly laundered, smelling of lavender. Molly lay facing him once he'd switched off the remaining lamp. In the moonlight, his eyes were tipsy and inviting.

Molly felt her resolve evaporating. 'Goodnight. And thanks again for coming to help me.'

He reached out to smooth a strand of hair from her face. 'Goodnight, Molly Johnson.' His fingers grazed her cheek, leaving a tingle in their wake. His gaze dropped to her mouth. She held her breath, willing him to continue. He ran his thumb lightly across her lower lip. 'Christ. You are so beautiful,' he whispered. 'If there is anyone worth breaking the rules for it's you.'

Molly melted inside. She wanted to kiss him more than anything in this world.

'Please don't look at me like that,' he begged. 'I

can't offer you what you want. And you should be with someone...' Levi's breath was ragged. The energy between them was intensifying. He shifted closer. 'You should be with someone special. Not your boss.'

Her heart hammered in her chest. 'And if you weren't my boss? If we'd met under different circumstances?'

'But we didn't.'

Molly inched closer. She mirrored his actions, trailing the back of her hand lightly down his cheek, tracing the line of his jaw. 'But if we did?'

Levi nodded slowly in answer.

'Well, you're not my boss any more,' she whispered against his lips, desperate for him to kiss her.

Levi jerked away. 'Sorry?'

'I quit.'

'You quit?'

'Earlier today.'

'You did?' Levi sat upright. 'When? Why?'

'Before the avalanche.' Molly sat up too. Her timing left a lot to be desired. 'Well, you did ask me to leave.'

'Yes. Leave the house. Not the company. And only because I wanted to protect you from...' Levi left the sentence hanging. He dragged his hand through his hair. 'Look. It doesn't change anything. You can have your job back.'

'I don't want it back.' Suddenly, Molly knew what she wanted – she wanted to sleep with him. She was twenty-nine. It was time she broke the ludicrously long dry spell.

They stared at each other for a moment, the atmosphere charged. He was inches away. All she had to do was reach out to him.

'I still can't offer you what you want. I don't have time for a relationship.'

Levi was being very stoic, and she wasn't at all impressed.

'Fine. Have it your way,' she said, trying not to sound sulky as she piled the cushions high between them. He was simply exasperating.

14

I AM GRATEFUL FOR THIS LIFE

Molly woke the next morning feeling utterly shattered. She had not slept a wink. Last night had changed her. It felt like a new low. The wall of pillows remained intact. An unmistakable divide, like the old Berlin Wall, high, sturdy and impenetrable. Having tossed and turned all night, she had made up her mind. As soon as the path was clear, she was leaving. She slipped from the sheets and threw on a robe to prepare coffee for them both. She wouldn't have his last memory of her as being petty. As she wandered back into the bedroom with two steaming mugs, the movement woke him. Molly wondered what effect last night's emotional exchange, their rather honest and soulful declarations to each other, would have on him.

Hoping to hear an outpouring of regret, she set the coffee down on the bedside table and climbed on the bed, eager to find out.

He opened his eyes, realisation spreading across his face as Molly gave him a hesitant smile. 'Jesus. That was the best sleep of my entire life.' Levi rubbed his eyes with the palms of his hands. 'My *entire* life!'

She waited for more detail.

'What time is it? I must have slept for nine hours straight. Maybe even ten hours. That was so great.'

Molly glanced at her phone charging by the bed. 'It's almost ten o'clock.'

'What? I've never slept that late. Eleven and a half hours!'

What was this? He sounded like an advert for a sleep management programme.

'Christ. I feel amazing.' He yawned, stretching his arms out. 'Eleven and a half hours.'

And the incredible remorse? Tell me more about that.

'I think I could even have slept for a bit longer.' Levi ran his hands through his hair and took the mug of coffee from the bedside table.

Molly got the immediate hump but hid it very well. 'Give me a call next time you're suffering from insomnia.' She tried to stop her voice from rising as she slid away from him. 'I'll come right round.'

She heard Levi chuckle. 'If you knew me, you'd know that's quite the compliment. I'm a notoriously bad sleeper. Usually worse if I have to share a bed.'

The last thing she wanted to hear about was Levi sharing a bed with other women.

'I can't believe that happened. I've never slept like that. Ever.' He rubbed the side of his face.

'Are you always this obsessed with sleep? You know there's an app you can get to monitor it, if you're so concerned.'

Molly climbed back on the bed begrudgingly. Last night was the worst experience of her entire life. She knelt facing him.

'How do *you* feel?' he asked.

She could not hide the disappointment she felt. 'Okay. I guess.'

Levi regarded her intensely. 'How come you're working for me? Here in a ski resort? What about the company you said you ran? Or was that a lie?'

Molly swallowed, unsure of how much to disclose. She swept her hair behind her ear. 'I'm on a break from it. I'm here to seek inspiration. New experiences.'

'And you've got someone managing the company for you while you're away? Where are you based? What's it called? How many staff do you employ?' Levi managed between mouthfuls of coffee, sounding as though he'd come directly from the Inland Revenue to dot some i's and cross some t's. 'Isn't Christmas a busy period for you? I expect you're quite relieved to be going back to it.'

And I bet he's relieved I'll not be chasing him round the lodge like an excitable puppy, she thought miserably.

Molly was desperate not to pursue this conversation and was saved by yet another ping from Levi's phone. He glanced at it. 'It's Toby.'

'Oh.' She knew what was coming next.

'The path back to the lodge is clear. We're good to go.'

Good to go.

As in, good to go home.

As in, it's time to leave.

Game over.

She took a moment to process what he was saying and drew in a deep breath. It was almost as though they were being forced to evaluate their entire dayslong relationship in just a few seconds.

'I guess this is goodbye then. You'll go back to the lodge for Christmas, and I'll get myself back to... England.' She didn't want to tell him about Le Petit Ange; he might be tempted to look for her. Ask questions she'd rather not answer. If only she'd been honest with him from the start.

Much to Molly's relief, a sadness swept over his face. 'I'll never forget you, Molly Johnson.'

So much had happened in such a short time and in other ways, so little.

'And I'll never forget you, Levi LeRoux. Wait. Why do some people call you Angelo? You never did say.'

Levi chuckled. 'I guess you'll never find out. I'll miss you,' he murmured against her hair as he leaned over to hug her.

Molly had never felt so heartbroken and joyful at the same time. She'd never, ever forget him. 'I wish things could have been different,' she gushed.

'Me too.' Levi brushed her cheek with his lips, holding her tight one final time. 'I'd stay in this moment forever if I could.'

* * *

It seemed like seconds later that they were fully dressed and putting on their boots when there was a banging on the door. It was Toby holding two cases.

'Good news and bad news,' he announced. 'The good news is I found your cases, Molly. They were buried up to the handles, but everything should be okay inside.'

Relief flooded her bones. Ava's precious journal was inside one of the cases.

'The bad news?' asked Levi.

'The pass back to the resort is blocked. We can't get any staff through, and your mother is screaming holy hell because I made the wrong breakfast this morning. Apparently, she developed a gluten intolerance yesterday that I should have pre-empted. *And* she was planning on micromanaging the catering and outfits for the wedding extravaganza this week, but the wedding coordinator is stuck at the airport with all the fabric samples. She's demanding the caterer that she booked, Molly... comes back to do all the Christmas cooking. She's furious you let her go.'

Molly took a beat to percolate this information.

'So...?' Toby asked Molly.

Molly beamed at the universe interfering yet again with her plans, a ripple of hope blooming in her heart. She would love an excuse to be near Levi. No matter what she told him, she had feelings for him. A lot of feelings. After all, hadn't they'd both just declared that they'd do anything to prolong their time together?

Molly nudged Levi, who had not yet said a word, wondering how pleased he was finding this fortuitous turn of events.

Levi seemed to be glaring at Toby.

'So we need Molly to come back to the lodge,' Toby clarified. 'With us. Right now.'

Silence.

'As a matter of urgency,' Toby pointed out. It was the obvious solution and yet it would appear, from the way Levi was looking at him, it was the very last thing he wanted.

How embarrassing.

'Erm, under normal circumstances that would have been fine,' Molly said, wringing her hands together. 'But unfortunately, Toby, I quit yesterday. So technically, I no longer work for the resort and so...' She shrugged in lieu of finishing the sentence. Her cheeks were burning at the silence coming from Levi. He couldn't be making it more obvious.

'Can't you just ask the boss for your job back?' Toby bobbed his head towards Levi, smiling. 'I'm sure he'd be able to pull some strings. Please, Molly. We're desperate.'

Levi had a face of stone.

More silence.

And plenty of it.

The atmosphere was getting more tense by the nanosecond. So much for 'staying in this moment forever'. Molly fiddled with her sleeves, hanging her head, hoping to hide behind a thick curtain of hair.

Toby's confused eyes were ping-ponging from Levi to Molly. 'I tell you what,' he said, leaving the suitcases at the door. 'Why don't I leave you two to work it out? I'll get back to the house. Your brother is complaining the sauna isn't hot enough, and your father is lost without the Wi-Fi for his online golfing tournament. He's livid and expecting me to perform some sort of technical miracle. I have under an hour to recreate the world wide web using a coat hanger and a ball of string. And your sister is hiding from your mother. She's forcing me to tell all sorts of lies. I'm stressed to bits.'

Molly kept her surprise to herself at the casual way Toby was describing the family as they watched him leap onto his snowmobile and scoot off in a cloud of snow.

* * *

'Are you sure about this?' asked Levi as he pulled their warm coats from the drying rack. He had been unusually quiet.

'Yes. I'm sure we can behave like civilised adults around each other. Besides, I have nowhere else to go until the pass to the resort reopens, there are limited supplies here, and your family... who sound delightful, by the way... need a chef.'

'It's not that I'm embarrassed by our...' Levi said, looking the very picture of embarrassment. 'It's just that...'

'I understand,' said Molly sharply. 'You're the boss. I'm your lowly employee. I'm sure I can keep my hands off you for however long it takes to clear the pass.'

'That's not what I meant,' Levi pointed out curtly.

She zipped her jacket up forcefully and spun round to face him. 'It sounds like you are *ashamed* of me.'

'I am not ashamed. I just don't want to tell everyone about it. And to be honest, I don't know why you would want to, either. Isn't it a private thing?'

'What happened to wishing things were different?' Tears pricked at her eyes.

Levi reached for her hand. 'If anything, I think we'd be amazing together. You're smart, you're funny, you're insanely beautiful. I just don't have time for a relationship. That's all.' He stepped in closer. 'And if I'm honest, I do care about you. I care enough not to hurt you. Okay?'

Molly swallowed. 'Okay. And while we're being honest, I care about you too. I care enough to respect your privacy. There'll be no social media ugly crying reels, no announcements on TikTok and absolutely no mention on the French television network about my many failed attempts to seduce you.'

An unspoken truce was agreed. Levi gave her hand a gentle squeeze. 'Much appreciated. I'll just make sure we have everything and lock up.' Molly watched as he tidied the board game away, straightened a few books on the coffee table, rearranged the blanket over the armchair and bent to retrieve something off the floor. Really, was there anything more attractive?

'What's this?'

An icy feeling gripped her as she watched him pick up the solicitor's letter that must have fallen from her pocket.

He unfolded it, along with the photocopied list it accompanied.

'No. It's nothing. Don't read it!' she yelled. But it was too late.

Levi furrowed his eyebrows. It took him all of two seconds to scan the letter. Then he separated it from the list and read that too, his eyes moving back and forth with increasing incredulity. He pinned her to the spot with a hard, suspicious glare.

'Jesus, what are you playing at?' Levi flicked the

letters with the back of his hand before throwing them at her.

Molly had no words. How to explain that on paper you were trying to get naked in a hot tub with a billionaire – any billionaire – for money?

'Am I some sort of game to you? A box to be ticked? Now who's the one not being honest?'

Molly had no time to reply because as soon as he'd said his piece, he swivelled on his heel and left. He didn't even give her the chance to explain. At the slamming of the door, she stood staring at it, flabbergasted, devastated, heartbroken.

15

MEET THE FAMILY... AND OTHER TRAUMATIC EXPERIENCES

Molly arrived at the lodge five minutes behind Levi, red-faced and puffy-eyed. Exactly as she had left. Levi had helped scoop the snow off her snowmobile and fixed her cases to the trailer in frosty silence. He had tested the machine was working correctly before handing her the keys, but he had absolutely refused to listen to any explanation regarding the letter. The only words he seemed to have digested were inheritance, bucket list, billionaire, hot tub, *naked* and deadline. He wore an incredulous expression on his face every time they accidentally made eye contact, as though words failed him.

Toby was waiting on the steps but had the presence of mind not to question why it appeared as though Molly had been crying. *How embarrassing.* He helped her with the suitcases and indicated the back route into the lodge.

'Take your time. I'll cover the family until you feel well enough to join us.'

'Thanks. But just so you know, these are tears of frustration and anger and disappointment... with men... and life in general.'

Toby backed away from her like she was an unexploded bomb. 'Good to know.'

Molly thumped into her room and threw the cases on her bed. Because he was behaving like a stubborn idiot and cutting her off each time she tried to explain, Levi was assuming she was callous and manipulative and treating him as though he was just a box to be ticked. But, thanks to a string of unfortunate events, she hadn't done that. 'See what you've done, Ava?' Molly yelled as she emptied her cases and stuffed her clothes roughly back into drawers and cupboards. She spotted the journal lying on the bed next to the letter. She would never understand why Ava had written the completion of her bucket list into her will, nor why she had spent the best part of the year grieving and staring into space instead of just getting on with it. She folded the letter carefully, placed it inside the journal and shoved it under her pillow. The clock was ticking. With only three days to go, she needed to reply to the solicitor with a progress report, send him photos of the pages she had managed to complete so far and sign the papers he'd emailed her ages ago.

* * *

A short while later, Molly found herself alone in the kitchen, yet again, taking out her frustrations on a basket of vegetables. She wasn't looking forward to seeing Levi. She had no idea what to say to him or how to act around him. Yes, it looked bad. Yes, it looked like she was targeting a billionaire, but the bucket list challenge had been drinks with him in a hot tub. Whereas she had tried to seduce Levi, many, many times, in a variety of settings, so it was an entirely different... Molly stopped chopping. Even by her standards that line of reasoning sounded very weak. Never mind that Levi was a trained lawyer. Typical. But at least he could have read the letter properly instead of picking out the few incriminating words that made her look bad.

'Hi,' said a glamorous woman, waltzing into the room. 'You must be the chef. I assume you've been informed about my gluten intolerance. Can you make sure you serve all my meals without wheat? And if you're thinking of doing shared plates, then don't. I'm also wondering whether an alkaline-based diet might be the thing. My pH levels are all over the place. Do that too.'

Her manners were certainly all over the place. Molly glanced up from the chopping board. Before she could reply, the impeccably dressed woman continued.

'Now, I've heard all about your weird and wonderful meat sculptures, but I'm telling you now, that avant-garde nonsense won't be of any interest to me. I like my nutrition to resemble food, not people. This isn't the Museum of Modern Art.'

Ah. The sausage-meat face.

Molly felt herself blush. How unprofessional. 'Understood.'

'Ignore my mother,' Lucca said, sauntering over. 'She has a different intolerance every other day. What was it last week? Allergic to poor people?'

The stern-looking woman in her late sixties huffed at him over the top of her glasses. Molly noticed her slender fingers weighed down with a plethora of antique-looking diamond, platinum and gold rings, the expensive cashmere dress hugging her slim frame, subtle lowlights streaking her perfectly shiny bobbed grey hair.

'Molly, meet Valerie. The matriarch,' Lucca said, sweeping his arms dramatically towards his mother. 'I'd love to say wicked stepmother but I'm afraid I did actually smash my way out of there.' He grimaced. 'Her words, not mine.'

Valerie rolled her eyes at him. 'And I still haven't fully recovered.'

Molly waited for her to laugh the joke off, but she didn't. 'Nice to meet you,' Molly said, holding out a hand.

Valerie stared at the outstretched limb with confusion, perhaps even mild horror.

'Mother doesn't do touching or hugging.' Lucca shook his head sadly at Valerie. 'Not even with her own children.'

Ignoring her son, Valerie smiled tightly at Molly. 'I've heard a lot about you.'

'None of it true, I hope,' Molly joked, retracting the handshake. Lord only knew what Levi had said about her.

Valerie knitted her eyebrows together. 'Petra said you were very talented. My good friend was a guest at one of your lunches. I had been wondering if we could discuss potential catering for the wedding.'

'Mother. Leave the poor woman alone. She's literally just arrived back from a very traumatic experience.' Lucca gave Molly a sympathetic look. 'Snowed in with my brother for almost two days. It doesn't come more harrowing than that.' He winked at her. 'Did he make you sit in silence and watch him work?'

'Only while he had me wearing the gag ball and handcuffs,' she replied flatly. While Lucca howled with laughter and Valerie looked confused, Molly was thankful that no one could see the humiliating images her brain was currently showing her. She'd have been lucky to get as far as handcuffs. Levi had a will of iron when it came to resisting her.

'It's fine.' She wiped her hands on a teacloth, keen to get back on topic. 'I'd love to discuss wedding menus. I have quite a lot of ideas that—'

Valerie tutted at Lucca before training her piercing sky-blue eyes on Molly. 'You wouldn't be the main caterer. Good Lord!' She seemed to find the idea so funny that she had to grip the bench with one hand while placing the other to her chest, her laughter coming in small silent huffs. 'No. No. We'll be getting proper Michelin chefs in to do the actual food. You'd do the nibbles. To accompany the welcome drinks on day one, or possibly day three. It depends how good you are. Oh, and each day is colour coordinated so the canapés will have to reflect that.'

'Colour-matched food?'

'Yes. Though can you believe, I'm having trouble getting a caterer to commit to a Santorini theme? I mean, how hard can it be to do blue and white food?' She shook her head.

Blue food. The most natural of all the food colours. Molly had no words.

'And before you say it, not blueberries. I can't stand them.'

'Mother. Stop micromanaging and let her get on with dinner. *Merci*, Molly.' Lucca dragged his mother away from the open-plan kitchen to the living room area. 'Where's Papa?'

'Where do you bloody think? He's online golfing. Again. I mean, why does he even bother to come anywhere with us? I'd divorce him, if only I had the time. Now, be a darling and get me the number of those caterers who did that event for you in Chambéry.'

Molly tried not to eavesdrop but the place was so ridiculously open plan, she could hear every word.

'Have you tried talking to him?'

'Lucca. Don't be ridiculous. I haven't tried to talk to him in twenty years. I'm not going to start now. He never listened then. He won't listen now. Stubborn fool.'

Molly watched Lucca guide his mother to the far corner of the living area where Valerie proceeded to scroll through her phone. Three family members down. Three to go.

'Go on then, I'll have a margarita,' said a young woman, sweeping into the kitchen. She was immaculately groomed, skin glowing, not a single hair out of place, eyebrows microbladed into perfect arches, tinted lashes curling towards the ceiling and dressed for a weekend in Ibiza, even though it was minus forty outside. 'Two twists and an extra shot.'

'Does she look like a mixologist?' Lucca yelled, walking back over. 'Molly, this is my emotionally dysregulated sister Freda. She's a raging alcoholic. Please don't serve her anything.'

Freda whacked him on the shoulder. 'Ignore him. I'm not. But make it a double, please. I'm having a terrible day.'

'Life is so awful for you, *ma p'tite soeur*. Molly, imagine having to get up at noon, drink cocktails all day, scroll through your phone and then go back to bed. Tragic. How do you cope?'

This earned Lucca another wallop, this time to the stomach.

'I'm drinking because I have a lot on.'

'You sound like Mother.'

'Yes, well. If she wasn't intent on organising the world's longest wedding, I wouldn't be so stressed. Did you know she's insisting on a different colour scheme for each day?'

Molly rubbed the back of her neck, inwardly wincing. She felt very sorry for the wedding guests. It would be a lot of work to coordinate outfits and gifts with the theme.

'She's even thinking of doing mirror-image weddings. One here in France, and one in the States! Who are we going to invite? Rooby is furious. He's only got two close friends and one of his parents is already dead.'

'Speaking of the groom, where is your poor spouse to be?' Lucca was searching the fridge for something.

'He's not coming.'

'Couldn't bear to be in the same room as us for more than five minutes? Can't blame him, poor sod,' Lucca mumbled, his mouth full. He turned to Molly. 'Lord knows how, but my sister here managed to bag herself one of America's nicest bachelors. Poor Reuben. He has no idea of the madness he's marrying into. Where is he then?'

Freda's cheeks coloured. 'He's gone ice-fishing in Canada.'

'Wow. He could not have gotten any further away from you.'

This earned Lucca a punch in the arm as he continued to poke around in the fridge. 'Molly, do we have any more of these delicious snacks? That swim has made me ravenous.'

Molly pointed to another platter of hors d'oeuvres on the bottom shelf. She was enjoying this sibling exchange very much.

'Molly. Could you please bring the margarita to my room? I'd rather watch Netflix than listen to my annoying brother all day.'

'Sure. Salt or chilli?' Molly had already found a shallow cocktail glass.

'One of each, please,' Freda exclaimed, delighted. 'I'm in the annexe bedroom just over there.' She pointed to the east wing of the lodge.

Lucca shook his head. 'Welcome to the annual LeRoux family get-together, where we all ignore each other for a whole week, until the following year, when we get together to ignore each other all over again.'

Even though Lucca was smiling as he spoke, Molly noticed the heaviness in his tone. If she had ever been lucky enough to have siblings, she would not be ignoring them. A big, lively, family Christmas was right up there with her desire for a Michelin star.

'Have you seen Levi?' he asked, interrupting her thoughts. 'By the way, these are scrumptious. Seriously good.' He had devoured almost the whole tray.

Molly inwardly groaned. She would have to make some more.

'No. Sorry.'

'He'll be working, I guess. He's always working.' Lucca studied her. 'Your eyes are puffy. Did he upset you?'

Damn.

'No. Not at all.' She rubbed her eyes self-consciously.

'Good. Actually, I think I will have one of those margaritas too. Can you bring mine down to the spa, please?'

Toby wasn't kidding when he said the family would keep her on her toes. Molly busied herself squeezing fresh limes, running the lime round the edge of the glasses before dipping two of them in her French sea salt and one in the chilli salt she found in the spice cupboard. She assembled the cocktails, added lime wedges and ice and placed all three on a tray. As she approached Freda's room, she heard shouting coming from behind one of the other bedroom doors. A man's voice. Yelling about fairways and greens, driving for show, putting for dough and going long or going home. Then she heard Valerie loud and clear. 'Oh, do fuck off with all that golf shit, Armand. Nobody cares about your hole in one.'

Molly knocked on Freda's door. The young woman yanked it open, took the whole tray from her, rolled her eyes at all the shouting and shut the door.

When Molly eventually made it down to the spa with a new, hastily assembled drink for Lucca, he was in the sauna. She knocked on the door. 'I'll put your cocktail down on the... erm, this table out here.'

'That's okay. Bring it in.'

Molly hesitated. She didn't fancy seeing Lucca undressed. 'I'll just leave it here. Outside.'

'This isn't Finland. I'm not naked. Bring it in. Don't be shy.'

She blew out her cheeks. This family. They were so used to people obeying every command.

What was the proper etiquette?

She was just about to open the door when she heard a movement. Levi was standing a few feet away, arms folded. He was not happy. 'Ticking off something from your bucket list?'

How dare he!

'If you'll just let me explain. I know it seems bad—'

'No need,' he said, cutting her off. 'The letter was quite explicit. You'll obviously do whatever it takes to get what you want.'

Molly took a sharp breath. She couldn't believe he

was saying that to her. 'It wasn't like that,' she explained in a low voice.

'Forget it. The evidence would suggest otherwise.' His voice had a hard edge, his face even more so.

'The evidence does *not* suggest otherwise. I think, if you'd read the letter properly, you'll find that there's no mention of...' Her cheeks were on fire. 'Of *doing* it on that bucket list.'

'Doing it?'

He was going to make her suffer.

'You know fine well what I mean,' she murmured through tight lips.

'I'm afraid I didn't have time to read the small print but I'm pretty certain there was mention of targeting a billionaire. *Any* billionaire.'

'No. Well, yes, but you aren't the billionaire from the list because I wasn't naked with you in a hot tub, was I? It was a sauna. And a shower. And yes, we shared a bed. But fully clothed. With a giant wall of pillows.'

Stop. Stop it. Stop listing things.

'I'm not sure that's quite the legal loophole you think it is.' Levi folded his arms in a condescending manner.

'I'm just trying to explain that—'

'And if you think you can play me or my family for

fools, you can think again.' Levi was obviously in no mood to hear her out. 'As soon as the pass back to the resort is open, I'd like you to leave.'

Molly felt physically wounded by his words. How could a man sometimes so kind and considerate be this cruel and heartless?

'Fine. Gladly!'

'*Leave*, as in, you're fired.'

'You can't fire me because I quit! *Again!*' Without thinking, she picked up the margarita and threw it in his face.

At that moment, Lucca opened the sauna door. 'Oh good, my drink.' He looked from Molly to Levi. 'Ah. You're wearing it.'

16

STANDARDS SLIPPING DANGEROUSLY LOW

Molly was horrified at her actions. She'd never thrown a drink in anyone's face before and although it had felt fairly satisfying at the time, she now regretted it bitterly. There was a knock on her door. Molly answered it, dreading having to confront Levi. She was relieved to see that it was Toby. She wasn't so pleased to see him standing with a frown on his face.

'Sorry about this, Molly.' Toby shuffled self-consciously from foot to foot. 'Levi has asked that you don't dine with the family tonight.'

Molly had expected as much. 'Yeah. Sure. Fine. Thanks for letting me know.'

'We can always eat together if you want?' Toby offered. 'As long as you promise not to throw any drinks over me.'

Major cringe. 'He told you?'

'No. Lucca did.' Toby waggled his eyebrows. 'He's finding the dynamic between you and the boss utterly hilarious.'

Molly looked away in shame. *How unprofessional.*

'Listen, I can clear a bit of space in my room or there's a small area off the kitchen with a table and chairs we can eat at? I feel bad leaving you alone.'

Molly assumed he was just being polite. 'That's kind of you, but I'll be fine. I'm not hungry anyway. I'll serve up the food and come back to my room. Speaking of food, do you have the updated list of Valerie's new allergies?'

Toby tutted. 'She's left a list on the fridge for you. It's quite long, almost the length of the fridge. Would you be able to cook anything at all with pumpkin seeds? For her inflamed bladder. And she wants to know if you have anything that will stop Armand's acid reflux. She seems to think you've got a PhD in medicine the way she's throwing all these questions at me.'

'Well, my mother is a nurse but that's as close as I get to being a doctor. I'll see what the internet says.'

'Don't bother. The Wi-Fi has gone again and the

mobile signal is so patchy. That's why I'm being hounded for solutions like a human Alexa.'

'Okay. No problem. I'll try to text my mother. But they're on a cruise so I might not get an immediate response.'

* * *

Once Molly had put the finishing touches to the family dinner, she stood back to admire the table setting. She'd had to use her imagination as to how the super-rich liked to dine at their ski lodges and so she set up the table as though a Hollywood celebrity was in charge of styling. There were winter garlands, courtesy of the many Christmas decorations that adorned the lodge, many candle holders that she'd found in a storage room while reorganising the kitchen, and lots of battery-operated fairy lights that she wove throughout the decorations, up the candlesticks and along the whole length of the table. A red table runner and matching napkins completed the tablescape. The whole display was a festive feast of reds, greens and golds.

'Wow, that looks very *Hello!* magazine.'

Molly spotted Freda approaching. 'Mother will love that. She's all about the glitz. The whole of

Christmas is about the photos she shares on her socials. She's worse than me for pretending life is a continuous stream of one fabulously pampered day after another.'

'I'm hoping the food will live up to her high standards.' Molly carried through small silver platters with crowd-pleasing pyramids of tiny bite-size hors d'oeuvres, canapés, blinis and appetisers.

'She'll still complain about something. Are they *gougères*?' exclaimed Freda. 'Papa's favourites. Stuffed with goat's cheese? Someone has done their homework.'

Molly had pumped Toby *hard* for information on the family favourites and had gone all out to impress by putting a slight twist on each one.

'Is that cake salée, too? Oh, my word. You really are the best. Levi said you were an exceptional cook. Just wait until he sees all this. And are those devilled shakshuka eggs? They're his favourite.'

At the mention of his name, Molly's heart skipped a beat. 'Yes, sort of. I just did a Christmas version of everything.'

'It's so clever. I wish I was good at something.'

Molly regarded Freda. 'I'm sure you're good at a lot of things.'

'No. Nothing. I graduated business school and basically haven't done anything yet. I met Reuben at college, and I've been setting up home and getting engaged and shopping ever since. My brother is exceedingly generous. I just wish he'd let me work for him, instead of gifting me a ton of money I don't even need.'

Freda had the good grace to look shamefaced.

'I know, first-world problems, right?' she mused aloud. 'What's your story, Molly? How long have you been a chef? Don't you have family to spend the holidays with?'

At the thought of sharing her life story, the quickest and dullest of all memoirs, Molly shrugged. The idea of spending Christmas Day without Ava had been one of the reasons for wanting to work during the holidays. She could keep herself busy and try to block out the bleak memories of last Christmas. Her parents had been fully understanding. It had been a miserable time for them too, so it was no surprise they'd booked to go on a long-awaited cruise around the Caribbean. 'Nothing to tell, really. Catering college, setting up a business and then here.'

'You ran your own business? What happened? Did it go bust?'

'Not exactly.' How to explain your best friend and business partner recently dying on you? 'It's kind of on hold while I figure some things out. I'm a contractor here for the season.'

Freda grabbed a morsel from one of the platters. 'Well, you're too good to be a chalet chef, that's for sure.' She made a moaning sound. 'This is so delicious.'

Freda followed her back into the kitchen. 'I'm going to pour a couple of Christmas cocktails. Do you want one? I make a mean Santa's Spritz, or an espresso martini, if you prefer?'

Molly shook her head.

'Please. Go on. Just one. Don't make me drink on my own.'

'Sorry, I need to keep a clear head until after you've all been served dinner and dessert.'

'You're not eating with us?'

'Erm, no... I have some...' Molly pulled gently at her hair, twisting it round her finger. That familiar heat crept up her neck. 'I have a lot of things to do. Planning. Correspondence.'

Freda gave her a disappointed look. 'Shame. I really wanted to talk to you about how to make these. Rooby is always teasing me about not knowing how to cook. I'd love to just, oh, I don't know, surprise him.' She blew out her cheeks. 'He's so clever and talented, and I'm so useless.' Molly watched as Freda rallied, going over to the kitchen to fetch a glass. 'Sure you won't join me?'

'Hey,' said Molly. 'Why don't you sous-chef for me? I could really use the help.' She held out an apron hoping it might distract Freda from daytime drinking.

Freda held up a hand. 'Honestly, I have no clue. I wouldn't know my way around a kitchen any more than I could make a pair of diamond-encrusted Jimmy Choos from scratch.'

Molly liked Freda. 'Everyone has to start somewhere. Follow me.'

Freda put down her cocktail glass. 'Don't say I didn't warn you,' she said, putting on the apron.

Molly noticed Lucca hovering in the doorway. He had a grateful look in his eyes as he mouthed 'Thank you' before disappearing outside. Moments later, out of the kitchen window, she saw him following Toby over to a covered woodpile to collect logs for the fire. As the sun set behind the mountains, both men seemed on very friendly terms. She noticed Toby sling his arm around Lucca's shoulders as he pointed towards the sky.

How was it that some members of this family were fine when it came to treating staff like equals, and some weren't?

* * *

Molly stepped back from the dinner table, now laden with an assortment of delicious food, to admire her handiwork.

Freda clapped her hands together excitedly. 'I can't believe we did this. Well, it was mostly you but, still, how do you even know how to do that kind of stuff? And the smells. It's incredible. And the attention to detail. It's crazy. Look at those miniscule edible flowers. It's more like art than cooking.'

Molly rolled her eyes, but a trickle of pride glowed in her cheeks. She desperately wanted to impress Valerie, in order to make up for the 'sausage-meat face' incident. She also wanted Levi to know that she could be the consummate professional, no matter what low opinion he currently had of her. 'Okay. I'll put out the starters after Toby serves the mulled wine and everyone has finished with the hors d'oeuvres. Would you mind rounding your family up, please, while I get changed?'

'Again, I am so sorry I spilled all of that melted chocolate down you. Thank goodness you had more.' Freda gave Molly an apologetic grimace. 'And the cherry glaze. I'm sure it will come out of your hair after a good wash. I just didn't see you down there.'

If Molly thought she was accident prone around Levi, then Freda was in a whole different league. Teaching Freda how to make a basic chocolate mousse fondant from scratch had cost her a box of eggs, a bag of icing sugar, a block of dark cooking chocolate and a pan of simmering hot cherries. She had been lucky not to end up in A & E with third-degree burns.

'Don't worry about it. Cooking can be a messy business. As long as you enjoyed it.'

'It's the most fun I've had without a drink in my hand for a long time.' Freda patted Molly's arm. 'This means a lot. I really loved learning to make it. I'm going to make one for Rooby as a surprise on Christmas Day. He's flying in from Canada.' She pointed to the large brown splodge in a bowl, which was her attempt at the chocolate cake.

'I'm sure he'll love it,' Molly assured her. It was the worst fondant she'd ever seen. And she'd seen plenty.

It was while Molly was lighting the last of the candles that a loud banging sound plunged the whole house into darkness. Her festive table together with the roaring fire in the huge stone fireplace, however, shone brightly with twinkling lights. It looked even more magnificent in the dark. She raced over to the kitchen using the torch on her phone.

She could just make out where she was going and when she opened the oven door, she saw with relief that the roasting pork joint was sizzling away cooked to perfection, as were the vegetables. She checked the sauces in the pans and quickly placed lids on them, turning the gas down to its lowest setting. She would have to serve dinner more quickly without electricity.

Toby raced into the kitchen holding a torch. 'You okay?' he asked. 'There's been a power outage. I'll go see if I can get it back on.'

'Toby!' yelled a gruff voice in a heavy French accent. A man emerged from the darkness into the fading light of the kitchen. 'What's going on?'

'Monsieur LeRoux. I'm just about to check the generator. We should be able to get the power back up.'

'Good, I'm in the middle of an important game of golf.'

'You and that bloody golf. God forbid you end up spending the evening with your wife and family. Toby, I forbid you to put the power back on.' Valerie was click-clacking her way across the wooden floorboards towards them. 'Dinner is ready. I say we eat. Molly, did you prepare my meal exactly as specified?'

'Yes, Madame LeRoux.' Molly pointed to a selection of covered dishes. 'Even down to the sauces, entrées and desserts.'

Valerie arranged her face to look slightly impressed. While the men were discussing electrics and Toby was instructed by Armand to go check the generator regardless, Valerie leaned in. 'Not bad,' she said, pointing to the table display. 'And was that spinach artichoke dip I saw?'

Molly had added crispy bacon crumbs, Valerie's favourite. 'And a selection of your favourite crudités.'

Valerie's eyes widened as she clapped her hands. 'Let's sit down, everyone. We'll get started on dinner. Lucca, you sit there. Freda next to me. Levi? Where's Levi? He can't still be working. Not in the dark.'

Molly was desperate to escape before Levi came to join them. She looked a right mess.

'Now, Molly, talk us through this feast. Starting with that huge pile of horse dung over there. I'm sure I said no to avant-garde. Or did you drop it by accident?'

Freda cleared her throat. 'Mother. That's my chocolate fondant. It took me all afternoon to make.'

Valerie eyed Molly. 'And then she threw half of it over you, did she?'

Molly wiped her cheek. 'Freda is a very fast learner. She was brilliant.' She had not expected to be regaling the entire family with a culinary breakdown, especially not dressed as a squashed trifle, her jogging bottoms covered in chocolate sauce, her hair in a top-knot covered in cherry glaze and icing sugar on her cheeks. She'd looked better.

'Actually, I was just about to change into some clean chef's whites and—'

'Nonsense. You look fine,' said Valerie. 'Besides, who have you got to impress here?'

Was no one in this family ever going to let her finish a sentence?

Molly ground her teeth. 'I'd rather not. I'll let you eat alone seeing as it's your first...'

'Join us,' boomed Armand LeRoux. 'Sit down. Can't have you sitting in the dark on your own.'

Lucca scraped out a chair and sat down. 'Well, I'm starving. I'd be happy to eat that pile of chocolate horse muck any day of the week, Freeds. I say, Molly, this looks spectacular.' Lucca's gaze roamed the table, back and forth, before settling on one of the silver platters. 'Are you responsible for these amuse-bouches, or did you have them sent up from the resort before the avalanche?'

'She made everything from scratch. I watched her. She's very clever.' Freda slung her arm around Molly's shoulder, causing her to stiffen. She hated being the centre of attention.

Lucca picked up one of the hors d'oeuvres and inspected it. 'These are like those aphrodisiacs everyone was raving about at the Cigar Lounge.' He popped it in his mouth and groaned. '*Merde!* They're delicious.' Then, as though a penny was dropping, his eyes widened. 'Do you work for the catering company that my brother has been looking into buying?'

Everybody turned to her.

'It's not just a catering company. We have Le Petit Ange restaurant too. We cater lots of different events as well as for the ski resort.'

'Who trained you? Who's in charge? Who is the executive chef?' Valerie demanded.

Molly looked at them. They all assumed she was the hired help.

'I don't work for anyone. I am the company. I own it.'

'Wait. You *own* Le Petit Ange?' Lucca asked.

'Yes.'

'My brother has been after that restaurant for years. It's where he earned his nickname, Angelo. Mother, do you remember?'

'I used to take you all there every morning during the holidays,' Valerie mused. 'They called him Little Angel, after the place, because he always helped tidy up. In fact, when he was ten, he promised to buy it for me when he was rich enough.'

Molly was struggling to see the angelic side of Levi. So far, he'd turned into more of a devil.

'It's the only restaurant in the whole of Val D'Amore he doesn't own.' Lucca looked beyond her, to Levi approaching. Molly sat up straight. This was not what she had anticipated. Especially not looking such a mess.

'Just in time, Levi.'

'Just in time for what?' Levi gave Molly a cold, hard stare. He was probably wondering why she was there when he'd specifically instructed her not to be.

'You owe me a finder's fee.'

'Do I?' Levi was still glaring at Molly.

'You know how you were struggling to track down the owner of the restaurant who makes all that yummy food and these delicious canapés? Well, you're looking at her.' Lucca tore his gaze from Levi back to Molly, a frown creasing his brow. 'You're also looking at her in the same way I would look at someone punching a dolphin in the face or trampling a baby kitten.'

Silence.

'Levi,' Freda injected. 'What on earth is going on between you two?'

'Nothing,' Levi and Molly replied in unison.

Levi shook his head slowly, giving Molly a sour look. 'And you didn't think to mention this to me, even though I spent an awful lot of time at the hunting lodge asking about your catering business? You let me divulge sensitive information and didn't think it appropriate to tell me you're its CEO? In my world that's very underhand.'

Molly bit her lip. She would find it hard to come up with an excuse under normal circumstances, never mind with the entire family watching her like a hawk.

'You told me you never mix business and pleasure. I was... I was waiting for a good time.' She had other things on her mind during her stay at the hunting lodge, or had he forgotten?

Levi looked thunderous at Molly quoting him. He yanked at the chair opposite her. 'How about now? Is this a good time? Seeing as you've decided to join us.'

Molly put a hand to her chest. He had such a forceful air. No wonder he always got what he wanted.

'That's enough. Leave the poor girl alone,' said Lucca. 'Let's just enjoy the food. And for your information, it was Papa who insisted she stay.'

'Don't be mean, Levi. Molly's been an angel to me all afternoon. Look what she taught me to bake.' Freda pointed to the huge lump of deflated chocolate slop sitting proudly on the counter.

Levi gave Molly a quizzical look.

The shame.

'It took me all afternoon, and a few goes, but we got there,' Freda said, lifting up her third glass of champagne in celebration.

Molly smiled weakly at her. It wasn't Freda's fault she had two left hands and a serious drinking problem.

'And I'm hoping to discuss the canapés for the wedding.' Valerie picked one up and inspected it. 'I hadn't realised how good they would be. I must swing by the restaurant some time. Let her stay.'

As Levi glared at Molly across the candlelight, she had a sinking feeling. This was going to be bad. Very bad.

17

SOCIAL HELL

As everyone settled down to their appetisers, Toby took a seat next to Lucca, explaining that he couldn't get the generator to work. Lucca offered to help him. Molly noticed again the ease with which the two men were able to talk.

'I'm not surprised. It's probably overloaded with the number of lights and decorations there are in this place. Do you want me to see if I can help?' Molly asked Toby. She'd do anything to escape this dinner.

Valerie shook her head. 'Leave the men to get on with it. I doubt you could help anyway. You're not an engineer. What would you know?'

It was all very dismissive.

'I don't know much about generators, but I do know—'

'Toby will fix it later, won't you?' Valerie said, cutting her off. 'Now, tell me about this restaurant. How much do you want for it?'

'It's not for sale.'

Valerie erupted into peals of laughter. 'Don't be silly. Name your price, girl.'

Molly was running out of patience with the older woman and wished she could find an excuse to leave the table. 'It has sentimental value and it's also my career and my home.'

'Everything has a price,' Valerie said, reaching over to dip a celery stick into one of the creamy dips. 'You'd be surprised what people are willing to sacrifice in return for lots of money. Isn't that right?'

To say that the ensuing silence was thorny would be an understatement, as those around the table appeared to inwardly question the matriarch's shallow belief system.

'Some people will go to extraordinary lengths,' added Levi.

Not wanting to get into a discussion about values and attitudes to money, Molly scraped back her chair. She doubted Levi nor Valerie would like what she had to say. 'It's not for sale. Now, if the generator is out, I guess we should move the food from the freezer and put it outside in the snow otherwise it will start to defrost.' The cupboards were well stocked and the freezer chests bulging with delicacies from around the world. Molly knew that they could be snowed in for months and she'd still be able to feed them, but there would be a day when it might come to crisp sandwiches or beans on toast, and she doubted any one of them could handle it. She surveyed the heavily laden table. The lobster tails, the Alaskan salmon and vacuum-packed Beluga caviar must be saved, or life would not be worth living. She glanced out of the window to see snow thwacking against the pane.

It was the last thing she wanted to do and apparently, she wasn't the only one. She got up but nobody followed her to help.

'Do what you must,' said Valerie, waving her away. 'It's all very inconvenient.'

* * *

It took Molly twenty minutes to lug things from the freezer to just outside the boot room door, piling them in the snow. When she returned, Levi was exuding frosty vibes aplenty, even though Freda and his mother were bombarding him with questions about the wedding, about employment in the company and about his love life.

Molly kept her head down while Valerie grilled him.

'Oh, come on. You must have women throwing themselves at you all the time.' Valerie was speaking to Levi the same way you'd fob off a child. 'I refuse to believe you spend all of your time working and none of it enjoying yourself.'

This was the most excruciating family dinner Molly had ever endured.

'I do enjoy myself. I enjoy work,' Levi replied tightly, leaning his elbow on the cluttered table. 'Please stop trying to fix a problem that doesn't exist. And don't think I don't know what this is about. I'm not going to allow you to marry me off to some second cousin with big teeth and a large forehead just to protect the family fortune.'

Valerie pretended to look innocent. 'I have no idea what you mean. It doesn't matter who any of you marry. Just make sure they are from the designated gene pool and preferably titled. And not too opinionated. Is that too much to ask?'

'We all know you are after grandchildren, Mother.' Freda chuckled. 'Something to do. I mean, seriously, how bored are you to want children to look after? You could just volunteer at a school or something. Buy an orphanage.'

'Pardon me for wanting the best for my children. I just want to see you all settled and happy instead of sowing your wild oats all over the place.' Valerie gave Lucca a piercing stare before she turned back to Levi. 'At least tell me you've met someone.'

Levi flicked Molly a look. 'No. No one special.'

Molly rolled her eyes. He was going to make her suffer.

'I'm very happy, Mother! In case you were wondering,' yelled Lucca down the table. He and Toby clinked glasses. '*And* I've met someone.'

This caused everyone to stop what they were doing.

'You have?' Valerie beamed. 'Who is she?'

Lucca looked from Toby to his mother. 'Someone we already know. Someone talented. Funny. Warm. Kind. Clever. Surprising.' He took a long swig of his drink. 'Someone just like me.'

Molly noticed two pink spots forming on Lucca's cheeks and wondered if he was talking about Toby. Surely Lucca's family would know if he was gay? But then, nothing would surprise her. Compared to her own family, this one didn't seem very close.

'Tell me who she is,' demanded Valerie.

Lucca shook his head, smiling enigmatically. 'Not a chance.'

'You're always gazing at yourself in the mirror,' laughed Freda, her eyes shining brightly. 'It was only a matter of time before you fell in love with your own reflection. I think you can legally marry yourself now. Is that a thing?'

Lucca was quick with a retort. 'I've always been madly in love with myself. Someone had to show me some affection growing up.'

'Who is she then?' asked Valerie again, topping up her drink.

'It's a secret,' Lucca said, winking at Molly as though she was in on it somehow.

Why? Why drag me into it?

'Good Lord, it's not that dreadful woman with the red hair who keeps hanging around, is it? There's something very hard about her. She's nothing but a glorified stripper. She's always inviting herself to my charity functions. If you're going to waste yourself on the hired help, then at least choose someone who's respectable.'

Molly didn't dare look at Levi.

Lucca straightened in his chair 'You're such a snob, Mother. I'm not telling you who it is. Besides, this family is full of secrets. Why should I be any different?'

Poor Toby. Molly wondered if that was the motivation for Lucca's discretion. Toby would never be accepted by Valerie into the family. He wasn't rich like them. He was a commoner like her. She dreaded to think what Valerie would say if Levi had given in to temptation. Maybe this was the real reason he had been so reluctant to start a relationship with her. It was just as well things had turned out as they had. Molly was not impressed with the way Levi was behaving and was going off him by the second.

'I don't have any secrets.' Freda pouted.

'Apart from the secret drinking problem that we all politely ignore?' Lucca held his hands up as Valerie and Freda began to protest.

Armand laughed at them arguing. 'Children. Who'd have them? Now, Toby, about that golf tournament. Can you sign me up?'

Within minutes, Lucca, Toby and Armand were back to discussing handicaps, and Valerie was back to meticulous wedding planning, every accusation having been successfully swept under the carpet. Molly took a peek at Levi while he was in conversation with Freda. At least he had dragged his irate gaze from her. He seemed furious about her being here.

'But I don't want *one* five-day, colour-themed jackass wedding, never mind *two*.' Freda was arguing her point to Levi. 'So please stop saying yes to everything Mother wants.'

'What did I do to deserve this? I'm just trying to help,' Valerie butted in. 'You do have family in both countries, don't forget.' The conversation round the table was heated enough without the matriarch throwing her weight around. 'The wedding is going to be in all the magazines around the globe. You have to keep up with trends, isn't that right?'

Molly noticed Levi agreeing with both his sister and his mother even though they were on opposing sides. She was distracted by laughter from the end of the table. Toby, Lucca and Armand were all easiness and light. Tucking into the food with gusto and liberally pouring wine. She noticed Lucca had his arm slung casually on the back of Toby's chair.

'How's your father?' Armand was asking Toby. 'Still golfing?'

'Yes, sir. I don't think he'll ever retire from the club.' Toby dabbed his mouth with a napkin. 'He loves the power too much.'

'And when do you think you'll take over running the business?'

Toby shrugged, lifting his glass to his lips. 'Not

until I'm good and ready. And definitely not until I've cracked Le Grand Couloir.'

All three started laughing, and suddenly, Molly realised that Toby wasn't simply the hired help; he was a friend of the family. Toby was from money. Toby was doing this job for fun.

'Did you know Levi did it at five years old?' said Armand, giving his son a proud look. 'At the time, he was the youngest to conquer Europe's most difficult ski run. No fear at that age.'

'He has no fear at any age,' added Toby, popping another of Molly's delicious creations in his mouth.

'Except for his fear of women,' said Lucca, raising a glass to Levi stuck at the end of the table surrounded by women. 'Isn't that right, bro?'

Levi slid his eyes to the men enjoying his discomfort and shook his head playfully. 'Only some women.' Molly had not expected him to then pin her to the seat with a heated look.

Awkward.

She scraped back her chair. 'Time for the next course, I think.'

'Levi, you're the nearest. Help Molly bring the plates in.' Armand turned back to Toby. 'I'm thinking of a golfing residential next year. The four-month one. Which professionals have you got lined up?'

This was clearly news to Valerie, who immediately began squawking at her husband. Levi gave a re-signed-sounding groan and stood up to follow Molly into the kitchen. It was very dark except for a large torch that Toby had put on the bench. The atmosphere was tense, and Molly's nerves were on end at Levi standing so close to her.

'Can you put these warm plates on the bench while I take out the roast pork for you to slice as thinly as you can, please?'

Molly noticed he was avoiding eye contact.

'The sharp knives are—'

'I know where my own knives are.' Levi yanked open the cutlery draw and let out a monumental sigh.

'If you'd let me finish a sentence for once, I could explain that I've put the block over there.'

'You've put the block of sharp knives over there in the dark where I can't see it? Genius.'

'It wasn't dark when I reorganised the kitchen, was it?' Molly said through gritted teeth.

'Nobody asked you to reorganise the kitchen, did they?' Levi gave her a determined look. 'Or was hiding things another box to tick off on your bucket list?'

'Forget it, I'll find it myself. And the salt and the garnish. I need to get them from the pantry.' Molly felt her way in the dark to the other side of the kitchen.

Within seconds, Levi was right behind her with the torch. She felt her body tingle. 'What are you doing?' she asked.

'Give me the knife,' Levi said, taking it from her as he shone the way to the pantry. 'After all, I couldn't help but notice you were more than a little psycho this morning. Plus, I'd hate to get stabbed in the back again.'

Molly swung round to face him. 'How dare you! You deserved that drink in the face, and I did not stab you in the back. If anything, you're the one who is at fault here,' she snapped. She pulled open the pantry door and stepped into a wall of darkness. 'Not giving me a chance to explain.'

Levi followed her in, almost standing on top of her in the tiny space. He placed the torch and the knife down on the shelf. 'Do it now then.'

'Do what now?'

'Explain. Explain how you led me to believe you were a guest when we first met.'

Flashbacks to them making out in the lift sprung to her mind.

'Explain how you waited for me in the sauna like a Venus flytrap.'

None of this was painting her in a great light.

'And finally, please do explain how you are only

here as part of some elaborate game you are playing with your business partner. I'm some box to be ticked off for a bet.' Levi's voice was scarcely more than a whisper, his words as hard as ice. 'I hope it was worth it.'

Molly stared up at him. She had no idea where to start. She desperately wanted to tell him about Ava. How all those events were linked. She put her hand on his arm and felt him bristle at her touch. Sadness swept over her at the thought of how much she'd upset him. Levi was not going to want to hear the truth, because all the accusations were true. Everything he had just said was spot on. Everything except one detail.

'I'm so sorry.' Tears prickled the back of her eyes as she searched his for signs of forgiveness. 'It's complicated.'

Levi stared back at her. 'Try me.'

Molly bit her lip. She could smell hints of sandalwood and lemon balm aftershave over his clean masculine scent. In the dim light, his hair fell across his forehead, casting shadows across his cheekbones. His full lips were drawn into a tight line. His eyes were dark and dangerous.

'It isn't what you think. I didn't set out to deceive you.'

'It looks *very much* like you set out to deceive me.'

'I know. I know it does, but it's not the way it happened. It isn't even *my* bucket list.'

'Whose is it?'

'Ava's.' Saying her name pinched at Molly's heart.

'Then why did you go all out to seduce me in the hot tub?'

Because I fell for you the moment I laid eyes on you.

'Why didn't Ava do it herself?' he snapped.

Molly swallowed. 'She's not here.' Saying it this way felt somehow easier than admitting she was dead and never coming back.

Her words hung in the air. She had to tell him. She drew in a sharp breath. Best to just blurt it out. 'Last Christmas, she took an unexpected—'

'You've been ticking off boxes since we met, haven't you?' Levi interrupted as though lost in a red mist of indignation. 'Crashing a wedding? The sausage-meat face? Even the burlesque costume and the goddamn camel was on it! And sleeping with a billionaire? I bet that would have ticked a big one off the list. Too bad you didn't manage it.' Levi was making imaginary ticking motions with his hand.

Molly flinched. He wasn't wrong but that was no reason to be so rude. 'If you'll just get down from your high horse for a second and let me explain properly...'

He wasn't listening. It was as though she had become invisible.

'And don't get me started on lying to me about your restaurant because, believe me, I always get what I want. You certainly won't be hired for my sister's wedding, which I assume is why you manipulated your way here in the first place. And I'll make sure that you and your business partner never contract with my resort ever again. In fact, I'll make sure none of our associates work with you either. Let's see how you like *that* game.'

Molly's head jerked up. 'This isn't a game. That restaurant is my life. It's my dream. You can't take it away from me. It's mine.'

'Not according to that letter, it isn't.'

'You can't take it.'

'Watch me.'

Infuriating. Utterly infuriating.

'What are you, twelve? Don't be so bloody childish.'

Levi stopped talking. His mouth gaped slightly open as though no one had ever spoken back to him.

'What's taking so long?' came a yell from Toby. They heard him making his way towards them. Molly dropped her hand from Levi's arm just as Toby shone his phone light at them. 'Oh, sorry. I didn't realise you were... I just came to check if...' He cleared his throat. 'But I'll leave you to it.'

Levi stepped away from Molly. 'Wait,' he instructed Toby. 'You take over here.'

'Sure,' said Toby, stepping aside to let Levi stomp past.

'I've got an important call to make.' He shot Molly a dark look. 'To my acquisitions team.'

Molly tutted loudly. 'You're being ridiculous. And unbelievably annoying!'

* * *

By the time a slightly taken-aback Molly had served the third of the five courses, the conversation had moved on from golf and weddings to plans for Christmas Eve and Christmas Day. Since his late return from making calls, Levi had missed two of the courses and not made eye contact with her once. She would find time after the meal to resume their conversation and tell him about Ava. She had never seen him so riled, but she hoped that if he knew the truth, he would understand and take back his ludicrous threats to ruin her business. His words had lit a fire in her belly. Something about him brought out a feisty side to her she was unfamiliar with. As though he'd woken a sleeping dragon. The more he purposefully ignored her, the more determined she became. She wouldn't be backing down without a fight.

'Rooby should be here by Christmas Eve. He'll want to go skiing both mornings,' Freda informed everyone. 'Then he'll want to chill in the spa. Then he'll want to eat a late lunch.'

'Well, that's settled then. We'll structure the two days around what Reuben wants.' Lucca was grinning at Freda. 'How does that sound for everyone?'

'Absolutely not,' said Valerie. 'I'm not skiing. I've got far too much to do. We haven't even gone through fabric samples for the wedding. Freda, darling, wouldn't you rather leave the boys to it and help me plan? It is your wedding, after all.'

'No way. I won't have seen Rooby for two weeks. We'll need to reconnect and spend every second together. Who cares about the bloody wedding? I'm sick to death of it. It can wait.'

This appeared to inflame Valerie. Her eyebrows shot up to her hairline, and her contorted face remained frozen.

'I'm not even sure why you're bothering to get married,' said Lucca. 'The two of you are never in the same country for more than a week at a time anyway. Is that why you drink so much?'

'That's enough, Lucca,' barked Levi. 'You're hardly the one to dish out marital advice. How many fiancées have you been through? Two?'

'Two and a half actually.'

Verbal fireworks ensued.

Toby gallantly waded in to try to keep the peace as the LeRoux family indiscriminately shrieked and yelled at one another. Glad of something to take her mind off Levi's threats to ruin her business, Molly had never been so distracted in all her life. She was used to quiet, respectful evenings with her parents spent chatting amiably and playing games. She watched enthralled as this family screamed accusations and hurled insults. She'd never seen a spectacle like it. It would be thrilling if Levi wasn't sitting opposite emitting an aura of furious energy.

It was while Lucca was reminding his mother what a terrible parent she was, and how she had missed every single one of his 'spoken-word political poetry satire' recitals at school when he was younger, that Molly noticed Armand remaining very passive throughout the arguing as though he was having an out-of-body experience. She then noticed a film of sweat forming on his brow and the colour drain from his cheeks. She flicked her eyes around the table. They were all animatedly engaged in yelling at each other. She sought Toby, only to find that he was just as bad, agreeing with each of them in turn, trying to prevent the conflict escalating.

Armand was quite a large gentleman who looked as though he had enjoyed more than a few decades of avoiding lettuce in favour of eating cheese and drinking fine wines. He looked as though he was on the verge of some sort of angina attack. Molly watched him mop his brow with his napkin, wondering if she should intervene. Nobody noticed her rise from her seat to collect the plates, as knives and forks clattered down. Not one person had commented on how delicious and well-assembled this third gravity-defying, molecular gastronomic feat of engineering had been, so absorbed in bickering and arguing they all were. Valerie looked as though she had simply pushed her food around her plate while she bickered with her offspring.

Molly made her way round to Armand and crouched down beside him. 'Are you okay, sir? Can I get you anything?'

Armand gave her a sharp look, his already small eyes narrowing. 'I'm fine,' he hissed out of the side of his mouth. 'It's nothing.'

Molly regarded him. He could be very dismissive. Like his son and his wife. 'Do you need aspirin? Are you on medication?' she murmured quietly. She poured him a glass of water. 'Drink this slowly.'

He looked incensed at the intrusion. A redness replaced the pallor in his cheeks. Before he could answer her, she rose quickly. 'Sorry.'

Molly scuttled into the kitchen, observing the family from afar. What a shitshow. At least Armand was now sipping at his water and seemed less agitated. Valerie decided to regale the family with tales of how many people she knew who had recently died and was disappointed to find that none of them had a clue who she was talking about. '...and that was the fourth husband she'd lost in as many years.'

'How careless. I wonder how many husbands you'll get through, Freds. We could start a new family tradition.' Lucca picked up a stuffed bell pepper and threw it at Freda. Freda retaliated by laughing heartily and throwing a whole breadbasket at him. The rolls of crusty bread spewed everywhere, knocking his glass of red wine all over Toby. He was drenched. Lucca found it hilarious.

Molly's own troubles aside, it was the best family dinner she'd ever been to.

'What a waste. That was a very expensive glass of wine,' Armand moaned as colour came back to his cheeks. He mopped his brow again and threw the napkin down on the table.

'Not the Château Lafite,' groaned Valerie, picking up the bottle. 'Who opened that? I was keeping it for the wedding. I bought it at auction. It cost me over twenty thousand euros.'

'You mean it cost *me* over twenty thousand euros,' said Levi drily. 'How many times have I said those auctions are a waste of time? They can see you coming a mile off.'

'Who brought it up from the cellar in the first place?' Valerie asked sharply. 'I deliberately ordered these crates to be kept separate from the others.'

'Don't look at me,' Freda snapped.

'Nor me,' said Lucca, holding up his hands.

Suddenly the arguing stopped. Everybody was staring over at Molly.

18

AN IRRATIONAL, UNSTOPPABLE LAW OF ATTRACTION

Molly woke up freezing the following morning. There was no heating. She threw on several jumpers over jogging bottoms and a thick pair of ski socks and padded through to the lounge area where Levi was already sitting with his laptop on his knees, in front of a roaring fire. She spotted Freda emerging from the archway at the far side of the room with a padded quilt around her shoulders.

'Where were you last night?' Freda asked her brother animatedly, walking over to the sofa in front of the huge fireplace and plonking herself down next to him. 'You just disappeared after poor Molly got all the blame for the wine, when I'm sure it was Lucca. You know what he's like. Anyway, you missed the best dinner I've ever tasted. It was amazing. I don't know how she did it, but Molly served up the best crispy pork dish I've ever eaten. It literally melted on my tongue. Like a snowflake.'

Levi continued tapping away on his keyboard.

'Busy working I presume?' she said. 'When's the electricity going to come back on? My phone is like, completely dead.'

Not looking up, Levi shrugged, his fingers tapping away, his focus on the screen. Annoyance flickered in Molly's chest. A simple 'don't know' would have sufficed.

Molly heard him complaining about the limited battery life left on his computer and had to stop herself from tutting. Freda was obviously trying to spend time with him. Toby was outside trying to fix the generator while Molly prepped for the day ahead. Without electricity, cooking was going to be difficult. Valerie had ordered a keto-based breakfast in bed and wanted to discuss the changes to the menu for the day. Valerie feared there wasn't enough tomato and cilantro bisque featured and wanted very much to enquire as to why.

Freda came over to her. 'Need some help?'

Molly didn't need any help. 'I'm just cooking breakfast for your parents.'

Freda's eyes lit up. 'Could you show me how to make eggs Benedict, please? It's Rooby's favourite. He would die if I learned how to make it. It would be incredible. He'd marry me regardless of my bonkers family.'

Yes. Of course it would be the eggs that would attract him. Not your extreme beauty or your fabulous glossy hair or your billions of pounds, thought Molly begrudgingly. She shook the terrible thoughts away. The incident with Levi in the pantry the previous evening had left her bereft. Even worse was getting the blame for opening the expensive wine. She desperately wanted to explain to Levi properly, hating that he had such a despicable opinion of her. She had not been able to sleep a wink. Rising early, she had knocked on his door early this morning and had heard him moving around but he had refused to answer. Then, against her better judgement, she had yelled rather loudly through his door, 'As soon as you've finished sulking, come and find me!'

Levi seemed to bring out the worst in her. She smiled dutifully at Freda. 'Of course I'll show you.'

Molly noticed Levi glancing over while she and Freda got to work. Freda's frequent squeals of delight, the hilarious dropping of ingredients for Molly to mop up and the sporadic yelps of pain as Freda re-

peatedly failed to listen properly were attracting attention. Freda was finding new and inventive ways to
burn herself.

Lucca now approached them. 'Freda, our lovely
parents are arguing again. When you've finished self-
harming, could you have a word with Mother, please?
You know she never listens to me.'

'She won't listen to me either. Can't Levi do
something?'

'He hasn't a clue about this family. Why would he
even care? Look at him, he hasn't looked up from that
damn computer once. I just heard him organising an
airlift out of here if the generator isn't fixed within the
hour. He'll leave us all here to freeze to death. No, it
will have to be you.'

Freda stopped sautéing Molly's asparagus tips to
bite a nail, deep in thought. Molly caught the tips on
the verge of burning and took them off the heat just in
time. She considered reminding Freda that timing was
everything in the catering business but thought better
of it. Freda seemed as scatterbrained as they come.
Molly also suspected Freda was already a couple of
drinks deep. The Sauvignon in the fridge had gone
down considerably over the last hour. While Freda
hopped up to sit on the bench as though she was not
right in the middle of cooking, Molly busied herself

finishing off the breakfasts for Valerie and Armand and pretended not to listen.

'Thank goodness you're getting married. Otherwise, I think they'd be divorced by now,' Lucca said, leaning on the bench next to her. 'It's the obsession with golf and him finding every excuse to be away from her.'

'I'm not surprised he avoids her because all she talks about is the wedding. Perhaps they just need to spend more time together. Doing something that isn't golf or wedding related.'

Molly listened to Lucca and Freda come up with a list of ideas, each one rejected because of the lack of Wi-Fi or electricity.

'How about a candle-lit dinner?' Molly couldn't help suggesting. 'Set them up on a date. Give them a list of safe discussion topics and questions to ask each other. Or even make a game of it. Like a "Mr & Mrs" or something. If they get it right, they get the next course. I could do a tasting menu of ten courses.'

Freda's face lit up. 'Some of the questions could be to guess what's in the food,' she said. 'There could be a few tasks in each round. Seriously, I love this.'

'Molly, you're a genius!' Lucca exclaimed, coming round into the kitchen area to grab her and kiss her on the forehead. 'That's it. That's what we'll do. We'll invent a degustation game. Tell them it's their anniversary present so they have to do it.'

As Freda squealed, Molly noticed Levi had stopped tapping at his laptop and was watching the scene. She stepped quickly away from Lucca, wiping her hands on her apron. 'Okay. All we need to do is make sure they turn up for dinner and tell everyone else to make an excuse to eat in their rooms tonight.'

'No problem,' Freda said. 'Levi is eating in his room tonight anyway if he's still here.' She made a face at him. 'He has a conference call with Japan or something.'

'I'll let Toby know,' offered Lucca. 'I can also give you both a hand in the kitchen.'

'Perfect.' Molly was pleased to see Lucca and Freda smiling from ear to ear. 'Okay. Now that that's sorted, we can plan a menu and table setting when I get back from taking them breakfast.' She picked up a tray laden with freshly hand-squeezed orange juice, coffee, bowls of chopped fruit, eggs Benedict and a host of mini-French toasts pan-fried with herbs and cheeses, seeing as none of the kitchen appliances worked without electricity.

'We'll list all their favourite foods,' said Freda.

'Did you know your mother has developed a fear

of leafy greens? So nothing with kale, spinach or watercress. Or gluten. Or peas.'

Lucca rolled his eyes.

* * *

As Molly approached Valerie and Armand's room, she heard loud bickering. She knocked on the door and waited several minutes for Armand to answer it. Although he was forcing a smile, he looked red-faced and frazzled.

'I just wanted to say again how sorry I am about the mix-up with the wine last night. It really wasn't me who chose the—'

'*Merci beaucoup*,' Armand said flatly, cutting her off. He was clearly in no mood to hear her out, just like the previous evening. He quickly took the tray from her, but as he nudged the door shut with his hip, Molly caught a glimpse of Valerie standing at the far side of the room in her dressing gown, fragile-looking without make-up, face tear-stained, shoulders hunched, arms folded tightly, far from the elegant poise of last night.

They clearly had issues. Molly resolved to make tonight's dinner the best she'd ever cooked. But without electricity it would be a challenge. And most of the food would go off within days. She went to Toby's room to find his door open and him pulling on extra jumpers over his salopettes.

'We really need that generator working,' he said. 'The fire and cooker run on gas, but everything else is electric. The fridge, the freezer, the boiler for the central heating, the sauna, the pool, the TV, the phones, all need electricity.' Toby looked stressed. 'And that lot are no help. They don't even know what a generator is, never mind how to fix one.'

'I'll help. What do we need to do?' Molly offered. 'I'll just grab my snowsuit and gloves. Have you got a toolkit? Screwdrivers, monkey wrench, multimeter, that sort of thing?'

'Molly, that would be amazing but I haven't got the first clue what you just said.'

'I've got an old generator at the restaurant that keeps blowing. I'm sure we'll work it out.'

'You have no idea how happy I am to hear that. The resort maintenance manager reckons the power outage will last several days so we really need that generator up and running as soon as possible. Levi will go ballistic if his laptop runs down. He says he's calling for a helicopter and leaving. Then that's the family holiday ruined. They'll all leave.'

Molly did not want Levi to run off without having

the chance to explain herself properly. She needed to reverse his low opinion of her. And Lucca and Freda seemed so excited to help their parents, it would be a shame if they didn't get this chance. Valerie and Armand clearly had bigger issues going on.

Molly raced back to her room to grab warm clothes.

'We have to ski over to it. It's at the bottom of the small field.' Toby led her through to the back of the kitchen area where glazed, Georgian-style double doors opened onto the boot room which was freezing cold. Racks of boots, skis, helmets, gloves, padded coats, hats and poles were all lined up neatly. It was more like a showroom. Molly glanced around the uber-modern and stylish room, dominated by stone walls and a floor-to-ceiling glass window with a breathtaking Alpine view. The highly polished wooden floors and wooden box-shelves oozed elegance. She noticed several first aid kits, walkie-talkies, large battery-powered torches, a box labelled flares and even a stretcher. She spotted her oversized, hi-viz, ski resort padded coat with STAFF emblazoned on the back, and the ugly hat that matched it hanging alone on a line of pegs. She slid with some effort into the standard-issue bright-orange staff salopettes and fastened up some equally unattractive purple moon boots. She went over to the large, cushioned bench. Toby proceeded to fit Molly with the regulation staff safety gear. The coat, the hat and the salopettes were all horrendously lumpy and unflattering.

It was snowing quite heavily as they stepped onto the snow outside. 'We'll have to be very careful,' Toby said, taking her gloved hand.

Molly was not confident on skis. In fact, the moment he let go of her, she began sliding backwards away from him. She flapped her arms about, poles in the air.

'Dig your poles in,' Toby yelled. 'No! Molly, keep your arms down.'

'I'm try-*iiiiiinnnngggg*!'

'Don't ski backwards. We're going this way.' Toby pointed away from the house, but it was too late. Molly had gathered momentum and was sliding downhill backwards. She passed the large living room patio doors where Levi happened to look up. They made brief eye contact as she whizzed by, screaming.

The sheer embarrassment. What an impression to make. Skiing backwards wasn't even on the bloody bucket list.

Molly eventually came to a stop and dug her poles in the ground, just as Toby swooshed to a stop in front of her. He was laughing hard. 'I've never seen anyone ski quite like that before. Oh man, that's the funniest thing I've ever seen.' He lifted his goggles. 'You okay?'

Molly chuckled despite herself. 'Yeah. That was quite exhilarating, actually.'

They inched back up the hill. This time Levi was standing at the window. He gave Molly a sarcastic look and took his hand out of his pocket to sweep it in the air.

'Why is he making a tick sign at you?'

'Erm, no idea,' said Molly, facing away. Levi was suspicious of her every move.

Toby held on to her as they slowly zig-zagged their way over to the generator. The generator was piled high with snow and required a lot of unearthing. Once they removed most of the snow, Toby lifted off the front panel to reveal lots of tubes and wires. 'See what I mean? Who would have the first clue?'

Molly patted him on the shoulder. 'It's a propane-fuelled engine, same as mine. Here, look.' She pointed out the control panel. 'This is basically your standard battery-operated control for the engine. I'll just switch it off while we assess what's going on.' Molly got to work pressing buttons and poking around, checking fuel, the overcrank, oil and coolant levels. 'Well, at least we have oil,' she said, wiping down the oil dipstick with a cloth and replacing it. 'So it's not that. And we have plenty of fuel. I'll try turning it back on.'

Nothing happened.

'Hmm.' She wiped her sleeve across her forehead to remove the snow. 'We've got three coils, three cylinders and no spark.'

Toby looked on, giving her a helpless shrug as though she was speaking Arabic.

'I suspect it may be the kill circuit. Sometimes if the unit has been tampered with or overloaded, it can kick in.'

'I have no clue what you mean.'

'I mean, there are thousands of lights in the main house. It's over-the-top ridiculous. Look at them. As soon as the generator kicked in it probably shorted immediately.' Molly fiddled about at the back of the engine, muttering to herself. 'Found it. Now, all I need is some starter fluid.' She spotted a spray can and some cloths lying on the inside of the generator box. 'Great, there it is.' She took off the cover of the air filter and sprayed some of the liquid into the carburettor.

Within minutes, Molly had the generator running. They looked back towards the house to see the lights flickering.

Come on, willed Molly. She patted the generator. 'It might be a bit temperamental to start with. That's a lot of luxury lodge and a lot of unnecessary electrical demands.'

Except the massage chair. And the sauna. And the hot tub.

The lights flickered, went out again and then in a glorious blaze of colour, the whole house lit up like the Eiffel Tower. She could make out the family gathering at the window, waving in celebration.

Toby threw his arms around Molly, lifting her off the snowy ground. 'That was awesome. I owe you big time. Especially after yesterday.'

'Call it even for finding my cases,' Molly managed to say. Toby was squeezing the life out of her.

'I hardly think that makes up for the wine incident.'

Molly was confused. 'What do you mean?'

Toby put her down. 'I owe you for taking the fall for me last night.'

'It was you who opened the wrong bottles of wine?'

Toby shrugged. 'They all look the same to me. Besides, Lucca told me to get them from the crate.'

'Why did you let me take the blame?' Molly couldn't believe her ears.

'Because you've quit anyway. As soon as the pass is clear, you're leaving. It made sense. Plus, Levi obviously likes you otherwise he wouldn't have offered to buy another crate for the wedding.'

'But he's furious with me,' Molly cried.

'Sorry, Molly. I really need to keep this job.'

'Aren't you rich enough to not work here?'

Toby went bright red. 'It's not about that. Come on. Let's go. I need to chop more wood for the fire.' Molly watched Toby yank off his gloves and clip his boots into his skis.

She wondered why Toby was so keen to stay with the family, in a job that he didn't need to do, for little or no reward. Molly wondered if it had something to do with Lucca.

'No, don't thank me,' Toby was saying to the family members as they gave him a hero's welcome. 'I was just doing my job.'

'You're incredible,' gushed Freda, kissing his cheek. 'You've saved Christmas. You really have.'

Toby glowed under her praise as Molly stood aside to let them take turns patting his back. She marvelled at the gall of him. Men! Rich men! Rich, pampered, egotistical men!

'How did you do it?' Levi asked firmly.

Like a rabbit caught in the headlights, Toby visibly gulped.

'So we know what to do next time,' Levi said more loudly.

'Well, actually...' Toby kicked snow off his boot and mumbled. 'It was complex.'

'Pardon?'

Levi was like a dog with a bone. Molly was in awe. She would have done exactly the same thing if it had been her restaurant staff. She was all about fairness and respect in the workplace. None of which seemed in abundance here.

Toby flicked Molly a guilty look before continuing. 'Well, the engine crank sockets weren't working so I sprayed the cylinder thing with the spray.'

'Crank sockets?'

Toby went the colour of a winter berry.

'So, what you're saying is that it *wasn't* complex then?' Levi had gone into barrister mode. At this rate Toby would be found guilty and sent down for a substantial amount of time. Molly imagined Levi in a wig and gown. He'd make a magnificent prosecutor.

Toby instantly crumbled. 'It was all Molly. She fixed it. I basically held the torch.'

Molly blushed, tapping snow from her boots against the step. 'It was nothing, really. Just your basic sparkplugs and starter fluid. And it'll need an oil change at some point, but it should keep everything running until the power comes back on. We should turn a few thousand of these lights off though, just to take the pressure off it.'

They all looked blankly at her.

'You lost me at sparkplugs,' laughed Lucca. 'Anyway, well done both.' He slapped Toby on the back.

'Yes,' said Valerie, before looking sadly over at Levi. '*Someone* was almost airlifted out of here... Well, it doesn't matter now. Thanks to you we can spend Christmas together.' She leaned over to pat Toby on the shoulder, much to everyone's surprise.

Molly felt invisible. She hoped Levi would at least smile at her. She glanced over at him, but his face was a mask.

Valerie continued clucking. 'We might even find it in our hearts not to charge Molly for the wine yesterday.'

'Sorry?' Molly must have misheard.

'Mother,' Levi warned. His voice was low and threatening.

Valerie ignored him. 'That's the problem with staff these days I suppose. You don't know who to trust. Except you, Toby, darling. You'd never "mistakenly" open an expensive bottle of wine just so you could Instagram it.' Valerie was doing air quotes.

Molly looked at Toby. This was his chance to come clean. 'Toby? Do you have anything to say?'

Toby deliberately looked away, taking off his hat and gloves.

Unbelievable.

Molly took a deep, calming breath. 'As I told you all last night, it wasn't me. I didn't go down to the wine cellar. Besides, I haven't the first clue what makes a good wine because I'm not a trained sommelier.' She let out an enormous tut. 'But honestly, if you don't believe me and feel the need to take it from my wages, please do.'

She prayed that they wouldn't, but it came down to a question of pride. She hated them having such a low opinion of her.

Valerie gave her a sympathetic shake of her head. 'Where would you get that kind of money? I know how little the resort staff get paid and your restaurant business is clearly in trouble otherwise you wouldn't be here. No. We'll just have to put it down to a genuine mistake and you owing us one.'

Owing them one?

'Either that or you might have to sell your restaurant to us.' She let out a tinkling laugh.

Molly dared to look at Levi. His eyes darted about as though assessing everyone in the group. She couldn't tell whether he was less pleased about her offering to pay for the wine, or with her fixing the generator so that he could continue to spend Christmas with his beloved family of insane megalomaniacs.

They locked eyes. He seemed to look straight through her. Molly tilted her head, wondering whether to appeal to him. He opened his mouth to speak and then closed it again as though thinking better of it. He frowned and walked away.

This family could be so exasperating.

19

IF YOU WANT TO BE TRUSTED, BE HONEST

It was while Molly was scrubbing the charred remains of an unidentifiable lump from a baking tray, while trying to rid the place of an acrid, burning smell, at the same time as prepping individual lunches for the entire household, that she realised this was a family keeping secrets. Someone had obviously been trying to cook. She found an almost empty vodka bottle hidden at the back of the pantry among the dried pasta and bags of rice. *No prizes for guessing who might be responsible for that*, Molly thought to herself.

As she was wondering whether to confiscate it or put it back, she heard someone approaching and hastily shoved it in her large apron pocket before swivelling round to find Valerie in the doorway sniffing the pungent air with an unimpressed frown.

'Busy?' Valerie said, eyeing the bulge in her pocket. She frowned, waiting for an explanation.

She would have to wait for a long time.

'Yes. I am busy. I have lots of meals to plan and prepare. Is there something you wanted?' Molly tried to squeeze past her, but Valerie blocked her path. 'Do you have a new allergy to inform me of, Madame LeRoux?' Because Molly was certain that Valerie would have to start inventing new ones, seeing as though she'd exhausted the current Food Standards Agency official list.

Valerie checked behind both of her shoulders. 'You're probably wondering why I came to your rescue earlier.'

Molly frowned. 'Did you? It sounded like you were accusing me of a crime I didn't commit and then expecting me to be grateful not to pay for it.'

Valerie tutted. 'Don't be silly. Of course it was you. Now listen,' she said in a low voice. 'I need you to repay the favour. I need you to do something for me. Something very sensitive.'

Molly did not trust herself to respond.

'I need your help accessing a phone. I'm not sure

how to get into it without a password. It's locked me out.'

'And how can I help with that?'

'You're young. You young people know how to get into phones. You live your whole lives with them glued to your hands.'

'I can try for you.' Molly had always prided herself on being helpful. Why stop now just because she had a bossy, mad woman in front of her asking for the impossible? 'Where is it?'

Valerie checked over her shoulders once more before explaining to Molly that the phone she was locked out of actually belonged to her husband, Armand. 'And I need you to get it for me.'

Molly couldn't quite believe what she was hearing. 'Let me get this straight. You want me to steal your husband's—'

'Shhh. Keep your voice down,' hissed Valerie.

'You want me to steal Monsieur LeRoux's phone, hack into it and then hand it over to you?' whispered Molly.

'Yes.' Valerie nodded vigorously. 'And then put it back before he notices it's gone.'

'And if I get caught?'

Valerie looked at her blankly. 'Don't get caught.'

'And if I refuse?'

'Why would you refuse?'

'Why wouldn't I refuse? You're asking me to break the law for no reason.'

A troubled expression covered Valerie's face. 'I'm worried about him. He's not telling me something.'

Molly's mind flew back to Armand and how ill he had seemed and how guarded he was over her question about medication. 'I'm sure if you ask him about it, he'll tell you.'

Valerie scoffed. 'You have no idea how deceptive and cunning French men can be. It's in their nature to keep secrets from their wives.'

Oh.

'But unfortunately for him, unlike French women, I do not turn a blind eye. I'm American. We are proud, outspoken and honest. That is what makes America so *great*.'

The irony that Valerie was whispering to her in a cupboard, out of sight, asking her to steal her husband's phone, was not lost on Molly.

'There must be another way. Have you checked his drawers and cupboards?'

There was a good chance Valerie would find his medication and Armand would have to come clean.

'That would be too suspicious. I haven't tidied his clothes for more than a decade. No, it has to be you. I will distract him from the online golf while you pretend to clean our room. Actually, *do* clean the room. And turn down the beds while you're at it. Hospital corners, obviously. And change the towels. Then bring the phone to me.'

Why not shove a broom up my backside while I'm at it?

'Why not ring his doctor? Or better still just ask him. Tell him you're worried about him.'

'Doctor? Why would Armand admit to the doctor he was having an affair?' Valerie pursed her lips. 'Unless you mean to see if he's asked for a Viagra prescription? No. I'm not embarrassing myself. I'd much rather you stole his phone and I can check through his messages for evidence.'

Affair?

'I'm sure he's not having an affair. I thought you meant... I can't possibly...'

'Do this and I'll give you the contract to cater the wedding,' Valerie blurted. 'All five days. It'll be worth a fortune, and that little restaurant business of yours will feature in every magazine around the globe.' Valerie spun round and walked quickly away.

Molly watched her go. Who wore high-heeled,

backless sandals and gold lamé in the house? Molly didn't know whether to despair more at the fact that once again she was unable to finish a sentence, or whether Valerie just assumed Molly would break the law for the sake of money. No matter how tempting the offer was, she wouldn't do it. Molly let out a slow breath. Maybe Lucca was right. Valerie had lost the plot.

'What was that about?'

Molly jumped a mile.

Levi stood with his hands in his pockets. He was wearing a loose-fitting shirt and tailored trousers as though for a meeting. Molly was relieved that he seemed a little less imposing than yesterday.

'Oh, nothing.' *Just your mother bribing me to break the law.*

'Didn't look like nothing.'

Cripes.

Molly felt her chest burning at the thought of even attempting to lie to him. A prickly heat shot up her neck to her cheeks. 'She just wanted me to get something for her.'

'What?'

Molly swallowed. 'She needs help with a technical issue.'

'What technical issue?'

'Not technical, a culinary issue. For the wedding.'
Molly put a hand to her chest. 'That's right. She is
having issues with the wedding.'

'Why is your neck red?'

Molly immediately slid a hand to her throat to
hide the prickly rash. 'No reason.'

Levi looked at her bulging apron. 'Bit early for
that, isn't it?'

'This?' She yanked the vodka bottle from her
apron. 'This is, erm, for the amuse-bouche tonight. I'm
not stealing it. Or drinking it.'

'And you just happened to take it into the pantry
with you?'

'Yes.' She placed it on the nearest shelf.

'It looks almost empty. How much have you put in
each one?'

'Each what?'

'Each appetiser.'

It was like having a conversation with Sherlock
Holmes.

'When it comes to pairing alcohol and food
items...' *Dear God, help me.* 'The food items, the appetisers, I'm preparing... For you and your family members. You enjoy alcohol a lot. So I'm soaking things
in it.'

It was as though Molly had forgotten how to be a chef. How to be human.

Levi frowned. 'Hardly appropriate. Where are they? Let me taste one.'

Molly felt a stab of anxiety. She gathered her long hair in one hand and piled it on top of her head, securing it with a band to give herself a minute to think up an excuse. Under his forensic scowl, she picked up the bottle, pretended to inspect the label and put it back in her pocket. She felt a light film of sweat form on her upper lip.

'They're in the freezer. You can't.'

'Show me.'

For fuck's sake.

'Haven't you got better things to do than harass innocent chefs?'

'No. And you're hardly innocent.'

Molly blushed down to her toes.

Levi looked taken aback. 'Sorry. I didn't mean like that. I meant... it doesn't matter what I meant. Carry on with whatever you're doing.'

'Wait.' For some indescribable reason she just wanted to be near him. To talk to him. To interact with him. Even in this almost unbearable exchange. With her heart beating double time, Molly reached out.

'There are a few things I need to mention. A few concerns.'

Levi raised an eyebrow. 'You're concerned? How do you think I feel?'

They were interrupted by the distinctive click-clacking of Valerie's heels returning on the slate floor of the kitchen. 'Molly, he's in the shower. Do it now before—' Valerie almost screeched to a halt. 'Angelo, darling, there you are. I need you. It's this wedding. I'm thinking white Mustang horses sprayed gold and vintage gilded carriages, but Freda is insisting it's old hat and animal cruelty. Come and talk sense into her.'

Valerie, with eyes bulging, gave Molly a hard stare. 'Leave Molly to get on. She has much to do. Important things to take care of, don't you?' She was all but shooing her away. 'Off you go. Hurry.'

Molly's jaw dropped at the dismissive fashion in which Valerie was wafting her away, like a fly hovering around food.

Levi's mouth tightened at his mother's gesture. He gave Molly an apologetic look before turning his attention back to Valerie.

'Actually, Mother, Molly and I were in the middle of something. Can this wait?'

You'd think Levi had informed her that he and Molly

were expecting triplets. But instead of getting the hump with her precious son, Valerie glared at Molly as though this was all somehow her fault. She narrowed her eyes, dropping them to the bulge in her pocket, before spinning swiftly on her heel and click-clacking away again.

Levi let out a slow breath and ran his hand through his hair. 'What's going on?'

Molly bit her lip, wondering how to tell him his uptight mother was batshit crazy with the morals of a snake. She wiped the back of her hand across her brow. Living with this family was becoming increasingly stressful. How were they creating problems at such speed? It was like living in crazy town.

'I'm not going to stand here while you think up a bunch of lies,' Levi snapped. 'When you're ready to tell me the truth, I'll be over there. Waiting.'

'Fine,' said Molly. 'Your mother thinks your father is having an affair and she wants me to steal his phone so that she can check his messages.'

'And you agreed?' Levi looked incredulously at her.

'No. Of course not!'

Levi's posture relaxed slightly. 'Okay, good. I'll talk to her later.' He glanced back at her as he walked away. 'And try to keep the drinking down to acceptable levels. It can't be that stressful working here. Show some professionalism.'

At that moment, Molly wished she *did* have a drinking problem.

* * *

Just before lunch was due to be served, Molly knocked tentatively on Freda's bedroom door. She answered, her eyes red and puffy.

'Can I come in?'

Freda sniffed. 'Sorry. It's not a good time.'

'I just wanted to check you were okay and to apologise for earlier.'

'Apologise? Why?'

'The wedding. Everyone seems to think I'm trying to win the contract for catering your wedding when I'm not. In fact, I wouldn't be able to do it anyway. I just don't want you to think I'm trying to manipulate you or to feel pressured or anything.'

Freda tilted her head and ushered Molly inside. 'Come in.' When Molly sat on the armchair, Freda flopped face down on the unmade bed. Molly glanced around at the many, many empty wine bottles and yet another empty vodka bottle.

'Wow. That's a lot of alcohol.' She strained to hear

Freda's muffled response. 'Sorry, what was that about the wedding?'

Freda sat up and trained her tear-filled eyes on Molly's. 'There is no wedding. Rooby broke it off.'

Oh.

'When?'

'Officially? An hour ago.'

'So, he's not coming to stay here for Christmas?'

'No. To be honest he tried to tell me before I left but I wouldn't listen. I thought he'd change his mind. But he hasn't. He's staying in Canada to reassess his life, and the wedding is definitely off.'

Molly wound an arm around Freda's shoulders and pulled her close. 'I'm sorry. You guys had been having trouble, I take it?'

'Yeah. It hasn't been right for a while, but I just figured it was cold feet over getting married. I thought once the wedding was sorted, he'd settle more.'

'What did your mother say?'

'I can't bear to tell Mother because she's so obsessed with the wedding, and she'll go ballistic that yet again I've ruined another perfectly good relationship,' Freda wailed dramatically. 'Decent men are so hard to find. I've literally been searching my whole life.'

Whole life? Molly reckoned Freda had to be around the same age as herself.

'He thinks I'm not passionate enough about him. He thinks I'm just going through the motions for something to do. Like I'm in love with *being in love*.'

'And are you?'

'I think so.' Her face grew serious. 'I just don't know what I want. I've been given everything I've ever wanted on a silver plate and now I have no idea what I want from life, how I want to spend it or who I want to spend it with.' She sat up straight. 'I sound like a spoiled brat, I know. But I can't help feeling empty. There's just this void of nothingness inside me.'

Molly closed her eyes. She could identify strongly with that last bit. 'Is that why you're drinking? To fill the void?'

'I know it won't help but I've gotten into bad habits,' Freda pointed out gloomily. 'I don't have anyone to talk to about it.'

'You could talk to Levi.'

For all his faults, he had proven himself to be an expert listener.

'Are you serious? He's never around. And neither is Lucca. We see each other once a year. They literally have no idea about my life or what I do for the other eleven and a half months. Which, by the way, is nothing. I literally do nothing.' Freda was twisting her bed-sheets forlornly as the words tumbled out. 'And Mother is just as bad. She buries her head in the sand at the first sign of trouble and doesn't want to know.'

Freda was painting quite a vivid picture of a dysfunctional family. Quite the opposite of what Levi had painted.

'How can I help?' asked Molly.

'You can't,' whined Freda. 'Unless you can find me something to feel passionate about? A purpose in life. Like you. It must be lovely to do something so creative for a living.'

'It is. Or at least it was.'

'You said earlier that you wouldn't be able to cater the wedding. What did you mean?'

Molly dithered. Freda had enough on her plate without Molly's woes. 'Forget it. There isn't going to be a wedding anyway,' she said gently. 'I'm so sorry that you're going through all of this alone. Why don't you freshen up and meet me back in the kitchen? We'll get tonight out of the way and then why don't we have a proper talk afterwards?'

Freda brightened. 'I'd really like that. Thanks, Molly. And is there any way you can sneak all these bottles outside to the bin for me, please? I can't let anyone see me like this. And please don't tell anyone about Reuben dumping me and the wedding being off.'

Molly rolled her eyes. 'Fine, but I'm not taking the fall for you if anyone catches me with this lot.'

'And just one more thing.' Freda had the good grace to look sheepish as she held out a Gucci handbag. 'If you could take care of this for me. Thank you so much.'

20

LOVE IS A MISUNDERSTANDING BETWEEN TWO FOOLS

The first person Molly bumped into as she tiptoed along the corridor with a giant binbag full of noisy, clinking empty bottles was Levi.

'Don't ask,' she said, heading off any sarcastic comments.

'To be honest,' Levi said, eyeing the bag, 'I thought there would be more. You seem the type who can put quite a lot away.'

If he didn't look so deadpan, she would have suspected he was teasing her. 'Do I?' With the exception of the hunting lodge and the Cigar Lounge, Molly had barely touched a drop. 'Maybe it's you. Maybe you drive me to drink.'

Levi's expression softened. 'I deserved that. Let me help.'

'Okay, here. Take this.' Molly handed him the Gucci handbag.

'What is it?' Levi weighed it in his hand. It was heavy.

'It's a bag of sick.'

'Jesus Christ.' It only took him a nanosecond to work it out. 'Are these from Freda's room?'

Molly hesitated a fraction. There was no point trying to cover for her. 'I'm going to see if I can help take her mind off drinking. I have an idea that might work.'

'What's wrong? Why does she need to drink? She's got a wedding to plan and loads of things to keep her occupied.'

'I think she could really use some brotherly advice. Maybe you could talk to her?'

Levi, slightly bewildered, held the bag at arm's length. 'I'll add it to my list.'

* * *

The next person Molly bumped into down the corridor was Armand. He looked terribly distracted.

'*Bonjour*, Monsieur LeRoux,' she said politely,

hoping he wouldn't notice the clanking bottles. 'Can I get you anything?'

It was almost as though he hadn't heard her.

'Is everything okay?' she asked.

His tone remained serious. 'Yes, thank you.'

'I wondered if I might ask you something. Personal.'

He looked at her blankly. 'How personal?'

'What were wedding banquets like when you got married here in France? Are they very different to America or Britain?'

It was as though she had flicked a switch.

'Ah, French gastronomy is the best. And weddings are no exception. You have the traditional foie gras and champagne tower of course.' Armand chuckled. 'We had the highest croquembouche anyone had ever seen. But it was the *magret de canard* that stole the show. It melted on the tongue. I can taste it now. And the plum and sloe jus. Heaven.' Armand stopped talking. As he fished about in his blazer jacket for his handkerchief to wipe his brow, she noticed the top of a tablet box peeking out from inside a pocket. It rattled as he searched.

'Are you okay?' she asked. 'Your breathing seems a bit laboured.'

He frowned with concern. 'Does it?'

'My mother is a nurse. We cared for my dad when he had a heart attack a few years ago. He's fine now, but we're always watching him like a hawk for signs of another.'

Armand flinched, as though he had seen a ghost. He grabbed Molly's arm as he dabbed his brow. 'Don't tell a single soul.' He marched off back to his room yelling, 'Can someone sort this bloody Wi-Fi out? I'm in the middle of a game!'

* * *

By the time Molly had dumped the bottles round the back of the lodge by the bins, made up all the beds, except in Levi's room, and Freda's who she overheard weeping, and tidied everyone's lunch dishes away, it was almost time to prep for the special parents' dinner. Lucca walked into the kitchen area looking ready to help. 'Something smells divine.'

Molly tossed him an apron. 'I wondered when you'd turn up. There's still quite a lot to do. It'll take all afternoon to prepare for the degustation tonight. I've managed to find out a few things from your father but there's a lot more I need to know about them for the plan to work.'

'We've got no chance of getting Levi to give us a

hand.' Lucca tied the apron strings loosely round his waist. 'He's working.'

All Molly could do was blush at the sound of his name. They had so much unfinished business.

'He likes you, by the way.' Lucca beamed kindly. 'I can tell.'

If only that were true.

'I think you'll find he hates me at the moment.'

'What do they say? There's a fine line between love and hate. Besides, no one else gets away with talking to him like you do. You seem to be immune to his grouchiness. Whereas it's like a red flag to a bull for me.'

Molly cleared her throat. 'Anyway, where's Freda? Didn't she say that she'd help too?'

Lucca looked out of the window. 'Maybe she went skiing with Toby. Or knowing those two, they'll be in the wine cellar.'

At the mention of Toby's name, Molly bit down an angry comment. He had hung her out to dry earlier and hadn't yet come to apologise. Something must have shown on her face because Lucca hesitated before changing the subject abruptly. 'Or the spa. Who knows where she is?'

'I'm here,' said a rough-looking Freda, dark circles

under her eyes. 'I went back to sleep for your information, my nosy brother.'

'Until two in the afternoon?' Lucca asked.

'We're on holiday. In the middle of a series of storms. With dodgy Wi-Fi.' Freda rubbed both hands up and down her face. Her skin looked grey, her eyes dull and her hair matted. 'Sleeping is pretty much all there is to do here.'

Sleeping and drinking through a broken heart. Molly sympathised.

Molly threw her a spare apron. 'Please tie your hair up. Wash your hands thoroughly. And then we'll get started preparing the rest of the degustation for your parents. I need to know all their favourite dishes.' She went straight to the blender and whizzed up a mix of salty and sweet ingredients, greens and fruit. 'Drink this.' She handed Freda a glass of green sludge. 'It's full of electrolytes. It'll give you a boost.'

Freda accepted the hangover drink with a guilty grace.

'Now, the plan is to tell a story across all ten courses. Starting with when your parents first met. We'll match the food to the questions in the game. Let's get planning.'

Lucca and Freda did exactly as they were told and before long, several dishes were being meticulously assembled. Molly had shown them how to poach, blanch, baste, sauté, reduce, infuse, ferment and pickle under her strict guidance.

'It's like watching someone perform open-heart surgery,' commented Lucca. 'You should open your own school.'

Molly invited them both to taste examples of each one. 'With tasting menus, the secret is to kind of roll the food around your mouth. Savour each unique aroma. Appreciate the balance of flavours on your palate. Give your brain a chance to explore each sensation, each texture.'

'This looks and tastes incredible,' commented Lucca, picking up a delicate multi-coloured roll, infused with mint and bergamot oil. 'You have such skill. It's a veritable feast for the eyes. No wonder people are clamouring to secure your services.'

Molly blushed and shrugged off the compliment. 'We'll do the hot courses as we serve later, but we still need wines to go with each one. Any ideas?'

Lucca grinned. 'Leave it to me. I'm a trained sommelier. One of my many talents.'

'One of his *only* talents. Unless you call international playboy a talent?' Freda said, throwing an olive at him. 'You literally just go from party to party across the globe.'

'I run a wine company. We cater big events. How is that being a playboy?' Lucca winked at Molly. 'Although it is a lot of fun. At least I have a job.' He threw an olive back at Freda.

'Wait. You knew that the wine last night was...' Molly couldn't believe the audacity.

'I'm afraid so, yes.' Lucca did not look even slightly embarrassed. 'And I have to say, it wasn't all that, was it?'

'But why didn't you say anything to Toby when he brought it up from the cellar?' Molly was growing exasperated with this family.

'Because I wanted to see what it was like.' Lucca shrugged. 'For professional reasons, obviously. And just as well, really. Freeds, honey, I think you should reconsider that vintage. I really do.'

'And are you going to tell your mother that you opened the wine on purpose?' Molly put her hands on her hips. 'Or at least come clean to Toby. He thinks it was all his fault. Although, he seems extraordinarily comfortable for me to take the blame.'

'Christ, no. Imagine the fuss! I'm in enough trouble as it is. Now, Freda, darling, what are you going to do with your life after the wedding? How many scrawny nieces and nephews am I to expect?'

It was as though Molly had become invisible yet again.

Freda stared out of the window as though in a trance. 'I'm still thinking about options. It's hard when you don't know which country you'll be living in. Or what you want to do. Where do I even start?'

Molly gave Freda a supportive stroke on the arm. She appreciated her predicament. 'You could start with picking up those olives.'

'Funny.' Freda laughed as though Molly wasn't serious and threw an olive at her too. 'I like you. I like you a lot.'

Exasperating. The lot of them.

'What will you do next, Molly? After the season ends?' Lucca asked her. He too was making no move to pick up the olives.

Molly stopped piping quince glaze onto tiny slivers of Manchego cheese and bent to pick them up herself. 'If your mother doesn't have me slung in jail for wine theft, I'll get my restaurant business back up and running. Before your brother can get his hands on it.' There were only two days left to get everything to the solicitor. With all the distractions this family were providing, it was beginning to seem less and less likely. She hoped she sounded more confident than she felt as she threw the olives in the bin. 'Please stop throwing food at each other.'

Lucca grinned in response. 'Well, if these dishes are anything to go by, you'll have no problem bringing clients in.'

If Ava had still been alive, it might be no problem, but Molly was certain running the business alone was going to be too daunting. She had no idea where to start with marketing, managing bookings and hiring equipment and staff. That was all Ava's field of expertise.

'I'm sure Freda will hire you for the wedding. Won't you?'

A pained look crossed Freda's face before she answered. 'Yes. Sure. Of course.'

Molly felt for her. Freda was going to have to admit that the wedding was off eventually. But obviously today wasn't going to be the day. 'I'm sure you don't need me for the wedding. There must be a thousand catering companies fighting for the contract.' Molly wiped her hands on her apron and received a grateful smile from Freda. 'Could one of you start peeling some potatoes, please?'

Neither of them made a move. Molly picked up her piping bag. The potatoes would have to peel themselves.

'Mother said you were hoping to get the Henri brothers in. They have three Michelin stars between them,' Lucca was saying, oblivious to his sister's mood plummeting. 'I will provide the booze of course, once we set the menus. And our dear brother can pay me extortionate amounts for overpriced wines. I was thinking, have you considered Monaco? I could probably get the Prince's Palace as a venue for the five days. People can fly or sail in—'

Freda let out a frustrated cry and slid off the bench. 'Can we stop talking about the goddamn wedding? I'm sick of it. It's all anyone talks about!'

Lucca and Molly stopped what they were doing.

'There are other things happening in the world,' she said loudly, stomping over to the fridge. 'There's a bloody war on, the planet's burning around us, and it looks as though Louis Vuitton are discontinuing my favourite crossbody bag.'

Lucca gasped jokingly. 'The one with the clean lines and sleek chain?'

Freda yanked out a bottle of wine and held it aloft. 'Yes. It's left me traumatised. Anyone care to join me?'

Lucca gave Molly a worried look as though wanting her to intervene, perhaps wrestle his sister to the ground and prise the bottle from her depressed, heartbroken fingers.

'Too early for me,' said Molly softly. 'And too early for any of us.' She raised her eyebrows at Freda. 'Besides, we still have the rest of this romantic evening to organise. Did you sort out the cards for the quiz?'

'Good idea,' agreed Lucca quickly. 'We'll get straight on it. Freeds, we'll leave Molly to crack on here. You come with me to finish the table settings and we'll write out the cards to go with each round of the degustation. We only have a few hours to go before dinner.'

Freda reluctantly put the wine back in the fridge. Molly watched Lucca guide her over to the dining table. He stopped to throw her a grateful look over his shoulder.

Was every member of this family unable to tell the truth?

Molly busied herself filling a plate full of canapés and leftover pork, gravy and roasties to take to Toby. Even though she was still mad at him, he'd had the good grace to avoid her. She suspected he was hiding in his room as per instructions. She left the siblings reminiscing in hushed whispers and knocked quietly on Toby's door. He answered immediately, took one look at the plate of food and scooped Molly into a hug. 'I can explain. I'm so sorry about not telling Levi about the wine.'

'I understand.'

'You can't understand.'

'Why not?'

'Because Lucca did it on purpose to wind Levi up. They have a thorny relationship.'

'You knew? Then why are you covering for him?' Molly saw Toby's cheeks redden. It was then that the penny dropped. 'You and Lucca...?'

'No. Lord no! But I do owe him a favour. He's the reason I'm here.'

Why was he blushing?

'Oh. You and Freda?'

Toby cleared his throat. 'It was ages ago. It's over. Ancient history. I just wanted one last chance to spend time with her. With them all. You can't tell her you know.'

'Why?' whispered Molly. 'You clearly still like each other.'

Toby winced. 'Freda has a fiancé in case you hadn't heard. And he's very wealthy and very well-connected. Besides, it was a holiday fling. Nothing more. No one knows. Well, Lucca does but that's it.'

'So you're carrying a torch for her but you haven't told her how you feel?'

'No. There's no point. She's getting married.' Toby looked sadly at the floor, scraping his foot back and forth. 'She's not interested in me. And even if she was, Valerie would never approve. I'm from *new* money. I probably shouldn't have come here, to be honest. It was a foolish hope.'

Molly raised her eyebrows. 'Maybe you should talk to her.'

Toby seemed lost in thought for a moment.

'You're welcome to join us in the kitchen.'

'Thanks, but I'll leave you to it. I've got some laundry and cleaning down in the spa to do. Valerie has suggested a deep clean. See? She thinks of me only as the hired help. And she's convinced someone has been up to no good down there,' Toby said, closing the door.

* * *

Molly scurried back to the kitchen but the two siblings were still where she'd left them, quietly guffawing over some past childhood memory.

'Sounds like it's going well,' Molly said, opening the fridge to get out an assortment of cream, eggs and fresh fruits to prepare the desserts.

'Where's Toby?' asked Freda. 'Didn't he want to join us?'

Molly shook her head. She saw a look of disappointment creep into Freda's eyes.

'It's about the wine, isn't it?' Lucca said quietly.

'Partly.'

'And why else?' Freda asked. 'Toby usually loves to join in. He's almost part of the family. It's why he comes to work here instead of helping his own family run their huge golfing empire.'

'I'm not sure,' Molly was quick to say. 'He said he had lots of laundry and cleaning to do.' *And a huge unrequited crush on you to hide.*

'Not like Toby to miss a chance to have you all to himself,' Lucca said to Freda, who instantly coloured. 'Talking of suitors, anything you'd like to share, dear sister?' Lucca put his hands on his hips.

'For the millionth time, we're just friends!'

'I meant about Reuben. And the lack thereof.'

'No.' Freda looked him squarely in the eye.

'Christ, this family and their secrets.' Lucca shook his head.

Molly looked at him. It was the pot calling the kettle black. When Freda was out of earshot she tilted her head at Lucca. 'Toby might have an unrequited crush on Freda, but how long have you been harbouring a crush on Toby?'

Lucca's face fell a thousand feet.

'Don't worry. I'd never tell.'

'Thanks, Molly. Is it that obvious?'

'No. I'm surprised your family don't know though?'

Lucca forced a laugh. 'They wouldn't care if I banged every female skiing instructor from here to Aspen, but if they knew my tastes lay elsewhere... I'm not sure they could handle it.' He gave her a pained look. 'Please don't tell anyone.'

Molly's heart went out to him.

21

LAST CHRISTMAS, I GAVE YOU MY TART

Molly lit the candles and switched on the twinkling lights while Lucca and Freda went to get changed into what would pass as waiters' uniforms. Molly was dressed in full chef's whites.

'Why is this table over here in the alcove and so out of the way?' Levi said, crossing the room, his laptop under one arm. 'There are only two place settings.'

'Yes,' said Molly, clearing her throat. 'I'll bring your meal to your room as requested.'

Levi inspected the table setting, the candles, the plates and glasses for two. 'It all looks incredibly romantic. And whose idea was this?'

'Lucca's.'

'My brother has ordered a romantic meal for two? How unsurprising.' Levi looked her over. 'Unless this is a bucket list thing. I suppose you'll be joining him?'

Molly gasped in surprise. 'Absolutely not.' She was growing tired of his leaping to conclusions. 'I know you have a very low opinion of me but come on, really?'

Levi didn't answer, his mouth set in a determined line.

She thought there was something odd in the way he was glaring at her. 'Wait. Are you jealous?'

Levi shook his head too quickly. 'No. Of course not. I have no idea what to make of you, that's all. I have no idea what you're up to in this house, with me, with my family. I just know that you're not being entirely truthful.' He slowly placed his laptop down, his eyes not leaving her face. 'Despite what you think, I read people for a living. I make business deals every day with people who have hidden agendas.' He was leaning closer to her. Molly was frozen to the spot.

She opened her mouth to retaliate but Freda came rushing towards them. 'They're coming! Quiet or you'll spoil the surprise.'

Lucca darted into the kitchen after her. They were both dressed in smart black clothes.

'What's going on? Why does the kitchen look like a

science lab?' Levi whispered back. He looked at what they were wearing. 'Did someone die?'

'Maybe, if we don't get our parents talking to each other,' whispered Freda. 'They're thinking of getting a divorce.'

'What? Impossible,' Levi said, frowning.

Lucca slung his arm around Levi, smiling. 'It's true. We'll be from a broken home. We'll end up as latchkey kids. Shunted from one house to another. Parents trying to buy our love.'

Levi shrugged his arm off. 'What are you talking about? They're a perfectly happy, solid couple.'

Freda coughed. 'Are you kidding me? Since when?'

Molly wondered whether to tell them about Valerie's suspicions and her own concerns over Armand's health when a familiar click-clacking rang through the lodge. 'They're here. Places, everyone. Levi, if you're staying, make yourself useful.' She threw a white chef's overcoat at him and hoped he would join in. After a second's hesitation, he flicked her an intense look. Despite her annoyance at him, it sent her pulse racing.

'We're trying to save a marriage. Come on, bro,' pleaded Lucca.

'I could use the help,' said Molly, trying desperately not to blush. Levi was wearing close-fitting jogging pants that barely left anything to the imagination. And her imagination was hellbent on making the most of it.

Levi rolled his eyes and put the coat on. The crisp, cotton jacket with its double row of buttons up to the neat collar suited him. He looked sexy as hell. 'Okay, Chef.' A warmth in his tone had replaced the usual gruffness as she saw him visibly relax. Lucca's words echoed in her brain. 'Where do you want me?'

Naked, sipping champagne in a hot tub. Molly shook the shocking thought away. She couldn't afford to take her eye off the ball. Pardon the pun.

'In the kitchen, please. I need you to sous-chef for me, starting with peeling the potatoes, then trimming the artichoke petals and slicing those shallots extra thin.'

He hesitated a fraction before giving her a half-smile. 'Yes, boss.'

Lucca caught her eye and raised his eyebrows a fraction as though to say, *What did I tell you?* She gave herself a mental shake.

'Here. I'll show you.' She would keep things strictly professional between them. She would focus on the delicate task of deconstructing her version of an innovative gazpacho with roast scallops on a bed of microscopic winter salad and not allow her eyes to stray. She was a robot. She would not react to him. It was a fool's errand because as soon as Levi stood next to her, she caught his familiar woody scent, putting her libido on immediate red alert.

He got to work speedily while Lucca and Freda introduced their confused and not entirely pleased parents to their plans for the evening. Molly and Levi listened from the kitchen.

'Where is everyone?' asked an irritable-sounding Valerie.

'Surprise!' Lucca said. 'We have a special evening planned for you both as a thank you.'

'Thank you for what?' Armand said gruffly.

'For being our parents, for being alive, does it matter?'

'What he means is,' interjected Freda, 'we wanted to do something special for your upcoming wedding anniversary.'

'It's six months away,' said Valerie in a harsh tone. 'And your father hasn't remembered it for the last ten years so why start celebrating now? And does it have to be so dark? I thought we had the electricity back.'

Armand studied his wife. 'You haven't a romantic bone in your body. You've forgotten how to love. That's why I don't bother.'

A thorny silence descended.

'Merry Christmas, parents,' Lucca said abruptly. 'Your loving children, well, the three you know about, hope you have a wonderful evening and would very much appreciate it if you could get along for at least the next two to three hours.'

'Christ Almighty. Is there really any need?' Valerie spat. 'And for your information, Armand, it hasn't been easy playing second fiddle to an art gallery and then to a golf stick.'

'Club, *ma chérie*. It's called a golf *club*. Perhaps if you took the slightest bit of interest, we could play together.'

'Never. I couldn't think of anything worse,' Valerie said frostily.

Levi gave Molly a grateful look as they hunched together over the bench, straining to listen. He whispered to her, 'Maybe this *is* a good idea.'

Lucca ploughed on, reading aloud from the card Molly had written for him. 'Tonight is a celebration of your wonderful marriage. A chance to rediscover things about yourselves as we take you on a culinary journey of your lives together. Each correct question will move you on to the next round and so on.'

'For the first round, we're taking you back to your wedding day,' Freda announced. 'Can you remember what you served your guests?'

Valerie rolled her eyes dramatically. 'Don't be ridiculous. No, of course not.'

'Like it was yesterday,' replied Armand at the same time.

While Valerie floundered, Molly nudged Levi into action. She pointed to a slate platter featuring a wide selection of amuse-bouches of all shapes and colours. 'I need you to gently place these flowers on top of the ones I pipe the purée on, please.'

Levi leaned very close to her, whispering back, 'What are they?'

'Each one represents every course they had at their wedding. But with a slight twist.'

Levi looked suitably impressed. 'How would you know what they ate? It was nearly forty years ago.'

'Research. Obviously. You're not the only one who's exhaustingly thorough. Also, Lucca has been pumping your housekeeper in France for information. She raked through an old box of mementoes and found the original menu. And I asked your dad earlier if he could remember, to jog his memory.'

She was pleased to see a smile tugging at Levi's kissable lips.

'Here, take these.' Molly bent down to retrieve two tiny ramekins filled with thinly sliced duck and shallots on a bed of mashed buttery potato. She took a pan from the stove and poured a drizzle of cherry brandy, sloe and plum sauce.

A cheer alerted them to the fact that the first round had been successful. Freda hurried through into the kitchen followed by Lucca. 'It's working,' he said excitedly, his eyes shining.

Molly gave them both a slate platter each. 'Instruct them to eat from left to right in order, then this one last. When they've finished, we'll give them a palate cleanser ready for the next round of questions.'

They watched Freda and Lucca go. Levi cleared his throat. 'This was a very thoughtful idea. I'm sorry for the way I've been behaving. I should never have accused you of...'

Molly held up a hand. 'It's fine. Let's just get through this meal and then we can talk. I still owe you an explanation for the letter you found. And then, when you realise you're wrong about me, you can apologise for being such a tosser.'

Levi's eyes softened as they exchanged a tender look. 'Okay. I'm guessing that's some kind of jerk. What's next?'

Molly had loved recreating this one. Freda had often heard her mother go on about how overjoyed she was to be expecting Levi but how difficult pregnancy in France had been due to her bizarre cravings for American food. Molly had managed to recreate the classic 1980s cheddar melt and the short-lived caramel pecan roll that apparently Armand had flown across the Atlantic especially for his wife.

'They must have been so deeply in love at the beginning,' Molly whispered as she assembled the miniscule, bite-size cheeseburgers. 'It's such a shame how couples drift apart. Can you sprinkle those with cinnamon, please, and lie a gingerbread toffee twist onto the sauce?'

Levi gave her an intense look but said nothing as he did what she asked.

* * *

It was somewhere around the sixth round that Armand and Valerie could be heard laughing. 'I haven't heard them laughing like that for a long time,' Levi declared. 'I guess I'm away a lot. I hadn't realised how far apart they'd grown.'

'Well, this next round is a take on the time they took you to visit your grandparents in Phoenix.'

'Are those Mexican hotdogs?' Lucca sneaked up behind them. 'I can still taste them. I ate so many I was sick, remember?'

Levi chuckled. 'Yep. Who could forget? You threw up over the back of Papa's head as he was driving.'

Molly watched the two brothers share a friendly look. Lucca put a hand on Levi's shoulder. 'That was the best trip ever, wasn't it?'

'I made a whole pile of them over there,' Molly whispered, pointing to the bench adjacent. 'Help yourselves.'

Freda walked over. 'Molly, you're a genius. I've never seen my parents enjoy themselves this much in, like, forever. Mother is actually *eating* for once.' She gasped. 'No way! Are they Mexican hotdogs? Like the ones Grandma used to make?' She rushed over to Levi and Lucca and began digging in. 'And mini fries? This is like the best tasting ever. Can you pass me one of those fishy things, please?'

'I suppose I'll be jetting in a supply of these from Mexico for the wedding?' Levi joked to Freda.

Freda instantly looked at Molly, who pretended to tidy away dishes.

Like a prairie dog, Levi's ears pricked up. 'What's going on? Am I missing something?'

Freda and Molly said in unison, 'Nothing.'

'Is everything okay?' Levi asked them.

Molly admired how astute and mentally quick

Levi was becoming around his family. She was finding his empathy increasingly attractive.

'Service,' Molly said to Freda and Lucca. 'Take these melted puddings before they go cold. Freda, you take the cake stand with all the desserts. It's the last round.'

Levi leaned towards her. 'It appears you know more about my family than I do.'

Molly felt the hairs on her arms bristle. He wasn't wrong. His close proximity was clearing her mind of ways to avoid telling him the truth. She needed to start with her own. She gazed into his dark eyes. She had his undivided attention. 'The reason why I'm here working at the resort is because my business partner had already signed off on the contract months and months before, when we had staff and she was hoping to expand the business, but—'

They were interrupted by Freda and Lucca approaching. 'Mother wants to see you, Molly.'

She gave Levi an apologetic look. 'I'll be right back.' Molly wiped her hands clean and went through. Valerie was sitting alone. She beckoned Molly close. Then closer until Molly was bending down a few inches from Valerie's face.

'Get the phone now,' she instructed. 'When he returns from the bathroom, I'll keep him talking. It's on the bedside cabinet charging. Call me into the kitchen when you have it, then you can put it back once I've had a look.'

Molly gasped. 'No. I told you I wouldn't.'

Valerie dismissed her with a wave of her hand as Armand approached. 'Nonsense. Just do it.'

'I will not,' Molly hissed defiantly. 'Why don't you ask one of your children to do it? Or would they also not approve?'

Valerie looked incensed. 'If you dare say one word—'

Armand stopped in front of Molly. 'Molly, *merci beaucoup*.' He bowed graciously and thanked her for a delicious meal and an entertaining evening. 'That was the best degustation I have ever had in my life. A real trip down memory lane. I don't know how you did it, but it was wonderful.'

'I'm glad you enjoyed it. You have coffee, liqueurs and a cheeseboard after your dessert, but please let me know if there is anything I can get you before I close the kitchen and retire my staff for the evening.'

Valerie scowled at her from behind Armand's back. Molly scurried to the kitchen to find the others in high spirits.

'What a great team we make. Who's for celebrating

in my room?' Lucca whispered. 'We'll leave the two lovebirds to it.'

'Good idea,' agreed Freda, downing a glass of wine. 'I'll bring a few bottles. Levi, you grab the brandy. Molly, bring some of those amazing desserts.'

'We'll sneak through the boot room, so they don't see us,' suggested Lucca, smiling.

Levi hung back. 'What did my mother want?'

Molly winced.

'She still wants you to steal his phone, even after such a lovely night?' He rubbed a hand down the side of his perfectly shaped face. 'How could she?'

Molly shrugged in answer. People. Such strange, unpredictable creatures.

Just as they were about to leave, they heard Valerie say clearly, 'It's no good. She'll have to go.'

Freda stopped suddenly in her tracks, causing Lucca, Levi and Molly to bump into each other behind her. They heard Armand protesting.

'Don't spoil this wonderful evening, Val.'

'I'm not spoiling it. You've seen the way she looks at him. It's for her own good.'

Molly froze.

'I have no idea what you mean. She's cooked all this delicious food, and you're dismissing her? Why, may I ask?'

Oh boy. Now it was Valerie's turn to fire her. She'd have to get in line.

'Because I can see the way Levi looks at her. Don't tell me you've not noticed. He'll fall for that innocent look of hers, but let me tell you, I know a gold digger when I see one. She's got to go.'

They heard Armand let out a hefty breath. 'She doesn't strike me as a gold digger, Val. Why do you have to be so negative all the time?'

'The wine? She lied about the wine, didn't she? She's shrewd, much cleverer than we've given her credit for.'

Lucca flicked Molly a guilty look.

'And I caught her drinking vodka this morning. A whole bottle of vodka hidden in her apron. She's clearly got a drinking problem.'

It was Freda's turn to glance guiltily at Molly. She mouthed an apology.

'And she lied about the catering business, about her restaurant, probably to manipulate Levi into buying it at a higher price. Petra told me she'd rung the number on the contract and was told the owner had died. Then all of a sudden, Molly turns up. Very much *alive*. And Petra was so desperate for staff, she went along with it thinking she'd made a mistake. Something is off. No. She has to go. That's final.'

While Lucca and Freda were making confused faces, Levi was frowning with concern at Molly.

'I think you're wrong, dear. She's a clever girl, yes. I mean, who else knew how to fix the generator? But I think you've misunderstood her. It's time you stopped interfering in our children's lives and started looking at your own.'

Molly stood rooted to the spot as an almighty row unfurled between the two.

'She is not good enough for this family. She can't ski. She can't make a decent espresso martini. She has no clue who the Wertheimers or the Meyers even are, for God's sake.' It sounded like Valerie was becoming hysterical, clutching at straws. 'And she won't have her own Centurion membership or offshore savings account or *kidnapping insurance*!'

'You're being utterly ridiculous,' Armand said with exasperation. 'Since when did you become such a snob?'

'If you won't send her away, then I will.' Valerie was breathing very heavily. 'In fact, I have an even better idea. I'll invite Clarice for Christmas.'

Molly had no idea who Clarice was but at the sound of Armand almost choking on his wine, she was deeply concerned for him.

'You can't invite Levi's ex-fiancée to stay with us. She'll think he wants to marry her after all.'

'Exactly.'

Molly shot Levi a startled look. Now *he* looked like he was having a stroke. They heard a chair scrape against the floor and what they presumed was a cloth napkin being thrown down onto the table as it rattled some cutlery.

'This is our last Christmas together as a family, Val. For pity's sake, don't spoil it.' Armand's voice cracked as they heard him get up to leave.

'*Sit back down!*' barked Valerie. 'You don't get to walk away from me. Not this time. Tell me who she is.'

'Who are you talking about?' shouted Armand angrily.

'The tramp you're seeing!' Valerie shrieked. 'Who is it this time?'

22

I ATTRACT LOVE AND POSITIVE ENERGY
INTO MY LIFE

'There's a lot to unpack there,' whispered Freda. 'Does that mean Papa is divorcing Mother? And that's why he thinks this is our last Christmas together?'

'There's no way he's having an affair. Why does she have to self-sabotage all the time?' Lucca snapped, shaking his head at Freda. 'At least we know where you get it from.'

'Never mind that. What the hell is she playing at inviting Clarice? I can't fucking stand her. If she comes here, I'm leaving,' Freda said to no one in particular.

'And I'll be coming with you. I hate that woman's guts after what she did.' Lucca gave Levi a hard look.

Levi frowned. 'She won't be coming anywhere near us. I'll make sure of it. I'll go and put a stop to it.'

Lucca put his hand out to stop him walking away. 'Then they'll know we've been eavesdropping,' he complained.

'Who cares? I'll go if he doesn't,' said Freda.

Molly was taken aback at how angry Lucca sounded. She was desperate to ask what had happened with Clarice but as the two siblings began bickering against the backdrop of Valerie and Armand yelling at each other in the next room, Levi tugged on Molly's arm.

He pulled her gently away to one side. 'What did my mother mean? Did your business partner die?' Levi asked softly. 'Recently?'

Molly had to look away.

'I'd never have threatened to take the restaurant from you if I knew,' he said, taking her arms and gently twisting her to look at him. 'Why didn't you say?'

Because I was desperate.

'Because that's not everything. And every time I think about it, I start crying and never stop.'

It was a highly inappropriate moment to be dredging up such trauma. Lucca and Freda were now arguing loudly about their parents' marriage. Armand was retaliating as Valerie accused him of all sorts.

'The hot tub, the wedding,' Levi said as though

pieces of a puzzle were falling into place. 'So the bucket list was something you were doing together?'

'No, not together. I'm way too socially awkward to do even half of what was on there. But Ava was almost finished when she suddenly took an unexpected turn for the worse. We had to move her out of our home into a hospice.' Molly heard her voice shaking. 'It wasn't until after she died that I found out she'd left me everything in her will. She wanted me to have her half of the apartment.' Molly sniffed. 'Anyway, it turns out that the way the will was written...'

'It included the restaurant as well.'

Molly nodded sadly, appreciating that Levi was a trained lawyer when he wanted to be. It didn't take him long to realise that the condition of the will was the completion of Ava's bucket list.

'And I'm guessing all the assets were frozen? Essentially locking you out of your own business?'

'But that is *not* why I wanted to sleep with you,' Molly whispered. She was staring up at him, every fibre in her body pleading him to have faith in her. 'You have to believe me. That was a genuine connection. I never meant to deceive you. I'd never do that to you. I'm not like that.'

Levi gave her an intense look, causing tears to prick at her eyes. Then he swept her into a hug. He cradled her head in one hand and pulled her in tight with the other. She sagged against him, taking immediate comfort from his warm, strong embrace.

Lucca stopped arguing with Freda to throw them a lopsided grin. 'Get a room, you two.'

Molly managed to stifle a giggle.

'We need to try and salvage this disaster.' Lucca gestured to them. 'We as in *all* of us.'

'Give us a minute,' Levi said. Molly thought she would explode with joy as Levi leaned towards her. He cupped her face with his hands.

Freda's eyes nearly popped out of her head. 'What are you doing?' she shrieked. 'Wait. Is there something going on between you two?'

Molly instinctively stood back from Levi and shook her head. She didn't want Levi to be embarrassed. His mother had already done enough of that.

Levi reached for her hand and pulled her back to him. 'Yes. There's something going on.'

Molly's head jerked up in surprise. 'You don't need to say that.'

'It's true, isn't it?'

Levi kept a tight hold of her. Her skin was on fire where he held her. His eyes, full of promise, caused her heart to melt. Valerie's words about Molly not being 'good enough' rang round her brain. Common sense was telling her to run a mile but the more time she spent with Levi, the more attracted to him she was becoming. Even if he did behave like a pompous, judgemental workaholic most of the time.

This news was not going to go down at all well.

'Now you have no excuse not to teach me how to cook.' Freda beamed at Molly. 'We can hang out together.'

'Listen,' hissed Lucca. They stopped talking. 'I can't hear anything.'

'Did they leave while we were yelling at each other?' Freda whispered just as her mother let out an agonising howl.

Molly, Levi, Lucca and Freda scrambled back through the kitchen and into the lounge area at great speed. They saw Armand slumped over the table. His glass knocked to the floor. His face drained of colour. Valerie stood staring at him as though none of it was real.

'Papa!' yelled Levi, sprinting towards him.

While the family panicked, Molly raced to Armand and rifled through his pockets. 'What are you doing?' screeched Valerie. 'Leave him alone. I don't care about the bloody phone!'

'His tablets. His spray. Where are they?' Molly asked her calmly.

Valerie responded with a bewildered look. 'Tablets? I have no idea what you are talking about. Leave him alone, I tell you.'

Molly ignored her and tapped Armand on the shoulder. 'Monsieur LeRoux, can you hear me? Monsieur LeRoux?' She put her ear to his mouth to check his breathing. 'Shit, he's not breathing. Ring an ambulance,' Molly told Levi. 'Freda, go to the bedroom and search for your father's heart medication. There should be tablets and a GTN spray. Lucca, help me get him flat on the floor.'

While Levi shouted into his phone for an air ambulance, Lucca leapt into action as they eased Armand from the chair. 'He needs CPR.' Molly glanced at each family member. 'He's gone into cardiac arrest. He needs CPR,' she repeated. Valerie immediately burst into tears. Lucca looked like a frightened child.

'Sorry. I don't know how to...' Lucca gasped helplessly. 'Papa! Papa! Please don't die.'

Seriously? No one knew CPR?

Molly got to work opening Armand's airways and doing compressions as an eerie silence fell. Levi dropped to his knees. 'How can I help?'

'Do you know CPR?'

Levi shook his head. He looked desperate. 'I did a course a million years ago. I'm not sure exactly...'

'Keep his airways open for me. The rest of you stand back. Give us some room,' Molly instructed. 'How long until the ambulance gets here?'

'Twenty minutes, maybe more.'

'Do you keep a defibrillator in the house?' Molly asked Levi calmly.

Levi shook his head.

'Are you sure? Lucca, go to the boot room. There's a shelf with first aid kits. See if there's a portable defib machine.'

'What will it look like?' Lucca shrieked. 'I don't know what it'll look like!'

'Stay calm. Either a large unit with defibrillator written on it or a small pack with AED on it. Hurry.'

Molly continued compressions but Armand remained unresponsive. Time seemed to stand still as she worked harder and harder on him. She bent at regular intervals to blow air into his lungs only for it to seep back out. If he didn't start breathing again quickly, his brain would be starved of oxygen and the consequences too awful to imagine.

'Found it!' Lucca yelled, tearing through the room towards them just as Freda came running back into the room with an armful of medicine boxes.

'Levi, take over compressions,' Molly ordered. 'Freda, give me the medicines.' Molly scanned the boxes for confirmation that Armand had a heart condition and tore the AED pack open, deftly switching it on and taking out the electrode pads.

Without being told, Levi ripped Armand's shirt open, exposing his unmoving chest. Molly grabbed a napkin from the table and gave it to Levi. 'Dry him.' They watched her take the razor from the pack.

'What are you doing?' squealed Valerie. 'Someone get her away from him. Levi, for crying out loud, tell her!'

Molly ignored her and quickly shaved two patches on Armand's unusually hairy chest, one on the upper right side and the other on the lower left side. She peeled off the plastic backing of the electrodes and stuck the pads to the shaved areas, then plugged in the cables and was relieved when the machine automatically began analysing his heart rhythm. She sat back, her eyes glued to the monitor's screen.

Valerie raced round the table and dropped to the floor, elbowing Molly out of the way. 'Armand, can you hear me? Armand!' She went to slap his face.

'No. Don't touch him!' yelled Molly, knowing it would interfere with the reading.

Levi, fast as lightning, grabbed his mother just as she reached for her husband. 'Mother. Molly knows what she's doing. Trust her.'

Valerie's eyes widened. 'But she's just a chalet chef, for God's sake.'

Taking no notice, Molly threw her arms wide. 'Everyone, stand clear. We need to shock him.' She pressed the button, and they watched as Armand's chest jumped. Molly swallowed. Seconds seemed to drag by as Armand showed no sign of breathing. She restarted compressions immediately. Sweat dripped from her forehead as she counted. 'Come on. Come on.'

Molly heard Freda crying, which seemed to set off Valerie, who howled into Levi's shoulder. Molly made brief eye contact with Lucca's tear-filled, disbelieving eyes. She sent a silent prayer up to Ava. *Help me save him.*

She bent to breathe air into his lungs and finally, Armand jolted and they heard a small choking sound as he took a breath, then another, then another. His eyes pinged open as he gasped loudly. He was alive! Molly checked the machine to make sure Armand's heart was beating regularly and collapsed backwards on the floor. 'You're okay. You're going to be okay.' She leaned over to the pile of medication and quickly rifled through it. 'The spray?' she asked Armand.

Armand reached for her hand and tried to nod. He opened his mouth, and Molly gave him a squirt of the spray under his tongue. Within seconds, colour was flooding back to his face.

'How long before the paramedics get here?' she asked Levi.

His phone beeped. 'That's them now,' he said, jumping to his feet.

Molly made eye contact with Valerie. 'He needs a blanket. We need to keep him warm.'

Valerie bent to kiss Armand on the forehead and got to her feet. Freda and Lucca sank to the floor and took a hand each. Amid the commotion, Molly ran to the kitchen to get a glass of water. She hurried back, grabbed the box of aspirin from his pile and took one out, crushing it.

Armand, his body now covered in a warm blanket, seemed to know exactly what she had in mind and patted her hand when she bent down. Freda lifted his head as Molly sprinkled the crushed tablet onto his tongue and put the water to his lips. Within minutes, two paramedics stormed through the house with a stretcher and first aid kits. Molly stood out of the way to let them check him over.

'Who did this?' said one of the paramedics, unpeeling the electrodes carefully. 'Was he unresponsive?'

Molly stepped forward. 'Yes. He was unconscious

for around three to four minutes. He took one shock and I've given him a spray of GTN and an aspirin.'

'Great job,' he said, eyeing the AED unit and Armand's chest. 'You saved his life.'

Levi was the first to throw his arms around Molly. His eyes were misty. Molly felt the adrenaline that had been soaring through her body suddenly crash. She felt weak at the way he was looking at her.

They watched, trance-like, as the paramedics unpacked equipment, did a variety of checks and spoke to Armand about the heart condition he had clearly been hiding from his entire family.

Suddenly, Freda was nudging Levi out of the way to throw her arms around Molly. 'Thank you. Thank you so much. And I'm so sorry about you taking the blame for the vodka.'

Molly raised her eyebrows.

'And the wine mix-up, I knew it wasn't you. And for burning the lunch yesterday while I was drunk. And for not telling anyone that the wedding is off.'

Levi looked incredulous. 'You all stood by and let Molly take the blame?'

'The wedding is *off*?' screeched Valerie. 'Since when?'

'Since Reuben dumped me this morning.'

'Why didn't you tell me? I've gone and booked

Hotel Du Pont on Lake Garda. It's the only way I could get Celine Dion to commit.'

Freda put a hand on her hip. 'See? No wonder Rooby got cold feet. He had no say whatsoever in his own wedding.'

Lucca cleared his throat. 'While we're at it, it was me that opened the expensive wine. Molly was covering for me and Toby.'

Just then, Toby ran through to witness the scene. 'What happened? I had my AirPods in.'

Levi looked furious. 'Not one of us has treated you with the respect you deserve, Molly. Shame on the lot of us.'

'Can we keep the family theatrics down, please?' boomed one of the paramedics. 'Your father's heart rate just shot up.' They worked diligently to strap him into the stretcher and repack their emergency kits. 'We'll ready him for transportation to Geneva HUG. It's the nearest hospital. They have a bed and a medical team on standby. Who's going with him?'

'I will,' said Valerie. She made eye contact with Armand, and they exchanged a knowing look. 'We've been married nearly forty years. He's not getting out of it this easily.'

Valerie walked over to Molly. She stood stiffly in front of her. 'I, too, am sorry for the things I said.'

Levi cleared his throat loudly.

'And the things I asked you to do.' Valerie looked down and clasped her trembling hands together. 'This is not the LeRoux family's finest moment. Thank you for saving my husband's life. We owe you.'

Molly shook her head. 'No, you don't. You absolutely don't. I hope he recovers quickly and that you get to have your family Christmas.'

Valerie tilted her head. 'You're leaving?'

'Petra messaged me earlier. The pass should be open tomorrow, and my replacement will arrive before the evening.' It was all very bittersweet but probably for the best.

Valerie looked genuinely sad at the news. 'But I didn't ask her to replace you. I know I said I would, but I didn't.'

Before anyone could say anything, the paramedics lifted Armand up and yelled instructions for everyone to stop bickering and open doors, and to pack his overnight bag and to gather all his medication to take to the hospital and to say their goodbyes.

'I'll come with you,' Levi said to his mother. It was only when Levi let go and walked towards Valerie that Molly realised he had been holding her hand the whole time.

Valerie smiled, then looked across at Molly. 'No.

I'll be fine. You stay here. I'll ring you from the hospital.'

'Are you sure?' he asked.

'Positive.' Valerie went around each of her children and hugged them tight, leaving them gobsmacked. 'Freda, call me, darling. I want to know everything that happened with Reuben.'

They went outside to wave them off. As the helicopter lifted into the dark night, a shooting star shot across the sky.

Thanks, Ava, prayed Molly silently.

23

KARMA HAS NO DEADLINE

'Fuck me,' exclaimed Lucca, plonking himself down heavily onto the sofa. 'What a night. Poor Papa. I hope he's going to be okay.'

'Me too,' agreed Freda, chewing her nail. 'Mother must be really worried. I thought she was going to tell us she loved us at one point.'

Levi stifled a chuckle. 'Shock does strange things to a person. That was quite the unsolicited outpouring of apologies and regret.' He pulled Molly down to the sofa next to him. 'You were brilliant. So cool under pressure. You knew exactly what to do and when to do it.' He gave her an admiring look.

'That's the benefit of having eight years of running a busy kitchen under my belt, a nurse for a mother and a father in recovery from a heart attack. I've been through this before. Armand is in good hands. The quicker he gets to hospital, the quicker he'll recover and be up and about. Usually within a couple of days.'

'Thank you, Molly. I needed to hear that.' Freda curled up next to Lucca and Toby on the sofa opposite. 'And sorry about your own father. Is he okay?'

'He's fine. He's recuperating somewhere in the Caribbean. He and Mum are on a cruise.'

'So you're on your own for Christmas?'

Molly deliberately avoided Levi's gaze. 'My, erm, plans kind of changed recently. I had intended to spend the day in the kitchen at the main resort hotel, but now I'll be free to...'

...spend the day on my own, trying to get the deeds to my apartment and restaurant back.

Levi tightened his grip on her hand.

'Do you have to leave tomorrow?' Freda pleaded. 'I was so looking forward to you teaching me to cook. I've really enjoyed it.'

Molly let out an involuntary snigger. 'I'm not sure we have enough eggs left. You went through sixteen this morning to make one poached egg. If I ever do open a cooking school, please never swing by.'

Freda laughed. 'See? I need you. You're the only person who's honest with me. Levi, ask her to stay.'

It occurred to Molly that she hadn't felt this level of warmth, excitement, frustration, abhorrence, worry or, indeed, overwhelming horniness, in a long, long time. She'd become a numb husk just getting by on a mix of gloomy despair and lethargy towards sorting out her business. And she had Levi and his bonkers family to thank for it. They'd woken her from the emotional coma she'd been in since Ava died. She glanced shyly at Levi. She was feeling all the feels, and it felt like her body was making up for lost time. Being snowed in here at the lodge, around this madcap family with all their drama, was infectious.

Levi put his arm around Molly's shoulder. 'I know I haven't been the easiest person to get on with. I'm truly sorry for being such a jerk about everything. But would you please consider staying for Christmas?'

'Is that because you suspect I cook the best Christmas dinner on the planet, or because you need me to save you from Freda's undercooked turkey and salmonella poisoning?'

'Both.'

Lucca groaned. 'Please, Molly. Please stay. Levi is so much nicer when you are around. I've never heard him so much as apologise to anyone *ever*. You *must* stay. Forever, if possible.'

Molly gazed at Levi sitting next to her, every bone

in her body screaming to say yes. 'I'd love to stay, but I have something very important to do tomorrow.'

'The bucket list? What's the deadline?' Levi asked.

'Tomorrow at 6 p.m. I'll never get it done unless I spend all day doing it.'

'Bucket list? On Christmas Eve?' Lucca exclaimed. 'Sounds fun.'

'We'll help,' offered Freda. 'But why the deadline?'

Molly explained about her friend, the list, the restaurant and the solicitor and was amazed to find her tear ducts intact. For the first time, she could talk about her situation without having an emotional breakdown.

'We can do that no problem,' Lucca assured her. 'Then you can email the evidence through before the deadline.'

Molly felt a swell of gratitude for the people around her.

Toby glanced repeatedly at Freda before Molly saw him pluck up the courage to speak to her. 'I'm sorry to hear that Reuben called the wedding off.'

Freda inhaled noisily. 'I think deep down I knew it was coming. I just didn't know what to replace him with, if that makes any sense. I'm trying to find my passion. Something that I'm good at.'

'Well, it's obviously not cooking,' laughed Lucca.

'Something will come to you. You've got a lot to offer,' Toby said warmly.

Lucca punched him on the arm. 'Stop hitting on my sister, dude. You've already failed at that many times. You need to know when to give up.'

Toby laughed. 'I'll give up when it's me she's walking down the aisle towards.'

Freda gasped in mock shock. 'Why, Toby, I thought you'd never ask.'

Toby grinned. 'I'm serious. Just name the day.'

Freda let out a huge yawn in response. 'I would but I think Valerie would have a stroke. Anyway, I'm done with love. It's too time-consuming. It's for weak-minded people who don't have the self-esteem to know that they are enough as they are.'

'But it's life-affirming and joyful,' Toby argued.

'Not for me it isn't. It's no-strings sex for me from now on.'

'That could also work,' Toby said hopefully, until Lucca threw a cushion at him.

'Dude. That's our baby sister. She might be an emotionally unstable drunk but she's not desperate.' Lucca laughed hard at his own joke until Toby threw a cushion at his head.

'Okay, that's enough excitement for one night.'

Freda stood up. 'Should we wait up until we know Papa is okay?'

'No. I'll ring the hospital now.' Levi took out his phone. 'You lot can go to bed if you need to. I'll instruct my PA to ring me if there are any changes. He's flying over to meet Mother and will be on hand for whatever they need. He's already booked her into a hotel by the hospital.'

'Great. I'm so tired.' Freda yawned again, setting off a chain reaction. 'I'll see you all at breakfast. Molly, bring the list. We'll tick them all off. You'll get your restaurant back, I promise.'

Levi made eye contact with Molly, causing her to blush. She wondered if he was thinking about the naked hot tub scenario. He got to his feet and hauled her up beside him. He whispered in her ear, 'I'll do whatever you need me to do.'

Molly felt every hair on the back of her neck tingle. Her entire future hung in the balance and yet one word from Levi and she felt strong and capable. And unfortunately, very lustful. He must have caught the way her pupils dilated, accentuating the bright sparkle in her eyes, because he visibly swallowed. 'Come with me.'

Once they heard bedroom doors closing and they were sure the coast was clear, Levi led Molly down to the spa area and locked the door behind them. She took a step towards him and, feeling brave, reached up on tiptoes. She closed her eyes and kissed him tenderly on the lips. 'As much as I appreciate it, you don't have to do this.'

When she opened her eyes, Levi was staring at her and, after a beat, he pulled her towards him. This time their lips slid hungrily back and forth, a heated exploration. Molly felt tingles fluttering in her stomach.

She slid her hands over his back, pulling him against her. She heard a low growl escape from him as their kiss deepened. Her head in a whirl, Molly tugged at the many, many buttons of his catering uniform. Why had she insisted on him wearing it? But this wasn't the time to question her excellent hygiene standards. This was the time to end her dry spell. *I mean, complete the bucket list*, she thought, trying to focus. *He's just here helping with the bucket list. Do not read too much into it.*

'Wait.' He broke from kissing, took her hand in his and led her to the massage chair.

'What are you doing?' Molly asked. This was definitely *not* on the list.

'Something I should have done the first time round.'

He unbuttoned her jacket, slipping it from her

shoulders. She followed his lead, marvelling at how quickly he shed the rest of his clothes. He stood naked in front of her.

'This makes a refreshing change.' She grinned. 'I like it.'

'I bet you do.' Levi smiled playfully. 'You've waited a long time for this.'

Molly giggled and tried not to stare as he helped her peel off the rest of her own clothes. She glanced down when she felt something nudge her bare stomach. *Gosh.* Were they all that big? It had been so long, she'd forgotten.

'Sit.'

She looked down at the massage chair. 'Don't I need a towel over myself?' After all, like Lucca had said, this wasn't Finland. She'd never been naked so much in her entire existence. Nor was she an expert on chair sex.

Levi shook his head, pressing a button to make the chair recline to almost horizontal. She lay down on it and felt the weight of him as he settled on top of her, their legs entwined. He held her wrists gently above her head and bent to kiss her lips, her neck, her breasts. She writhed beneath him, causing him to moan with desire. When she cried out for him, it was clear he was going to take his time. Her every nerve ending was on fire for him. He slipped easily from the chair and strode round to kneel in front of her. He pressed another button, and the seat tilted her up to sitting and began to gently vibrate. She gasped as he parted her legs, placing one on each arm of the chair, her womanhood fully exposed.

She very much doubted he was a qualified gynaecologist. And this would be unlike any examination she'd ever had. She opened her mouth to object.

'Relax,' he told her. 'Close your eyes.'

She took a deep breath and did as she was told while relaxing music filtered into her consciousness. Her body trembled with anticipation. She breathed in the warm scented air, lemon balm essential oils infused with calming ylang ylang. The feel of his hands sliding slowly up her thighs was unspeakably erotic. She felt him massage her with his thumbs, one massaging her lightly while the other entered her, sliding gently in and out. *Oh my.* Then, keeping her eyes tightly closed, she felt his thumbs spread the lips of her womanhood wide open.

She felt powerless, consumed with longing for his touch. She inhaled a sharp breath as his hot mouth made contact, his tongue flicking expertly against her.

A tingle throbbed rhythmically down below, matching the drumming of her heart. She was completely lost, helpless to the delicious sensation. Tangling her hands in his hair, she pulled him closer, revelling in his stubbled chin tickling her thighs, his mouth hungry for her taste. It sent sparkles throughout her entire body and just when she thought she'd explode, he applied more pressure, causing a strong pulsating beat to spread from her core out to every nerve ending. He grew more insistent, lapping at her sweet spot again and again until, like a dam, the orgasm burst through her. She threw her head back, freefalling over the edge as her whole body quivered to a thundering climax.

She bucked against his mouth but still he held her in place, his tongue an instrument of exquisite torture as wave after wave of white-hot ecstasy shuddered through her. As she cried out, her whole body collapsed, sated with endorphins, completely and utterly spent.

She opened her eyes slowly, gazing at him in wonder. Molly was sure she had sparkles shooting from her eyeballs like fireworks. They stared at one another for what seemed like an eternity before Levi got to his feet. He held out a hand and pulled her up. He was the perfect height for her. She could barely stand up though, never mind speak. Her legs had turned to jelly. She instinctively looped her arms around his neck.

The feel of his naked body pressed against hers felt so right. Everything about this moment felt destined to be. Magical. Dreamlike. Perfect.

'I love the way you look at me,' she said, her voice scarcely more than a whisper as he held her tight. Was it possible to fall in love with someone you barely knew? Based purely on their ability to deliver orgasms that had you as high as a bath of cocaine? With a contented whimper, she breathed, 'That was amazing.' She trailed the back of her fingers tenderly down his cheek and over his jawline. She'd never felt so giddy, so open, so honest with a man. She was in a complete loved-up haze. 'I'm falling in love with you,' she murmured against his lips. As soon as the words were out, she regretted them. She gasped. 'I'm sorry. I shouldn't have...'

Levi's eyes grew dark and intense. Time seemed to stand still. He nodded slowly. 'I'm falling in love with you, too.'

It took a few moments for them to digest what they'd just said to each other. Levi was first to speak, a smile tugging at his lips. 'Now, let's see what we can do in the hot tub with the champagne.'

It turned out that quite a number of things could be done in a hot tub with champagne, and none of them to do with drinking it!

24

BARKING MAD

The following morning Molly woke from the deepest, most restful sleep of her life wrapped in Levi's arms, with a delicious ache all over her body. She felt an inner glow. She would never be the same ever again. Last night had changed her. It felt like a new beginning. For the first time since Ava's death, she felt *hopeful*. For the second time that week, she found herself in bed with the man of her dreams wondering what effect last night's soulful union, their life-changing, mind-blowing sexual experience, would have on him. She propped up on her elbow and nudged Levi awake, keen to find out.

He opened his eyes and smiled at her. 'Jeez. What

a night. That was so great. So, so unbelievably great.'
Levi rubbed his eyes with the palms of his hands.

Encouraging start.

'I've never experienced anything quite like it.'

Even better.

'I feel incredible.'

Molly looked at him, beaming from ear to ear, and
tutted playfully. 'You're talking about sleep again,
aren't you?' She glanced at her phone charging by the
bed. 'Before you ask, it's almost ten o'clock. You've had
nine whole hours.'

Levi reached over to kiss her. 'You are so good
for me.'

She wriggled out of his arms. 'Time to get up. We
have a lot to do.'

'Have you always been this bossy? How did I not
notice?'

'Too busy working and being grumpy?'

Levi feigned heartbreak.

Molly rang the solicitor's office as soon as she was
dressed.

'It's me, Molly Johnson. I'm ringing to let you
know I'll be completing the rest of the tasks today and
emailing the signed papers, photos of the journal and
witness signatures to you before the deadline at
6 p.m.'

For once, Monsieur Fournier sounded a tiny bit compassionate. She quickly clicked off the call and raced through to the kitchen to find Freda poking in cupboards, gathering pans.

'I'm only trying to help speed up breakfast,' she joked. 'I have everything under control.'

Molly looked in the pedal bin to see a pile of broken eggshells.

Freda held her hands up. 'I only broke four eggs. That's it. And I dropped the flour. Why do pancakes have to be so difficult to make?'

By the time Molly had taken her through the three basic steps to making the perfect pancake, steps that a six-year-old could master, Freda was squealing with delight. Levi and Lucca gathered round the table to tuck feverishly into Freda's stack of warm pancakes, drizzled with maple syrup, topped with crispy bacon and a side jug of hot melted chocolate.

'These are delicious,' exclaimed Levi.

'Freeds. You've nailed it!' Lucca said with his mouth crammed full. 'You've found your true calling.'

Freda was beaming. 'Do you really think so? I mean, I do love the restaurant business. Who doesn't like to eat out every night?'

'There's a bit more to it than that,' chimed in Molly as she flitted around collecting plates, refilling dishes.

Freda gasped. 'I could help you run your restaurant. If you'll let me. I have a business degree. I'm sure I could put it to good use.' She looked pleadingly at Molly.

In that moment, Freda reminded Molly of Ava. Bubbling over with enthusiasm. Was she ready to open herself up to new friendships and a new business partner?

Closing her eyes and taking a calming breath, Molly heard herself saying, 'Okay. Sure. Why not?'

Freda shrieked with joy as Molly put the dishes down on the table, her body trembling. 'But I can't pay you for a while. Not until my funds are released and we get some business in.'

Lucca wiped his lips. 'I can help you there. Who do you need?'

Molly shrugged. 'I've always dreamed of getting endorsement from the Bisette sisters but they're impossible to get hold of. Ava and I tried for years.'

'Sophie and Magda?' Lucca said, whipping out his phone. He tapped a few buttons and handed it to her. She could hear it making a call. 'Do it now.'

Molly thought she was going to die. She was about to speak to her culinary icons. Everyone listened silently as Molly took the phone with shaking hands and, somehow, managed to explain who she was and ask whether the Bisette sisters would be interested in giving her a chance to show them what she was capable of. Sophie Bisette agreed to visit the restaurant in the coming months. She instructed her to get back in touch, and that any friend of Lucca LeRoux's was a friend of theirs.

'Oh. My. God. Lucca, thank you so much,' Molly whispered, giving him the phone back.

Levi slapped him on the back. 'Who knew you were so well connected?'

'You would, bro, if you'd only hang out with me a bit more than once a year.'

'Fair point,' said Levi sheepishly.

'Okay, what do we need to do now, Molly?' Freda said, wiping her hands on her apron just like she'd seen Molly do. 'Looks like we have a restaurant to save.'

They all stopped eating to look at Molly. She reached into her pocket and laid the list flat on the table, smoothing it out with her hand. Seconds later, they were all howling with laughter.

* * *

As she was about to clear away the breakfast plates,

the first of the challenges was almost ready to be ticked off.

'Sorry, what was that, Molly?' Levi asked, grinning at her.

Molly repeated herself.

'Molly,' laughed Freda. 'Would you like some more pancakes?'

Molly felt her cheeks burning as she responded.

'What is happening?' asked Toby, walking in late and eyeing the pancakes eagerly. 'Molly, why are you barking? What's going on?'

Poor me, thought Molly as Lucca's eyes widened mischievously. He waved the list around, laughing. 'Molly, you absolute sweetheart. I've always admired you, Molly. So, which one do you want to tick off next, Molly?'

Molly barked repeatedly. 'Can everyone stop saying my name, please?'

This made everyone say her name even more until Levi, choking with laughter, ticked it off the list. 'Where's the journal? I'll do a witness signature. Toby, can you take a photo of us round the table, please?'

'I think Ava and I would have got along very well,' said Freda, looking down the list. 'She sounds really good fun. You must miss her.'

Molly closed her eyes and took a deep breath. 'Every single day.'

'Let's eat up and crack on,' said Levi, taking the piece of paper in his hands. 'I think we can combine a few of these. And to be fair, you've done most of the really hard ones already.'

Again, Molly felt her cheeks flame as she looked at the first item on the list.

* * *

By teatime, Molly had solved the mystery of the missing hat, spent the day blindfolded and was completely and utterly exhausted by constantly referring to herself in the third person.

'Can Molly take a quick break now, please?' she asked, shivering as she felt along the wall back to where she hoped Levi was waiting.

'What happened?' she heard Levi ask her. Until five minutes before, he'd stuck to her like glue since blindfolding her after breakfast.

'Molly somehow managed to lose her personal bodyguard. The one who swore to stick by her side all day. And now she's tired. She needs an alcoholic beverage, and she needs to change out of these wet clothes.'

There had been a slight incident when she'd gone to the bathroom downstairs, come out, taken the wrong turn and ended up in the spa where she accidently pulled on the cord that released the bucket of ice-cold water.

'She would also like to know where the hell you were when she needed you?'

Levi chuckled. 'So sorry. I took a call from the hospital. I literally turned my back for a second and you'd gone.'

'Can you untie Molly now, please? She's fucking fed up with being blindfolded and no longer gives two flying shits about the bucket list.'

Levi tried not to laugh as he untied the blindfold. 'Christ. This is a bit tight, isn't it?'

'Well, it certainly is headache-inducing,' said Molly through tight lips. She had never felt so exhausted. 'Okay. That's got to be almost everything on the list by now, surely.' She'd decided not to tell Levi about conquering her fear of highly-strung, overly controlling American mothers. She wasn't 100 per cent sure that would ever happen, but Monsieur Fournier didn't need to know that. She glanced down at the list. 'Except...'

That eighth challenge was becoming a huge elephant in the room. A woolly mammoth.

'Let's see it.' Levi held out his hand as Molly, with her eyesight fully restored, handed the list over.

Ava's Bucket List (RIP)

Drink champagne with a billionaire while naked in
a hot tub overlooking the Alps

Bark loudly every time someone round
the table says your name

Crash a wedding and give an
uplifting toast

Ride a camel dressed in
a costume

Speak in third
person all day

Solve a mystery

Conquer a fear

Fall madly in love

Spend the day blindfolded

Make your own face out of sausage meat

Publicly eat vanilla pudding out of a mayo jar
(with gusto)

Spend ten minutes naked in a sauna standing like
the Vitruvian Man

'Your friend was certainly looking out for you, wasn't she?' he said quietly.

Molly stared at the list. She hadn't dared to cross out *Fall madly in love*. She quickly folded it back up, hoping he hadn't seen it. 'These were supposed to be for *her* to do.'

Levi gave her a tender look. 'But I'm not sure they were meant for *her* to finish.' He took her hand. 'For what it's worth, I think you can cross off number eight.'

Molly melted. Properly melted.

'Come on. We don't have long to go before the deadline. Let's send these photos of you falling over the sofa blindfolded to the solicitor.'

Molly sat wrapped in a towel next to Levi as they quickly uploaded everything to the laptop, including the one of the camel, the sausage-meat face and a signed affidavit from Levi testifying that Molly did indeed complete the remaining tasks, with the exception of photographic evidence for those requiring nudity, on the grounds of common decency, and he even invoked some clause in the Human Rights Act.

Just as she went to press send, the Wi-Fi died. 'Don't worry. It's been dropping in and out all day. It'll come back on.'

Toby, Freda and Lucca came to join them. 'Have you sent everything across? Did you get your business and house back?'

'The Wi-Fi is out. Mobile data isn't getting a signal.' Molly was starting to panic.

'Don't worry,' agreed Toby. 'It'll come back on soon.'

'Yes, it will. It was working before because I've posted on my socials about my new job working with you,' said Freda, all excited. 'There's been so much interest already. So I'm thinking soft launch between Christmas and New Year and hard launch after. I've called in some favours.'

'You have? Already?' Molly tried to hide her alarm.

Lucca waved his phone at her excitedly. 'And I've got you your first catering booking for the New Year! It's a high-end event in South Africa. My friend's thirtieth. Safari themed.' Lucca gave Freda a high-five slap of the hand. 'They'll fly you both out there. Business class obviously.'

'We have a booking? Without running it by me first? But who would manage the...' She saw the joy shining from their faces. 'Doesn't matter. Well done. Thank you.' Molly had wondered how the three of them would work together. A million miles an hour apparently, with no corner of the globe off limits, and lots of jet-setting. She felt her palms starting to sweat. *This family!*

Twenty minutes crawled by, and Molly sensed she wasn't the only one beginning to worry. She whipped out her phone and called Monsieur Fournier, the solicitor.

'Hello, Monsieur Fournier. It's me, Molly Johnson. I just wanted to warn you that the Wi-Fi isn't working... Hello? Hello? Monsieur Fournier?'

With wide eyes, Molly redialled. The line was crackled and patchy. 'Monsieur Fournier. It's Molly Johnson. I have all the evidence you need, but the Wi-Fi isn't working. Can you hear me?' Molly strained to hear the reply. 'No. No, I *do* have everything, it's just that... Yes, I know that the deadline is in less than two hours. I have witnesses. I can put them on the phone. What do you mean email the proof? How many times do I have to tell you? The Wi-Fi isn't working! I know it's Christmas Eve. Can't you keep the office open a little longer? The signal will...'

Infuriating, insufferable man.

'He hung up,' Molly said miserably. 'I couldn't get a word in edgeways. He's not a relative of yours by any chance?'

Levi sprang up and raced into the kitchen with his phone clamped to his ear. He darted back to the lounge several minutes later, just as Molly was explaining that Monsieur Fournier insisted the legal requirements rested on her signature. Her signature on the forms she hadn't emailed back to him. The forms he'd been asking for repeatedly, for months.

'Shit. I'm going to lose everything and it's all my own stupid fault.' Tears sprang to Molly's eyes as she stared out of the window. The snow was coming down. Toby had just received word that the pass was still blocked. How could she stumble like this, at the last hurdle? 'I'm so sorry, Ava,' she whispered.

'What about me? I was looking forward to starting my new job!' moaned Freda. 'I manifested it. I put it out into the universe. The universe responded. I have the launch outfits picked out and everything.'

'Think. Think,' murmured Molly. 'We need internet. And mobile signal. I know! The roof!'

'Great idea!' squealed Freda.

'I'll get the ladders and some rope,' barked Lucca. 'Molly, you climb up there, I'll hold the ladders, secure the rope to something and Freda can climb up and hold on to you while you send the email.' He beamed. 'What a team! Come on, girls, we've got this.'

Levi shook his head slowly, frowning. 'Fascinating. Truly fascinating.'

They stopped chattering.

'What?' Molly asked. 'What's fascinating?'

Levi was struggling to hide his amusement. 'The three of you have put your heads together, and that's the plan you've come up with? To climb on the roof, in this treacherous weather, and wave a phone about in the hopes you can get a signal?' He folded his arms and looked at the three of them like they were naughty children. 'Do any of you even know the rudimentary elements of how mobile signals or the router or the wired ethernet connections work?'

It sounded very much like a rhetorical question and so Molly didn't feel the need to answer it. If her life ever depended on explaining exactly what 5G was, she wasn't sure she'd make it out alive.

'There's a good reason he's the billionaire and we're not.' Freda giggled. 'I wish I'd had the foresight to invest my inheritance in Bitcoin the way he did.'

'Molly, grab your coat and your phone,' said Levi, rolling his eyes at Freda while he picked up his laptop. His phone was still glued to his ear. He was barking out orders with military precision. 'Toby, get my coat, radio the helipad at the resort and clear us for landing please, and ready the jet for immediate take off. Molly, where's the solicitor's office?'

Christ, she loved watching him be bossy and capable.

Molly took out the letter. 'It's just outside of Paris.'

'Toby, tell the Civil Aviation Authority we need to land in Le Bourget within the hour.'

'You can't be serious?' Molly asked. It was more of a squeak. It didn't seem real, but she grabbed her coat anyway. 'I'm still soaking wet.'

Levi gave her an exasperated look. 'Then get changed. We literally have no time to lose.'

'And there's something else.'

They all looked at Molly.

'I have a fear of sharp, pointy objects, in particular, rotating blades. I can't possibly get in a helicopter with you.'

'But you're a chef,' he said, trying not to snigger. 'Isn't handling pointy objects and whizzing things up in blenders half the job?'

Molly shrugged, nodding. It was almost as though Ava was doing this on purpose.

25

'YOUR TIME IS LIMITED, SO DON'T WASTE
IT LIVING SOMEONE ELSE'S LIFE.'
STEVE JOBS

Molly glanced at her phone. There were less than two hours to go. Within fifteen minutes, she was dressed in thermal leggings, an oversized sweatshirt, snow boots and padded coat, hat, scarf and gloves and was racing through the lodge, hand-in-hand with Levi, out into the freezing cold. The snow had eased off, and the helicopter was only just visible in the fading light. Its gigantic rotor blades glinted menacingly in the torchlight. It was nothing compared to the ice-cold fear that was gripping her chest.

'Are you sure you know what you're doing?' she yelled at him as he swung open the door and helped her into a tiny cockpit. He slammed it firmly shut behind her, raced round, and jumped in next to her. She watched, dumbstruck, as he flicked switches, checked the fuel, checked the engine. She jumped a mile as the blades rotated forcefully to life, shaking the craft to its core as Levi radioed in that he was taking off. It looked very much like he was just flicking any old random switches for show. Levi stopped what he was doing to take her face in his hands.

'Trust me.' He leaned in to kiss her thoroughly on her cold lips. The heat from his touch sent a bolt of reassurance surging through her veins.

Within seconds, they were high in the air. Molly stared at Levi piloting the helicopter as they hurtled towards the Val D'Amore helipad. 'I didn't know you were a pilot!' Molly yelled through the headset. 'Are you sure you're licensed to fly?'

'Bit late to ask me that now, isn't it?' Levi laughed. 'Just relax. I know what I'm doing. Trust me.'

Of course he would be a pilot. Of course. Wasn't there a rule where all billionaires must be able to pilot aircraft, sail superyachts and drive the world's fastest cars?

'We'll have to take my jet.' He pointed to a silver aircraft waiting on the nearby landing strip. 'Don't worry, I'll get you to the office before it closes.'

His jet? This was getting worse. Big-ticket splurging on Gulfstream jets, private tropical islands and solid gold busts of Buddha were a world away from her upbringing.

'I guess with us spending so much time together as regular people, I totally forgot you were a...' Molly stopped herself just in time. It was unfair to label him a billionaire when there was so much more to him than his bank account. She liked to think people wouldn't judge her in the same way, just because her own modest account was currently holding less than €400.

Levi chuckled through the headset. 'You'd probably believe me if I told you I'd just bought my own space station.'

'Absolutely I would. I imagine you did that right before you took a shuttle to Mars.'

Levi smirked. 'I have a holiday home there. All we billionaires do.'

Molly loved that he was so laid back about his status as one of the world's wealthiest men. In her eyes, it was more disconcerting that he was also one of the world's most *attractive* men. But he was also kind and thoughtful (and an unbelievably generous lover, but she would hate to keep going on about him). She marvelled at how deftly he flicked switches and bellowed numbers and altitudes down the headset to the control tower. It was certainly doing wonders to cure her fear of rotating blades. In some ways, she was finding this experience almost pleasurable. Levi flashed her a confident grin. He was self-assured. Cool under pressure. He had really competent hands, if that was a thing. Long, slender fingers. Not too long but just—

'Okay, brace yourself. This landing is going to be tricky.'

* * *

The race from the helicopter to the private jet was seamless. Or at least it would have been had Molly not had such a tight grip on the chopper's door handle and refused point blank to move. Fear at the sight of the jet, the roar of its engines and the bitter gale outside rocking the helicopter from side to side had rendered her incapable of moving. It was only Levi's soft voice that coaxed her out. There were even two cabin crew in resort uniforms standing to greet them. The engines were running, and Molly was relieved to find out that Levi wasn't flying the plane. Just as well because she was clinging to him like a tree frog. It took off mere minutes after they'd been seated on either side of a small table and had fastened their seatbelts.

It was deliciously warm on board. Still trembling,

Molly took off her coat, hat, scarf and gloves. She shook her hair out and glanced at her reflection in the jet window. *What a mess.* She must have gasped because Levi was trying not to smirk. 'I've seen you look worse.'

Molly looked around at the plush surroundings, her jaw falling slightly open at the soft cream leather seats and sofas, the polished walnut interior and the gold fixtures and fittings. It was the most elegant mode of transport she'd ever seen. She could not look more out of place if she tried.

'Opulence is one of the perks.'

'I bet it is,' whispered Molly. 'Is that a giant TV screen? And a bar? OMG, look at the size of that!'

Levi twisted around in his seat. 'The bathroom?'

'No. The world's biggest air fryer over there. It's massive. I love those things. Best invention ever. Can I see the kitchen? What sort of menu do you do? Is it bespoke?'

'Touting for business already?' laughed Levi, bringing her down to earth with a bump. They now had just over an hour to get to Monsieur Fournier's office.

'If I still have a business to run. Do you think we'll make it? Does this aircraft have Wi-Fi? I could email the proof ahead of us, just in case.'

Levi's face grew serious. 'That solicitor was very rude to you.'

Molly swallowed nervously. 'He was. Although it is Christmas Eve. And he is French.'

'Don't make excuses for him. I heard the way he kept cutting you off.'

'Yeah. That seems to happen to me a lot.' Levi had the good grace to look sheepish. 'That's why I like to keep to myself. In the kitchen. Out of the way.'

Levi held his hands up guiltily. 'Maybe it's time to be more assertive.'

'I'm not sure I have it in me any more. You know, because *life* and all that.'

'I've seen you with my family. Not many women can hold their own against my mother. You know exactly how to be assertive. Just apply it to every other area of your life. And Lucca told me you've been keeping an eye on Freda. I really appreciate you making the effort with her.' Levi put his elbows on the table and made a steeple with his fingers. 'She's very bright. She'll be an asset to your business.'

'My little "food hut"?' Molly smirked. 'Does this mean you aren't going to fight me for it?'

Levi shook his head. 'Of course not. I think you'll make a great success of it.'

'You do?'

'Your idea to run the restaurant as a bijou cooking school and a fine-dining experience is highly lucrative. With increased staff, you could still cater Lucca's celebrity events *and* scale up the takeaway service. The sky's the limit with the number of contacts we all have between us, and your skill and creativity.'

It sounded too good to be true and for the first time, Molly dared to believe she could do it. Excitement ripped through her. She would build Le Petit Ange's brand in Ava's memory and make a huge success out of it. She glanced at the time on her phone. 'What if we don't make it?'

'We will.'

Levi had such a reassuring manner. Molly sagged back into her seat and tried to resend the email. She received an immediate out of office in return. She showed Levi.

'The office will be open. I've already sent word to say we are en route.'

By the time the cabin crew had been round several times to ask if they would like a drink or a snack, and Molly had politely declined each time, the pilot announced they were preparing for landing.

'That was so quick,' Molly said, fastening her seatbelt. 'I can't thank you enough for all of this.'

Levi fixed her a look. 'You saved my father's life.'

Molly chewed her lip. 'I just did what any hero would have done.'

'You helped my sister through a troubled time.'

Molly shrugged. 'We've all been there. Doesn't hurt to be kind.'

'You covered for Toby so that he wouldn't be sacked.'

Molly tutted. 'It's not like he needs the money. He just has a huge crush on Freda.'

Levi looked amazed. 'Does he?' He tilted his head. 'Not just a crazy-talented chef. You're genuinely a very astute, smart, caring person.'

Molly blushed. 'Speaking of astute. What's the deal with Lucca and you? Does it have something to do with your ex-fiancée?'

Levi rolled his eyes. 'It's all in the past but yeah, it really ruined our relationship.'

'Can I ask what happened?'

Levi stared out of the window. 'Clarice told me Lucca had tried to seduce her. Lucca denied it but I took her side.' He took in a deep breath. 'But it turned out that he was right, and Clarice was lying.'

Poor Lucca.

'Why would she do that?'

'Apparently, Lucca had caught her cheating on me, and she tried to blackmail him into keeping silent.

When that didn't work, she accused him of coming onto her to drive a wedge between us.'

'She cheated on you? Who with? One of the Hemsworths?'

Levi smirked. 'Truthfully, she felt ignored. I was always too busy for her.'

Surprise, surprise.

'Why didn't you tell your parents? Valerie obviously has hopes you'll get back together.'

'Because Clarice is my mother's best friend's daughter. We all grew up together.'

'And Lucca has never quite forgiven you?'

Levi shook his head sadly.

'Well, it is the season of goodwill. You should definitely talk to him. I'm a great believer in the healing powers of Christmas.'

'Why does that not surprise me? How are you so nice?' As the wheels touched down on the tarmac and the jet came to a halt, Levi unbuckled his seatbelt and held out his hand to her. 'Come on. Let's get your business back.'

* * *

After a twenty-minute dash from the airport in a shiny, black, expensive-looking chauffeur-driven car,

Molly and Levi stood outside Barrowfield, Fournier & Fils Solicitors. The street was dark, save for a few streetlamps. It was deserted. All of the lights in the building were out. Levi rapped forcefully on the door. Molly checked the time. They had ten minutes left to reach Monsieur Fournier.

No answer.

Levi tried again while Molly rang his number.

No answer.

Molly felt crushed, especially after the magnificent rush and excitement of the journey with Levi. He had been positively heroic. She grabbed his arm. 'I'm so sorry. You went to all this trouble for me, and he's not even here. I'm so, so sorry.'

Levi lifted her chin. 'Don't be. Whatever happens you'll be fine. You'll start a new business. You'll find a new place to live. You'll live the happy and adventurous life that your friend wanted you to. And you'll do it because of who you already are. Not because of someone you think you should be.'

Molly felt her body glow from within as she gazed at him. He reached out to wipe a single tear from her cheek, leaning down to kiss her gently on the lips. It was a kiss so tender, so soft, that Molly wasn't sure if it was really happening.

The sound of a door being unbolted interrupted

the moment. It creaked open to reveal an old man. 'Miss Johnson, I presume?'

Molly nodded. 'Monsieur Fournier?'

The man before her wore a crumpled brown suit. He looked old and tired. And grumpy. Molly wanted to assert herself but something about the man appealed to her better nature. He looked worn and lonely.

'Thank you for staying late. I appreciate you might have family waiting for you.'

A sorrowful look crossed his face. '*Non.*'

'Erm, well, here are the documents you requested. And the photos. And a signed affidavit from Levi, erm, my lawyer, Monsieur LeRoux, to confirm the bucket list has been completed.'

Levi straightened and took his arm from around her shoulders but not without the sharp eyes of Monsieur Fournier catching the movement. Levi cleared his throat. 'Yes. I am representing Miss Johnson's case.'

Monsieur Fournier let out a tired grumble. 'What case?' He ushered them both inside out of the cold with a confused expression. He led them down a musty hallway, into his office. It looked straight out of the 1950s. He went over to a large wooden desk piled high with files and papers and lifted a folded cardboard wallet off the top. 'Here are all the necessary documents, deeds, keys and a copy of the will. Sign here, please.'

Molly took the papers. 'Is that it? Aren't you going to check that I've done everything?' She pulled Ava's journal from her pocket and flipped it open. 'I mean, look, here's a photo of me riding the camel dressed in burlesque. Well, no. Don't look at that one. Here's me covered in sausage. And look, here's me wearing a blindfold and... Let me find the videos on my phone of me barking.'

'You have been busy, haven't you?' Monsieur Fournier looked disbelievingly at her. 'But why? As I tried to explain to you, multiple times, I might add, the will stipulates that you only have to *try* to finish the bucket list.'

Molly traded a confused glance with Levi.

'Do you mean to say that Molly – Miss Johnson – only had to *try* to complete the list? As in, if she'd tried only one thing on the list then that would have been enough to satisfy the terms?'

Monsieur Fournier tutted. 'At last. Someone is listening to me. You'll make a good lawyer someday.'

Molly was glad that Levi chose to ignore the undercurrent of sarcasm.

'But... but why didn't you tell me that in the first

place?' Molly was astounded. Had all of this been for nothing? It couldn't be possible.

'I did. And I kept writing to you. Several times.' He handed Molly a copy of the letter.

She quickly scanned it. Now that he had pointed it out, it was as though the wording was changing before her very eyes.

'Blah, blah, blah,' murmured Levi, reading over her shoulder. 'The recipient, Molly Johnson, must try to complete everything remaining on the bucket list before Christmas Eve at 6 p.m. of the following year otherwise blah, blah, blah... all of the assets pertaining to Ava's estate will go to her next of kin.' Levi's head jerked up. 'He's right. He's rude but he's right.'

Monsieur Fournier coughed. 'Apologies. My manner is not what it was. Ever since I lost my wife, I have been a cantankerous old buffoon. All those years spent slaving away at work instead of making the most of my time with her. In fact, Ms Johnson, you are my very last client. Well, strictly speaking Ava is my last client. And for what it is worth, I would have waited for you.' Monsieur Fournier smiled forlornly at Molly. 'She was my goddaughter, you see.' His eyes misted over. 'Her dear parents are my oldest friends.'

'You were at the funeral,' gasped Molly, squinting at him.

'You gave a wonderfully heartfelt speech,' said Monsieur Fournier. 'I know how well you took care of her. And I know how much she wanted to help you rebuild your life afterwards.'

Molly had broken down halfway through her speech and she would never forget how kind and patient the congregation had been, sitting quietly while she gathered the strength to do her best friend proud. They'd shared a whole life. And when it came towards the end, Molly chose to walk together in the darkness with Ava than alone in the light. There was nothing she wouldn't have done for her.

'When she came here to draw up her will, you were all she could talk about. You were her best friend, her soulmate.'

Molly was embarrassed to find tears once again pooling in her eyes. 'That's very kind. We did everything together.' Her voice caught in her throat. 'I don't know how I'm going to live without her.'

Levi put his arm around her shoulder. A comforting, caring gesture.

Monsieur Fournier watched them, his voice wavering. 'If there's one thing I've learned in my seventy-six years, it's that friendship is at the heart of everything meaningful. It's the most powerful energy there is. But Ava was very clear about one thing. She wanted you to embrace life and all it has to offer.' He glanced at Levi and gave him a brief nod. 'Make new friends. Live life. Don't spend it hidden away in the kitchen working.' He leaned towards Molly, his voice soft as a feather. 'Have fun. Shine brightly. Be bold. Fall dangerously in love.' He flicked his eyes back to Levi. 'Because some people leave it too late. Never put these things off.'

* * *

After they said their goodbyes to Monsieur Fournier, and he'd rejected their offer to spend Christmas with them, Molly and Levi got back in the car. Levi held her while she cried.

'Will I ever stop crying?' she asked him.

'Even if you don't, there's a continuous drought in parts of Africa where you could do some good. Water the plants, fill reservoirs with your well of endless tears.'

Molly let out a half chuckle, sniffing as she sat up straight. 'You're right. It's time to stop crying and start doing. Although, speaking of the future, now that I have my business back and I'm no longer your chalet chef and you don't have time for a relationship – which, by the way, you mentioned on many, *many* occasions – where does that leave us?' She took a deep breath. Now was the time to be bold. She locked eyes with Levi. 'Is this goodbye for us?' Because she knew without a doubt that if this was goodbye, she would cry until she became nothing but a shrivelled husk and died of dehydration. Africa would have to find someone else to fill their wells.

Levi held her hand. 'Weren't you listening to a word that poor man just said? Ava is clearly counting on you to live a full and adventurous life. And here you are. With a billionaire to play with for Christmas. You can literally do whatever your heart desires.'

'Really? Because my heart only desires one thing.'

'I hope you're talking about committing to a relationship. Because, like me, you did mention it on many, *many* occasions.'

'Yes. Yes, I am.' Molly leaned in to kiss him. A warm, loving, soulful kiss that would have stretched on forever if the chauffeur wasn't doing his job properly.

'Sorry to interrupt,' he announced over the car speaker. 'Your jet is ready for take-off, sir.'

Levi murmured against Molly's lips. 'Please say you'll protect me from my dysfunctional family.'

'Not a chance. We're spending every minute with them. Playing games. Bickering. Listening to them go on and on. Your siblings have many issues between them. It's going to be great.'

Levi gave her a soft look. 'Can't wait.'

They boarded the luxury private jet for the second time within as many hours. As soon as they took off, Levi looked up from his phone. He had developed a dangerous glint in his eye.

Molly felt a surge of butterflies in her stomach. 'What is it?'

'The pass has reopened. Lucca, Toby and Freda have taken the minibus down to the resort. They're spending the night at the Cigar Lounge Christmas Eve party. They'll see us for Christmas dinner tomorrow, back at the lodge.'

'How nice for them.' Molly's pulse raced. She and Levi would be alone at the lodge.

Alone.

Totally alone.

'And, well, you know we have no more challenges left to do on the list...' Levi didn't get to finish his sentence because Molly had thrown herself at him across the table. When they came up for air, Levi murmured in her ear, 'Why don't we start a new bucket list of our own? Full of firsts for *both* of us.'

'Good idea. What do you want to put on it?' she said, trying to catch her breath. Levi really was a magnificent kisser. She saw his eyes flicker towards the bathroom.

Oh.

A primeval, lustful surge ripped through her. She may as well have had a neon sign above her head. *Take me now, up against the toilet cubicle.* She was out of her seat and dragging him by the hand before he could even elaborate. They burst through the bathroom door, locking it behind them.

Levi scooped her into his arms as though she weighed nothing. Sizzling chemistry exploded the moment their lips collided, sliding feverishly, hungry for more. Levi pulled her closer, his hands roaming her back. Molly scrambled to straddle him, pressing her body against his. She moaned with passion against his lips as she slipped her hands under his top, his warm skin making her hot with desire. She arched into him, desperate to feel every inch of his body against hers.

'What about the crew?'

'They'll have seen worse. They're very discreet. Besides, this bathroom is soundproof. It doubles as a safe room.'

Molly's heart lurched, instantly jealous at the thought of Levi with someone else. Although knowing they were also safe from a terrorist attack was a small comfort. These billionaires thought of everything.

'Not terrible behaviour from me,' he assured her. 'Lucca and Freda treat my jet like their own private Uber.'

Molly couldn't hide her relief, beaming at him as she tore at his top while he unbuckled his jeans. She threw off her sweatshirt and stepped out of her leggings, trembling with urgency. He peeled down the straps of her bra, deftly unhooking it at the back. It practically disintegrated in his hands, causing him to groan with delight as her breasts tumbled out before him.

She slipped her finger beneath his waistline, tugging his jeans down as their kiss deepened, gasping as his erection sprang free. 'Merry Christmas,' she said huskily as their bodies came together in a heated frenzy. 'I'm hoping you meant we should join the Mile High Club. Because this is definitely a first for me.'

Levi chuckled. 'I was actually going to ask you to show me how to use the world's biggest air fryer. Apparently, they're the best invention ever.' He trailed a slow hand over her hot skin, down her stomach, to remove her knickers.

'Oh my God. I'm mortified,' she squeaked as his

fingers slid unexpectedly between her legs, making her pant with longing.

'Don't be,' Levi growled. 'This is also a first for me. You're unpredictable. I never know what you'll say or do. I've never felt this excited with anyone in my life.'

Molly was flabbergasted. He couldn't possibly mean her. 'Me?' she breathed against his neck. She kissed a trail from his Adam's apple up to his earlobe. 'Do you mean it?'

A harsh breath caught in his throat as their eyes collided. In one fluid movement, he spun her round to face the mirror while he kissed his way along her shoulder, sending tingling sensations down her arm, one hand massaging her breasts, stroking her skin, the other between her legs, creating waves of all-consuming desire to pulse through her. 'Look at yourself. You're not just incredibly beautiful, you're a powerhouse of raw determination. You have heart and soul and an abundance of dramatic talent that has people in awe of your creativity.'

OMG. She'd never felt such a #bosslady in her entire life. He was right. She could listen to him go on all night. Like a sexy, never-ending, inspirational TED talk.

She beamed at his reflection as he reached into a nearby cabinet and pulled out a foil condom wrapper and deftly ripped it open with his teeth. With his body pressed into hers, they locked eyes in the mirror as he entered her. They were on a private jet. Flying through the night sky, full of stars. It was thrilling. It was daring. It was better than a hot tub. Levi let out a moan as though he couldn't hold out a second longer. She squeezed herself round him. One thrust, then another. And another. Until a flush of warmth spread throughout her body. Sweat was forming on their faces, the mirror steaming with the heat. Levi leaned one hand against it as he held her tightly, his breathing growing faster and more audible until with one final thrust, he cried out her name.

It took a few minutes before either of them was able to speak. She'd never wanted to hold on to the hands of time more, so that they could stay in this moment. This perfect moment.

Levi held her gaze in the mirror, his eyes soft with love. They made a very striking couple. Molly stared back at the woman she'd become. Confident. Bold. Sexy as hell. Gone was the gaunt, haunted look. She arched back against him, looping her arms round his neck. Exposing herself completely. This was her life now. It was going to be wild, adventurous, fulfilling. You only live once. She was going to do it right. And then some.

Levi gave her an adoring look. 'Do you think you could get used to this life? I'm not the easiest man to be with and I'm incredibly busy *all* the time, but I really want this to work. I really want to be with you.'

His words sounded like music to her ears. Something inside her knew they'd make each other happy. It felt like destiny. 'Even if it means we ignore each other and turn into bitter, grumpy workaholics?'

'Yes. Although technically, we'll be bitter, grumpy billionaires. What do you say?'

Could she run a successful business and start a brand-new relationship at the same time? Could she cope in this world of extreme wealth and decadence? Could she put up with his pain-in-the-neck mother?

She spun round to face him, a grin spreading from cheek to cheek, her heart bursting with joy. She could more than handle him.

'Honey. You had me at grumpy billionaire.'

* * *

MORE FROM JO LYONS

Another book from Jo Lyons, *Girls Gone Rogue* is available to order now here:

https://mybook.to/GirlsGoneRogueBackAd

ACKNOWLEDGEMENTS

So many writer and reader friends helped me get this book to publication. Huge thanks to all of them and enormous thanks to my wonderfully talented editor Francesca Best for her brilliant support and the entire Boldwood team for welcoming me into the family. Special thanks to copy editor Jennifer Kay Davies and proofreader Susan Sugden for helping get it in shape and the clever Alex Allden for making it look fabulous.

I'd like to thank all the lovely women at Comedy Women in Print, especially Helen Lederer and my fellow long/shortlisters who have been excellent cheerleaders. All at Curtis Brown Creative for their support and encouragement during the many, many writing courses that I have become addicted to – yes, I'm looking at you, Jenny Colgan. When I started out, I had no idea about how to save a cat. Now I know things like every character needs an arc and a book will never be finished, only ever abandoned. Constant tinkering is not an option.

Last but not least, my awesome and talented writing tribe and beta readers who help fix all the terrible first drafts: Jayne, Jess, Julia, Farrah, Cristal, Amanda (aka The Coven), Nichelle, Kim, Keith, Claire, Cara, Joanna, John (my Curtis Brown writing tribe). And a special thanks to all my fabulous friends who cheerlead me on: Jennie W who kindly offered to be first reader, Alice, Nicky, Linds, Wendy, Helen, Deb, Genize, Shauna, Mrs B, Mags, Paula, Maria, Shelley, Scottish Kate (and her fabulous Tillyfruskie farm cabin), Janine, Anna Foster for narrating the Girls series so brilliantly and my sisters, especially Philippa and my niece Gabs who listen to me go on and on and fecking on (I know, difficult to believe) and my lovely aunties who encourage me to keep going. And the Lyons boys who always have my back and never moan that I now live in a crazy fantasy world, talk about my novels incessantly and have completely abandoned the housework. I am living the dream!

I could not do any of this without them. I have enormous respect for anyone who sets out to write a book and gets to the end without wanting to hurl themselves off the nearest cliff. Be nice to writers – we are ALL in varying states of emotional collapse.

ABOUT THE AUTHOR

Jo Lyons is the bestselling author of uplifting, laugh-out-loud, warm-hearted romantic comedies, and was shortlisted for the prestigious Comedy Women in Print Awards in 2021. She spent years working abroad in sunny destinations like Turkey, Spain and the south of France at a vineyard (trying her best not to drink them out of business).

Sign up to Jo Lyons' mailing list for news, competitions and updates on future books.

Visit Jo's website: www.jolyonsauthor.com

Follow Jo on social media here:

facebook.com/Jo-Lyons-Author

x.com/JoLyons

instagram.com/hinnywhowrites

goodreads.com/jolyons

tiktok.com/@jo_lyons_author

bsky.app/profile/jolyons.bsky.social

ALSO BY JO LYONS

Standalone Novels

A Billionaire for Christmas

The Girls Series

Girls Just Want to Have Sun

Girls Gone Rogue

Girls Take Vegas

Boldwood
EVER AFTER

xoxo

JOIN BOLDWOOD'S
**ROMANCE
COMMUNITY**
FOR SWEET AND
SPICY BOOK RECS
WITH ALL YOUR
FAVOURITE
TROPES!

SIGN UP TO OUR
NEWSLETTER

HTTPS://BIT.LY/BOLDWOODEVERAFTER

Boldwood

Boldwood Books is an award-winning fiction publishing company seeking out the best stories from around the world.

Find out more at www.boldwoodbooks.com

Join our reader community for brilliant books, competitions and offers!

Follow us
@BoldwoodBooks
@TheBoldBookClub

Sign up to our weekly deals newsletter

https://bit.ly/BoldwoodBNewsletter